SARAH HENSTRA is a professor of English at Ryerson University, where she teaches courses in gothic literature, fairy tales and fantasy, and women in fiction. Some of her best story ideas come from classroom discussions. She grew up on the wild, wet west coast of Canada but now lives in Toronto with her two sons and a poodle named Nora. *Mad Miss Mimic* is her first novel and was shortlisted for the Canadian Library Association Young Adult Book Award and the Amy Mathers Teen Book Award, and was also a Global TV Morning Show Bookclub selection. You can find Sarah at www.sarahhenstra.com.

MAD

MISS

MIMIC

SARAH HENSTRA

razOr
bill

RAZORBILL

an imprint of Penguin Canada Books Inc., a Penguin Random House Company

Published by the Penguin Group
Penguin Canada Books Inc., 320 Front Street West, Suite 1400,
Toronto, Ontario M5V 3B6, Canada

Penguin Group (USA) LLC, 375 Hudson Street, New York, New York 10014, U.S.A.
Penguin Books Ltd, 80 Strand, London WC2R 0RL, England
Penguin Ireland, 25 St Stephen's Green, Dublin 2, Ireland (a division of Penguin Books Ltd)
Penguin Group (Australia), 707 Collins Street, Melbourne, Victoria 3008, Australia
(a division of Pearson Australia Group Pty Ltd)
Penguin Books India Pvt Ltd, 11 Community Centre, Panchsheel Park, New Delhi – 110 017, India
Penguin Group (NZ), 67 Apollo Drive, Rosedale, Auckland 0632, New Zealand
(a division of Pearson New Zealand Ltd)
Penguin Books (South Africa) (Pty) Ltd, 24 Sturdee Avenue,
Rosebank, Johannesburg 2196, South Africa

Penguin Books Ltd, Registered Offices: 80 Strand, London WC2R 0RL, England

First published in Razorbill paperback by Penguin Canada Books Inc., 2015

Published in this edition, 2017

1 2 3 4 5 6 7 8 9 10 (RRD)

Copyright © Sarah Henstra, 2015

*Publisher's note: This book is a work of fiction. Names, characters, places, and incidents either
are the product of the author's imagination or are used fictitiously, and any resemblance to
actual persons living or dead, events, or locales is entirely coincidental.*

Manufactured in the U.S.A.

LIBRARY AND ARCHIVES CANADA CATALOGUING IN PUBLICATION
Henstra, Sarah, 1972–, author
Mad Miss Mimic / Sarah Henstra.
Originally published: 2015.
ISBN 978-0-14-319237-4 (paperback)
I. Title.
PS8615.E597M33 2017   jC813'.6   C2016-900953-X

eBook ISBN 978-0-14-319238-1

Library of Congress Control Number: 2016933005

Visit the Penguin Canada website at **www.penguinrandomhouse.ca**

The London Examiner

MAY 7TH, 1872

An Act of the Black Glove?

ARCHIBALD MAVETY, SPECIAL REPORTER

>─◆>─O─<◆─<

THE EXPLOSION THAT destroyed more than a dozen ships on the Thames River late last week set off a flurry of accusations and arguments in Parliament today. Determining blame is, of course, a matter of much urgency. In an exclusive interview with *The Examiner*, police confirmed that the incident differs from the other explosive attacks that have terrorized our city in recent months. This blast occurred in the nighttime when most of us were safely home and abed. Its target area was deserted except for a few unfortunate sailors and docksmen (may God rest their souls). Most striking of all is the absence of any note claiming responsibility for the action.

The case has been further complicated by the rescue, from the scene of the disaster, of a gentleman's daughter whose family has asked that her name be withheld. Unlike certain journalists writing for other London newspapers, this reporter is committed to honouring that family's wishes in this most distressing of times. I should like to state for the record, however, that the salacious and mean-spirited reports linking the young lady to the sudden disappearance of Francis Thornfax, the Lord Rosbury (the newest member of our House of Lords), have no bearing in fact whatsoever and must only reflect the poor taste and faulty moral compass of their authors.

ONE

*T*here are things I cannot say in any voice.

I was born Leonora Emmaline Somerville, but I am not at all sure that is still who I am.

Oh, I could tell you the facts as you will find them in *The Examiner* and *The Times* and the *Morning Post*. I could tell you which *Illustrated London News* artist depicted the burning masts most faithfully, which Royal Academy painter best captured the hurricane of light reflected on black water. But I could not tell you where to find me in their pictures, or even which of the facts are reliable when it comes to me.

"Miss Somerville," they called me to my face at Hastings House, and "Mad Miss Mimic" when they thought I could not hear. Which is the more accurate name for me? My sister always said that one's station determines who one is. Certainly she believed it her life's noblest task to secure my station through a good marriage. She did believe it, and she did try—I must grant her that at least.

My aunt Emmaline says that your story decides who you are. But what about the chapters I did not write? Those scenes in which I stood by, watching in horror, but found nothing to say? Those moments when my tongue froze, and I tasted ashes and could not produce a single word?

If I am not visible in the pictures of the Thames disaster, it must be because I am still under water. I've long given up thrashing for the surface and fighting for breath. The current turns me in its bed like an efficient nurse, shifting my limbs and nudging me and whispering me to sleep. Sweeping me down, down, out to sea.

Oh Aunt Emma, how can you ask me to recover the traces of my story from the wreckage? I am still in the river, caught here in the undertow of grief.

Spilled slops, and a housemaid's illness. A lowly beginning for a tale to be sure! But looking back I think that must be when it really began for me. A morning in early March—a cold morning between winter and spring, the kind with dull grey light outside the window and rain hissing down the chimney onto the coal-grate. The kind of morning that asks you to linger in bed instead of rising to greet the day.

I was only half-dressed when Hattie's accident happened. My lady's maid, Bess, had gone to fetch my hairbrush from my sister's room. A sharp clang of metal on wood echoed from the service stairs, followed by a feminine cry of distress. Afraid that Bess had fallen I ran down the hall to assist her but discovered Hattie instead. The servant girl was stopped halfway down the narrow staircase, struggling to right a copper bucket and gather the hearth brush and tray she'd dropped. I hadn't seen Hattie often in my eighteen months at Hastings House. The lower servants kept their own schedules and stayed in separate quarters. Hastings is large for a city home: a cold, cavernous maze of a house with thirteen bedrooms, a greater and a lesser hall, and two libraries in addition to the usual parlours, eating rooms, nurseries, and kitchens. The regular staff of eleven grew to sixteen or twenty when my sister planned one of her parties. So I knew nothing of Hattie's background or character—to me she was only a shy housemaid, maybe thirteen or fourteen years old.

The spreading stench told me the contents of the tipped bucket: the girl must have just finished emptying the family's chamber pots. I shivered in my chemise and would have turned back to avoid embarrassing her, but I was surprised by the violence of Hattie's trembling and the whiteness of her knuckles as she gripped the banister for support. The slops pail slid farther from its precarious balance against her knee. It looked like she might fall. Hastening to Hattie's side I steadied the pail and seized her round the waist. She was so thin that I could feel all her ribs.

"Sorry, mum," Hattie gasped, and then she paled even further: "Oh, I ain't to be seen by the family carryin' slops, mum! I beg you, mum, please leave me."

"Shh," I soothed her. "Shh, now." I was composing a joke about my baby nephew's soiled diaper, which had rolled nearly to the landing, and I might even have attempted to tell the joke for Hattie's sake, but we were interrupted by the appearance of Mrs. Nussey through the door below us.

"Hattie! What is the meaning of this?" The housekeeper hiked her skirts and lumbered up the stairs.

I smiled at the woman, about to tell her that I wasn't the least bit upset, that the poor housegirl was near to fainting from shame and fear.

But Mrs. Nussey was gaping in open-mouthed horror at my feet. "Miss Somerville! Your slippers are ruined. Do remove them at once!"

"S-sorry m-m-m …" I stammered. "I only m-meant …" But my tongue had fixed itself like a bar of lead in my mouth. I sat down right there on the stairs and tore off my urine-stained slippers.

"Whatever are you doing, wandering about undressed?"

I kept my head down so that my hair would fall and screen the flush on my cheek.

Concern sharpened the housekeeper's voice: "Miss Somerville, are you quite well? Shall I call for Dr. Dewhurst?"

I shook my head and, so that she would not fetch my brother-in-law, I forced myself to meet Mrs. Nussey's eyes. And there it was, plain as day: that expression I knew so well but still cringed every time to witness. The eyes darting all over my face, the mouth tight with anticipation. Wary but fascinated. *Waiting.*

What was I to do? I knew that if I did not speak for her Hattie would be punished—unfairly, since she was obviously ill—but my embarrassment and fear of self-exposure made me creep, barefoot and shamefaced, back up the stairs. I winced when I heard the housekeeper's slap and Hattie's suppressed cry, but I did not turn around.

TWO

This small episode, awkward and distressing as it was for both the servant girl and me, might have passed from my mind altogether if Hattie's illness had not overcome her again only a short week later. Thinking back on it I am amazed that the poor girl managed to postpone her collapse long enough for Christabel and her friends to finish their luncheon and depart for Mayfair Street.

The visiting ladies had been discussing my case. "She does very well today," fat Mrs. Cauldhame observed, turning her heavy-lidded gaze my way. "So lovely in that yellow frock. Is that the fabric from the shop in Broad Street?"

"Special order, from Frankfurt," my sister said. "The shade brings out the shine in her hair, does it not?" Christabel put a hand to her own hair, which was finer and blonder than mine. My sister was six years older than I but, at twenty-three, Christa was still childlike in her looks: wide-eyed, smooth-skinned, pretty. The softness of her figure after two children, rather than making her matronly, only added to the impression of girlish charm.

"Beadall! More sherry for Mrs. Greer." Christa had spied the butler through the parlour door. "And do check with the housekeeper and all the maids again," she called after him. "I shall be furious with you if Mr. Thornfax's card has arrived unnoticed."

My sister may have appeared soft, but five years as Mrs. Daniel Dewhurst, mistress of Hastings House, had not taught Christabel to *be* soft, at least not with servants. Maybe it was because the Dewhursts didn't own the house—it belonged to our widowed aunt, the Countess of Hastings, whose preferred residence was her summer estate in Kew or, when she came to London, her smaller house in Gordon Square— but whatever the reason, my sister played her role to the hilt. Her idea of a ladies' lunch saw everyone in the house scurrying from kitchen to parlour like a parade of ants with her endless demands. The tea wasn't hot enough. Another log on the fire at once: it was positively *freezing* in the parlour. A clean serviette for Mrs. Cauldhame, who'd smeared gravy on hers, and hadn't Christa specifically asked for *white* rolls with the ham? Where was that little portrait of the collie we used to keep at Holybourne, and wasn't there any blackberry sauce for the pudding?

With every glass of lemon cordial the ladies' cheeks had pinked brighter and they'd laughed harder at their own jokes. Mrs. Greer had dropped her spoon on the rug and nearly tipped out of her chair trying to retrieve it.

"Yes, she does very well today. Silent as the Sphinx." Mrs. Cauldhame's chins bulged as her tongue darted out to lick sugar from the corner of her mouth. I thought of the cane toad in the hothouse at Kew Gardens and felt a shiver ladder up my spine.

"Well, but, she must have *some* conversation, mustn't she?" said Mrs. Greer. "Such silence could be taken as … unnatural, could it not?"

I straightened in my chair to stop my corset pinching my ribs. Christabel would dismiss me soon, I thought. It was important for me to be seen, she believed, and not be always tucked away in back rooms like a nasty secret. But she didn't like for me to be noticed too directly.

I was certainly being noticed now. Mrs. Greer said, "Miss Somerville, let us practice, my dear."

Mrs. Cauldhame croaked her approval. "Yes, let us practice with her! Miss Somerville, say after me: 'What light through yonder window breaks?'"

Christabel glared a warning at me. "That will not help," she told them.

"No, I have it," said Mrs. Greer. "Say, 'O Romeo, Romeo! Wherefore art thou Romeo?'"

"Leonora doesn't parrot the words of others," my sister said.

"Mimicry. That is her affliction, is it not?" Mrs. Cauldhame leaned forward so that the vast swaths of her bodice buckled and rolled along her lap. I recognized the look on her face, the same expression I'd seen on the housekeeper's last week: polite concern barely masking curiosity, fascination, and anticipation.

Christa was pale. "Not precisely, Mrs. Cauldhame."

"She stammers, except when she copies after another person's speech," insisted Mrs. Cauldhame. "I had it from Dr. Dewhurst himself, you know, at the Spauldings' dinner last month."

"N-no. I don't p-p-p"—I couldn't manage *parrot* and had to switch to Mrs. Cauldhame's word—"c-copy, not word for w-word."

The woman was partway correct. I did stammer. From earliest memory, in fact, I have suffered from a severe dysfluency of speech. My stuttering was a constant worry to my poor father, whose career in the church was, after all, built upon his skills in public speaking. When I moved to London after his death last winter to be introduced to society, Christabel had had one condition: I was not, under any circumstances, to speak to guests. "Better a wallflower than a crippletongue!" she was ever fond of declaring.

Now my sister stood, turned, and gripped the back of her chair. Her skirts swirled round her legs like water sucked down a drain. For the briefest of moments I imagined she would lift the chair and hurl it, cushion and all, at Mrs. Cauldhame. Or at me.

The butler's return brought us relief just in time. Christa snatched the card from his tray and read it while the ladies watched. Then she ballooned back into her chair, fanned the card at her chest, and sighed.

Beadall tipped the decanter to Mrs. Greer's glass and was dismissed.

"Well?" said Mrs. Greer. "Tell us! Is it as we hoped?"

"Mr. Thornfax is coming to the party," my sister affirmed. "And he sends his regards especially to Miss Somerville, whom he sincerely hopes will be well enough to attend!"

Mrs. Cauldhame snapped her fingers once, twice, thrice, until Christa passed the card to her. She read it and chortled. "Oh, dear Leonora, and in his own hand, too!

Mr. Thornfax could mean very good news for you indeed, I think."

Mrs. Greer emitted a little moan. "That man is an Adonis! I confess, I daren't stand next to him for fear of a swoon."

"Look here, in yesterday's *Examiner*. His profile is featured in the society pages." Too impatient to call Beadall back, Christa bustled to the sideboard herself and swept the newspaper into Mrs. Greer's lap.

Mr. Francis Thornfax was a new business partner of my brother-in-law, Daniel—not a fellow physician but a merchant seaman, returned to London just six months ago from the Orient. He was the only son of a politician of some distinction, the Lord Rosbury, and he was said to have amassed a great fortune importing goods from India and China. Over the last twelve weeks or so Mr. Thornfax had come to dinner at Hastings House twice to dine with the Dewhursts, but had more often visited us casually when he called on Daniel to discuss pharmaceutical supplies for his surgery or details of the new venture they were undertaking.

I was, of course, never allowed to speak to Mr. Thornfax on these occasions. But whenever she'd been given sufficient warning Christa would have me gowned and beribboned and positioned somewhere along the man's sightlines as he traversed the house. And then, at breakfast two days ago, Daniel announced that Mr. Thornfax had asked after me.

"And what did you tell him?" Christa demanded. "Not all, I hope!"

"He wondered why she wasn't engaged," Daniel said, "so I gave him the broad outlines of the thing, yes."

"Dr. Dewhurst! You never did!"

"Thornfax has seen the world, Mrs. Dewhurst. He knows that if a girl as pretty as Leonora sits on the shelf after a whole season in town"—here he patted my hand in apology—"something must be amiss. And he's been home long enough to have heard tales."

My sister groaned. "All my work is ruined. Undone again, as ever."

"I wouldn't give up just yet," Daniel reassured her. "In fact the man was entirely unfazed. Said something along the lines of not giving a fig for society's opinion. He is a lionheart, Francis Thornfax. He might just take her, if only we can get him to stay ashore long enough."

And now Mr. Thornfax had sent his card and would be coming to our party next week.

Mrs. Greer's lips moved silently as she read the newspaper profile. Then she gasped. "Only hark this, Miss Somerville: 'After years of business at sea and abroad, the gentleman is now poised for adventure of a different kind. Mr. Thornfax declares himself intent on settling back in England and raising a family.'"

"Better and better," Mrs. Cauldhame declared. "Just look at the girl! Those rosy cheeks, those wide eyes, that exquisite bosom—she needn't say a word, only smile at him and present her lips to be kissed."

"I would present my lips to him in a heartbeat, if only Mr. Greer would look the other way," Mrs. Greer said, driving her companions into seizures of laughter.

THREE

*Y*es, it was a humiliation to be discussed in such a manner, as if I weren't even in the room, as if I were deaf as well as silent. I'd lived through one social season in London already, so I was well used to humiliations of this kind, but I could not claim complete immunity. And so, hot with embarrassment and clutching my shawl over my *exquisite bosom*, I declined the offer to brave the spring chill and ride up and down Mayfair with the ladies in Mrs. Greer's sociable-carriage. Instead I did my best to hasten the assembly of hats, handbags, rugs, and furs, fetching Christa's shawl from where I'd spied it earlier in the dining room to save her maid Emily another trip upstairs.

Then I loitered by the parlour window, watching in a kind of exhausted relief as the carriage with its pair of high-stepping horses finally circled the drive and disappeared through the front gates. The discarded newspaper lay on the sill, and my eye fell on the name of my maternal cousin Archibald Mavety. Archie was a journalist, I knew—but surely he would never stoop to writing for the society pages!

No, the paper had been folded out of order, and I was looking at an ordinary news column:

Who Is the Black Glove, and What Does It Want of Us?

ARCHIBALD MAVETY, SPECIAL REPORTER

ALL LONDON IS shocked and horrified by the spate of explosions in recent months, violent blasts deliberately engineered to occur in public buildings, at crowded occasions. Each of these attacks is accompanied by a note or a letter claiming that responsibility lies with the BLACK GLOVE. And beyond that: nothing. The letters offer no description of this mysterious entity, no accounting for his actions, no demands, the fulfillment of which might put an end to the violence.

Archie had a tendency to get round to his subject very slowly. My eye skipped farther down the column:

It is a matter of historical record that London and its trade routes were plagued by several powerful and lawless opium gangs in the days before the Treaty of Nanking. Has a similar band of thugs re-emerged to haunt the modern world? Police say there are regular gang-related skirmishes in the city's harder areas, though they cannot, at this time, confirm any arrests of persons confessing to involvement in any of the explosive attacks.

My reading was interrupted by the drumroll of a china plate clattering across the floor and settling, miraculously unbroken, at my feet. I turned to find the housegirl Hattie spread-eagled on the rug.

I called for help but no one answered.

I dropped to my knees beside the girl's head and touched her cheek. "H-Hattie?" I tried. Shadows ringed her closed eyes, and her lips were pale and cracked. I bent my head and waited, my heart thumping, until I was certain I felt her breath on my cheek. She smelled of stale straw and ammonia, a barnyard odour that sent me straight back to the village of Holybourne where I used to play with the other parish children. I took Hattie's hand between my own. The odd thought struck me that she too could have come from such a village, could even have been one of my playmates in the hedgerows and cow-barns.

I didn't realize I'd been holding my breath until Hattie's eyelids fluttered, and I gasped with relief. "Hattie, you've fainted. A-are you h-hurt?"

The girl moaned, coughed a little, and said, "I don' want another dose. I swear it to you, mum. But as soon as I pass my hour I gets so poorly, I haven't strength near to stand."

"I sh-shall find Dr. D-Dewhurst for you," I said.

Her eyes flew open. "No, mum, please! Only hold me here till Tom arrives," she said, and clutched my hand.

"Tom. The d-doctor's boy?" Daniel employed a young man from London's East End named Tom Rampling, two or three years older than myself, who fetched and messaged for him, repaired equipment, and assisted with chemical experiments—but I hadn't realized that Tom treated the patients, too.

"Yes'm. I promised him. He's helping me to ... not to—"

Hattie broke off in a fit of coughing and shivering. Sweat shone over her face.

"I'll f-fetch him at once," I told her.

I found Tom Rampling in the kitchen emptying an armload of kindling into the bin under the stove. He must have cleaned the stove just before refuelling it, because coal dust had soiled his shirt and dulled the dark hair that curled over his collar.

I cleared my throat, and he turned. "What is it, milady?"

I had never spoken to Tom Rampling before. The young man was rarely in the house and never in the rooms I frequented. He worked mostly in Daniel's surgery and more recently in the laboratory the doctor had set up in Mr. Thornfax's warehouse on the Thames. I was surprised by his deep, gentle voice and the solemn way he regarded me. His eyes were closer to grey than blue, the colour of a winter sky. My words died in my throat.

He crossed over to me. "Are you well?" he said, softer still, as though I were a bird he might frighten away.

I recalled myself. Naturally Tom Rampling would have heard of my affliction and would approach with care. "H-Hattie," I said, and I motioned him to follow me.

He stopped at the parlour door and frowned at the servant girl's prone form. Hattie seemed to have fallen back into a doze. Tom dug two sooty fingers into his breast pocket and pulled out a folded apothecary envelope. "Give her this, please, milady."

Inside were several white pellets. "M-morphine pills?"

A harsh sound from Tom's throat drew my gaze to his face, which had hardened into a sudden scowl. "You're quick enough to recognize it," he said. "A common remedy in your family, I'm sure."

I stared at him, unable to account for this shift into rudeness. "My father t-took it for his p-pain, before he d-died," I tried to explain. "But Hattie needs food. B-broth, cocoa."

He didn't seem to notice the stumbling of my words. "Hattie needs *this*. And she needs it soon." Tom looked down at his soot-covered boots as if he were considering whether to take them off or walk across the parlour rug in spite of them and dose Hattie himself.

"Please, c-call Dr. Dewhurst. He will know what to d-do."

"No."

"P-pardon?"

Tom crossed his arms. "I won't call him."

"V-very well then, I sh-shall." I moved toward him, expecting he would step back at once and let me out of the room. Instead, at the last moment, Tom raised an arm to block my exit, and I flinched back from a collision only just in time. My skirts swished against his shins.

Tom's long, tapered fingers made a print where they pressed on the wallpaper. He smelled of woodsmoke and blacking. My mouth dried, and my heart beat faster at his audacity in defying a mistress of the house. If he hadn't seemed so worried for Hattie I would have suspected him of baiting me, of trying purposely to upset me like the stable-boys at Holybourne used to do in hopes I would amuse them with one of my outbursts.

I watched Tom's throat move as he swallowed. The grey eyes searched my face. "Miss Somerville, please. Not him, of all people. Not now." He sounded somehow impatient and afraid at once.

I shook my head; he wasn't making sense. But in any case I found that speech had deserted me again and—more confusing still—I could not seem to wrench my gaze away from Tom Rampling's face. The fine planes of his brow, his cheekbones, his jaw—the pale skin wasn't sallow but warm, as if he were somehow illuminated from within. His nearness heated my skin like fireglow.

"Please," he repeated, and blinked and shifted his stance. His free hand came up to brush aside a strand of my hair. I was shocked at the touch, but this time I knew he wasn't baiting me. In fact I had the impression that Tom hardly realized what he was doing.

"You forget yourself," I said, at last. I didn't stammer, exactly, but my voice carried none of the sternness I intended.

Tom blinked again, frowned, and swiped at my cheek with his sleeve. "I've gone and smudged you," he muttered.

"Rampling, where are you?" My brother-in-law's voice boomed out from the hall behind us. Tom dropped his arm, stepping back from me just as Daniel's portly form rounded the corner. "Ah, there you are!" His brows shot up at his assistant's soiled clothing, and he *tsk*ed. "Have you been at the stove again? What have I told you about doing that girl's work for her?"

"Hattie's taken poorly, Dr. Dewhurst," Tom reported, so smoothly and levelly that I wondered if I'd entirely imagined his rebellion of the previous two minutes. "Miss Somerville found her and called for help."

Daniel crossed the room and bent over to press his thick

fingers to Hattie's sternum. "Well, well." He puffed, struggling upright again. "Pick her up, Mr. Rampling, if you don't
mind, and convey our poor girl to the surgery."

"At once, sir."

My brother-in-law patted my shoulder. His smile pressed
deeper dimples into his round red cheeks. "Now don't
frighten yourself, Leonora. Hattie will be restored by teatime,
I assure you."

I returned Daniel's smile, but my reassurance was
shattered when I happened to glance back at Tom Rampling
gathering Hattie's limp form into his arms. I met in those
grey eyes so thunderous an expression that for a moment it
was hard to draw breath, and I was filled with a disquiet I did
not understand.

FOUR

My father had been the minister at the Church of the Holy Rood in Holybourne, a small village fifty miles from London. Growing up at the manse Christabel and I lived comfortably but never lavishly. Father's dear old valet doubled as our butler and carriage-driver, and after we girls outgrew Mrs. Dawson, our nurse, we kept only one regular maid in addition to the cook. In my last years at Holybourne after Christa was married, whenever Father felt well enough for his parishioners to come to dine, it had fallen to me to oversee the turning out of rugs and drapes, the choosing of a menu, and the ordering of a vintage appropriate to the occasion. Now that I lived with my sister and her family at Hastings House my tasks were vastly simpler. In fact I had only one duty: to stand still and submit to being dressed and tressed to Christabel's satisfaction by the maids.

This occupation, light in description, was nevertheless burdensome in execution, as it consumed the better part of the week leading to my sister's card party. A ball was too extravagant for March, Christa and her friends had decided. Better to force Mr. Thornfax to court me at a casual evening of card-playing, where the music wouldn't overwhelm the conversation. Besides, they'd reasoned, Christa would have to invite every young lady of our acquaintance to a ball, and a gentleman new to the circle would feel obliged to dance with each one of them in turn. At a card party we might have Mr. Thornfax to ourselves.

Christabel had yanked from the wardrobe all of my gowns from last season and heaved them, one by one, across my bed. She'd wiped the glow of exertion from her brow and grimaced at the jumble of criss-crossed pastels. The deflated dresses looked to me like disappointed young maidens, crossed in love or unsuccessful in seduction, wilted and jilted. Well that was me, wasn't it, despite my sister's—and my wardrobe's—best efforts last year? Still husbandless.

Looking at the pile of silks I'd sent a silent plea out to Mr. Thornfax. Marriage to a man like that would mean independence, status, and a home of my own. More importantly it would mean invisibility, and therefore freedom from society's constant gossip and judgment. *Be as stout-hearted and bold as Daniel says you are*, I prayed, *not like the others. Take me, even if I should shock you.*

Within an hour the seamstress and her assistants had arrived to tear the pile apart and refashion the outdated gowns with lower waists and necklines. Fewer bows and more buckles, Christabel ordered. Less lace and more ruffled-ribbon trim. All week, whenever I was not standing on a box with my arms extended at my sides, strung with tapes and stabbed with pins, I was slumped before the mirror in

Christa's dressing room as the maids experimented on my hair with heated irons and starch spray.

As my physical appearance was so central to my purpose at Hastings House, I do not think it would be too immodest for me to describe it as it was finally shown to me, there in the looking glass, on the evening of the party. The gown Christabel had chosen for me was pine-coloured crepe de Chine with cream ribbon at the neck and waist. She claimed the green matched my eyes, but in truth they tend more toward hazel. My brown hair was brushed to its best shine, coiled, pinned, and adorned with a silk blossom. Cream-coloured gloves, silk slippers, and a string of pearls from our mother's jewel box completed the ensemble. For my part I was quite satisfied with how it all looked.

But my sister came in behind me, peered over my shoulder into the mirror, and frowned. "Ugh. You look positively common, Leo." Her nose wrinkled. "Bess! Come tighten her stays!" So I was undone and retied until my ribs ached within the restrictive undergarment. Christa adjusted my décolletage herself. "Oh, do stop blushing like a child! Your bust is your best feature, you know, and you had better make the most of it. Lord knows poor Thornfax won't get his fill in conversation. The least we can do is to offer him something to look at."

"I can s-speak to him," I said. "Dr. D-Dewhurst said he won't mind."

We were interrupted by my nephews' nurse, Greta, who had brought Christabel's little boys round to bid good night to their mama and auntie. Three-year-old Bertie had been allowed to sample some of the treats our cook was preparing for the party and was now very sulky about not being permitted to stay up with the "big people." Greta held baby Alexander for us while we kissed his cheeks, so that we would not wrinkle our gowns.

When we were alone again Christa reached out and flicked my lips with her fingernails, surprising me into a squeak of pain. "You will *not* speak to Mr. Thornfax," she said, "no matter what Daniel might have said. Keep your stumbletongue to yourself until he falls thoroughly in love with you. Then it will seem to him nothing but a charming quirk."

"He is s-stout-hearted. He w-won't mind."

"You listen to me, Leo!" She pinched my chin hard between her thumb and forefinger. "Dr. Dewhurst has managed to broker Mr. Thornfax's interest. In his great generosity to you, Dr. Dewhurst has argued the advantages of becoming brothers as well as business partners. But that is all. You and I both know how easily it will crumble if you fail to keep a handle on yourself." Christabel pushed herself from the vanity and brandished the hairbrush at my reflection like a club. "I swear to you, sister, I will cut your tongue from your mouth if you let Mimic attend this party!"

Stumbletongue, Gargle, Crippletongue, Mutemouth— none of my sister's names for me was ever uttered with quite the same ire and revulsion as Mimic.

I knew Christa hated Mimic, and to be perfectly fair to my elder sister there were times Mimic had made her life very miserable indeed. Embarrassed her before her friends. Tattled on her, thwarted her plans. Scared off potential suitors—in fact one young man she'd liked very much had had to be sent away from our house thanks to Mimic's interference. More recently, of course, it was my own suitors who tended to bolt. Last spring a nice young gentleman named Mr. Greenlove had frequented Hastings House until the afternoon Mimic made an appearance. Mr. Kelso and, disastrously, the Duke of Manchester had similarly been driven off. Christabel's only consolation was that the fine scruples of these gentlemen had ensured that news of Mimic's existence had not travelled far beyond our household. Of course, there were always a few ladies—Christabel's friends, mostly—who made it their business to know our troubles.

My aunt Emmaline, the Countess of Hastings, had a very large fortune. The knowledge that Christa and I were her only heirs was widespread enough to guarantee that more young men would emerge from the woodwork to call. But as my sister was fond of reminding me, "Madness will take the shine off gold." Where Mimic reigned neither fortune nor beauty would be enough to secure me a spouse.

For now at least, Christabel had evidently finished with the whole subject. Emily had brought her a glass of water and her little bottle of laudanum, the opium tincture that Daniel prepared specially for her frequent headaches. Christa squeezed the rubber bulb, her lips moving as she silently counted out the correct number of drops into her glass.

As she drank it down her eyes caught mine in the mirror, and she turned to squint closer at my face. "Freckles? Oh, Leo," she wailed, "'tis only March! Why do you insist on walking without your parasol?"

She ordered Bess back to powder my nose again. Next came rouge for my lips and cheeks. Then pearl ear-bobs, a smart little silk hat from her own collection instead of the

flower, a dab of rose scent on each wrist, and a lace handkerchief folded into the cuff of my glove.

"Now you are a town lady, at last!" Christa sighed. "Look
there, what a pretty parcel for an eligible gentleman!"

I looked in the mirror. There was no denying my sister's
artistry. I was ivory-pale—except for my bosom, still reddened
from Christa's tugging. I looked a good deal older than my
seventeen years.

How do you do, Miss Somerville? I greeted myself. This
Miss Somerville was indeed a parcel of sorts—an empty box,
or a blank page for someone to write his fantasies upon. I
swallowed. How easy it had been to assemble the costume
and don the mask. How easy then it should be to play this
role. Only my eyes seemed overly shiny, my pupils dilated—
whether from dread or excitement I could not say.

Christabel insisted I stay upstairs until called so that my
entrance would make a bigger impression. I chose a novel
from the drawer of my bureau, but I was too nervous to
concentrate on the story and instead found myself staring out
my window at the lights of Daniel's surgery. A candle flickering on one of the sills lit the face of a young boy looking
at a picture book. My brother-in-law saw his patients in a
converted carriage house directly across the courtyard behind
the house. The main consulting room doubled as a surgery
where he performed minor medical procedures. Upstairs, in
a loft reached by a spiral staircase, beds were laid out for those
who had no place else to recover.

I'd spied the same small boy just yesterday being chased
by Tom Rampling. The boy had darted out the surgery door
and tried to outrun the doctor's assistant. Perhaps Daniel was

treating him for some illness—though judging by his vivacity, I thought, he must be well on the mend already.

Tom had caught him up, twirled him round, and tickled his ribs until he shrieked with laughter. A broad grin had transformed Tom's face from its cool seriousness to something entirely new—a radiance, a warmth—that made me remember by contrast the frowning disdain he'd shown me during our confrontation in the parlour.

At last Bess came to fetch me downstairs.

"Ah, there you are, Leonora!" Christa trumpeted as I crossed the threshold into the Great Hall. The gentlemen within earshot rose from their seats at the card tables, and I curtsied in answer to their bows. Only a small number of the guests were actually playing at whist. The idea of a card party was to circulate, gossip, and flirt—and anyhow half the ladies' gowns were too elaborate for comfortable sitting.

My sister led me round the room for hasty introductions to the newcomers on our guest list. The Fayerweathers, an elderly couple recently returned from Bath, remarked on how well I'd grown since they'd last dined at Holybourne. Mrs. Fayerweather had a beaked nose under her swooping, wide-brimmed hat and a voice that reminded me of the chatter of squirrels. I must have been very young when the Fayerweathers visited Holybourne, for I had no memory of the woman. After she'd reminisced about our "poor dear mother, God rest her, and curse the scarlet fever, and you poor dears were only such tiny things when she was taken," Christa moved us along to Dr. Johnstone, a surgeon friend of Daniel's.

Once we'd exchanged the usual niceties, he and my brother-in-law resumed the conversation they'd been having before our interruption. "Have you solved your dosage problem then?" Dr. Johnstone inquired.

"It's complicated," said Daniel. "The strength of the drug appears to depend in part on the patient's emotional state, and even the location at which it's administered."

Dr. Johnstone frowned. "An environmental factor? That doesn't sound like morphine at all. Which solvent have you been using to purify it?"

Daniel chuckled. "No, you won't fiddle it out of me that easily! How can I hope to win a patent if I give up the formula to every medical man who asks me?"

Dr. Johnstone's face fell, but he covered it by giving Daniel a congenial slap on the back. "If I were you I'd forget the patent and start selling at once. A bright label, a romantic name—that's all you really need! 'Dewhurst's Celestial Dew' or some such."

Daniel shook his head. "Any middling chemist can glue a label on a bottle. This is different, Johnstone. It will put all the cordials and nostrums out of the market entirely. Cheaper to produce, four or five times more powerful. No ill effects on digestion, no wasting or prolonged stupor—"

"So you've claimed, so you've claimed," said Dr. Johnstone. "Well, we are all standing by with bated breath, Doctor."

"Mr. Thornfax! You approach us at last!" Christa's greeting was amplified by her relief at the opportunity to change the subject.

Daniel threaded his arm through the taller man's. "Thornfax. Back me up, will you? Johnstone here insists that securing a patent is a waste of our time."

"I'm afraid I couldn't speak to that, one way or another," Mr. Thornfax said, smiling round our circle. "My expertise lies rather on the supply side of the equation—the raw materials, so to speak." He reached past Dr. Johnstone to clasp Christabel's hand and bent to kiss it. "My radiant hostess."

Christa giggled and, when he released her, leaned her head against Daniel's arm. Her husband patted her hair and bent to kiss her pink cheek.

"So it *is* a derivative of opium, if that man has a hand in the enterprise!" Dr. Johnstone crowed.

Still Mr. Thornfax ignored him. "And her fair sister," he murmured, taking my hand in turn. "Good evening, Miss Somerville."

Francis Gabriel Thornfax. An angel's name, I thought, for an angel's visage. My sister's friends had not been overstating the gentleman's handsomeness. Mr. Thornfax had clear blue eyes and honey-coloured hair framing his strong-boned, open face. He towered over the other men in the room, and his broad shoulders filled out his tailcoat most becomingly. He was twenty-eight years old and by all accounts rich as a prince.

"Are you boring the ladies again with your pharmaceutical prattle?" he teased the doctors.

"Oh, mercy, yes. Do make them stop, sir!" Christa said, clasping her hands and casting her eyes heavenward. "Tell us of pirates in the Orient. Or shipwreck!" she breathed.

"Shipwreck's a tender subject for you these days, isn't it, Thornfax?" Dr. Johnstone interjected.

Mr. Thornfax met the man's gaze at last. He arched an eyebrow. "'Twasn't a wreck, exactly. But if you call the loss of a vessel worth fifteen thousand pounds 'tender,' then yes, I suppose it is."

My sister paled. "Did you lose a ship? Oh, I didn't mean to make a joke of it."

"Not at all, not at all," Mr. Thornfax assured her. "A chemical explosion at sea. It was the crew I mourned, of course, more than the ship. Some of my finest men."

"Nitroglycerin, as I heard it," said Dr. Johnstone. "What the devil were you doing transporting that stuff after all the reports of its destructiveness? Dewhurst, I hope *you* weren't behind it. That compound's effectiveness on heart patients is still a matter of some debate, you know. Certainly not worth risking human lives in the procurement!"

My brother-in-law frowned and was about to make a retort when Mr. Thornfax put a hand on his shoulder and said, "I agree, Johnstone. The sacrifices we make for science are not to be treated lightly, nor in casual conversation.

"Now that is enough of ill fortune!" he continued. "Miss Somerville looks positively parched. I will not rest until I have seen her safely glass in hand." He offered me his arm and led me away from the two men and my beaming sister.

We drew many admiring glances as we crossed the room together. I was glad for his suggestion of something to drink. It was a distraction, and I should be able to hum wordless agreement over my glass in response to everything my companion said. But Mr. Thornfax stopped me just short of the punch table and bent his golden head to mine. "You know, Miss Somerville," he murmured, "it occurred to me just now that I've never had the pleasure of hearing your part in a conversation. I thought I had better pry you away from your charming chatterbox of a sister."

I leaned away, offering him my most winning smile, but my stomach clenched in alarm.

"What do you think of the party?" Mr. Thornfax offered, by way of an invitation.

I stared at his handsome, expectant face and saw no cunning or ill will, no intention to test the affliction of which Daniel had warned him. Yet Christa had ordered me not to stammer or not to speak at all. Frantically I tried to conjure an answer containing none of the syllables that typically tripped me up. As I knew from bitterest experience, though, there were no safe syllables when I was put on the spot. I withdrew my hand from Mr. Thornfax's elbow and brushed an invisible wrinkle from my skirt.

He peered into my face. "Are you well, Miss Somerville?" Helpless, mute, I shook my head.

He took my gloved hand in his. "Please do not be uneasy with me. I wish you to be just yourself, you see." His voice, as I'd noted before on his visits to Hastings, was a most pleasing baritone, all modulated refinement on the surface but suggestive, too, of untapped depth and power. Up close, pitched for my ears alone, it put me in mind of the sound a lion might make when he was choosing not to roar. A tawny purr, in which Mr. Thornfax now said to me, "I believe in seeing things for myself, Miss Somerville. 'Tis the only way to discern fact from fantasy on any subject. Would you not agree?"

But here? In public? I sensed all eyes upon us. I knew as well as my sister did that everyone at this party had high hopes of a scene, hopes fuelled by vague and fantastical rumours of my madness and uncontrollability. Everyone watched, and everyone probably hoped I would flee Mr. Thornfax, or scream at him, or be sick on his shoes, or sprawl at his feet like poor Hattie.

"Are you quite all right?" he said again.

"Quite, sir. But I'm wary of refreshment, lest I should burst my stays!" No hesitation, no stuttering marred my statement.

Mr. Thornfax blinked.

"If you could only see the architecture that holds me inside this gown. 'Tis a marvel of modern engineering." Not a single syllable was out of place.

Another blink. "You ... you sound exactly like Mrs. Dewhurst," he observed.

"You flatter me, sir. But do remember that I am *much* younger than my dear sister. Cleverer too, I daresay, though I'll thank you not to tell her I said so."

He stared, then broke into a laugh and made me a short bow. "Younger and cleverer: noted and committed to memory." He stepped back and looked me up and down in frank appreciation. "Prettier too, since we are speaking truth for the record. I am a great admirer of your ... architecture. And I'm very glad to have met you properly at last!"

But Mr. Thornfax hadn't met me, of course. He'd met Mimic.

FIVE

*M*imic had leapt in to rescue me from trouble. She'd allowed me to adopt my sister's voice and manners wholesale, so that I could say whatever Christabel would say—or whatever I might imagine her to say—in precisely the way Christabel would have said it.

When I am particularly uncomfortable or anxious about my stutter, I sometimes fall into mimicry of another person's voice, and the stuttering disappears. I know not how I perform this mimicry so perfectly, nor why my tongue can untangle itself in other voices but never in my own. Neither do I have perfect control over when, or whom, I imitate. It could be a voice heard long ago, words long forgotten but suddenly recalled somehow and rearranged to suit the occasion. It is this unpredictability that had prompted Christabel, when we were still small girls at Holybourne, to personify my phenomenon and name her "Mimic," as though my speech were governed by a mischievous devil or evil sprite quite under its own power.

I was relieved that this time at least Mimic had chosen an imitation that made sense. Christa and I were siblings raised in the same house. It wasn't impossible our voices should bear a resemblance, even if it was an uncanny one. I was lucky this time. Mimic could just as easily have taken on Bess's country manners, or the dressmaker's foreign accent, or the street cant of a nameless beggar I'd passed on the sidewalk without consciously noticing.

At the refreshment table Mr. Thornfax chose grapes and gooseberries for me, and a little cake with soft cheese. Mimic continued in easy conversation with him, veering only briefly into the voice of a fat woman standing behind us in the queue for the punch bowl and then, luckily, landing on Christa again. A keen glance my way was the only sign that Mr. Thornfax had noticed.

When we rejoined my sister, though, I had to bite down hard on my tongue to keep her from discovering me. Even if I considered Mimic's presence a rescue, I knew that Christa would consider it a travesty.

"Such enthusiasm for charity, even I cannot keep track of it all," she was saying to a group of ladies. "To some of his urchins he even offers employment if they are well enough. You might see our Hattie about, or young Will at your carriage step. Dr. Dewhurst loves them practically as much as his own little sons!" One of Christabel's favourite topics in company was her husband's doctoring of London's penniless classes. "'Tis a strain on our resources, but what is our purpose on this earth except to ease the suffering of those less fortunate?"

"Leonora! There you are." I turned to see my cousin Archibald Mavety, a short, neat man with thinning blond hair and a snub nose. Tonight Archie had dressed with characteristic flamboyance in checked trousers and an orange silk cravat.

Risking rudeness I turned my back on Christa's circle and lowered my voice—Mimic's voice—to introduce him to Mr. Thornfax. Archie quirked his brows at me when he recognized my sister's way of speaking, but he had the good grace not to comment for the moment.

"Mr. Francis Thornfax," he said instead, clasping my companion's hand. "You are the son of Charles Thornfax, the Lord Rosbury, are you not?"

"Indeed," replied Mr. Thornfax with a polite smile.

Archie grinned at me and narrowed his eyes at Mr. Thornfax. "And are you as stout in your conservatism as that honourable gentleman?"

Mr. Thornfax's smile faded a bit. I inched the men away from my sister. Christabel would fly into hysterics if she heard our cousin goading Mr. Thornfax in this way.

Archie waved his hand. "I am a journalist, sir. 'Tis my professional duty to know who's who in the House of Lords. Rosbury spoke just this week against the campaign to stop importing opium into England. 'An economic impossibility,' he called it. For him 'tis all a question of profits, of supply and demand. For him the thuggish violence, the public menace posed by drug gangs like the Black Glove, doesn't even signify!"

"Are you quoting to us from one of your own articles?" Mr. Thornfax said, frowning. Then he glanced at me and his face relaxed. "Mavety, is it? I see you do know your business. But in that case I'm sure you're already aware that I do not share my father's politics. Or his companionship, for that matter." His face wore that easy, open smile again, and it was impossible to say whether the mocking edge in his voice was directed at himself or at my cousin.

"Are you saying, then, that you would *support* an opium ban?" Archie persisted. "Even if it meant an end to your profits as an importer?"

Enough was enough. "Pray excuse us cousins for just a moment, sir," I said, and marched Archie halfway across the room. "What are you doing? Leave him alone, won't you? You don't even know him."

"What are *you* doing?" Archie shot back, poking me playfully in the shoulder. "You should leave Christabel's voice alone. It doesn't suit you at all."

Mimic pulled forth Christa's best whine: "Don't be so cruel, Cousin. I deserve your support if I deserve anyone's, do I not?"

Archie gave a theatrical shudder. "Do stop, Leo. It's absolutely terrifying. Can't you find a nice Frenchwoman or—I know what! Do Mary Mathilda. How I loved your Welsh accent!"

Archie was teasing me. He knew I couldn't call up a voice on purpose like that, not at his convenience or at mine. Mary Mathilda had been my aunt Emmaline's chambermaid when we were younger. When I was ten years old, staying with my aunt at her Kew estate, my cousin was expelled from Cambridge for something he'd written in the student newspaper. Aunt Emma had invited him to stay for the summer, and I spent many a happy day with Archie riding round in the pony trap, frogging in the pond, and building signal fires in the fields. We even put on plays for Aunt Emma—my role mostly pantomime, of course—using the scripts she'd saved from her time as a stage actress at the Adelphi Theatre. Archie knew all Mimic's tricks—knew the entire panoply of voices through which I might cycle in the course of an ordinary day of play and adventure.

I cast a glance round the party, taking in the lace, the jewels, and the high-piled French hairstyles. Nobody was staring at me for the moment. Dr. Johnstone was now seated at a card table, engaged in some heated debate about the rules of the game. Mrs. Fayerweather was laughing at something Mr. Greer had said to her, her broad-brimmed hat flapping so wildly that a nearby gentleman leaned away in alarm. Still dismay seeped through me. It was all very well for Archie to love Mimic: my cousin had early declared his intention never to marry, never to bend to society's rules. His dream was to travel the world, speaking always in the name of what he called journalistic freedom and truth.

But Archie was right about me, too. I wasn't suited to this. I couldn't possibly bring it off. At best I was a fool in motley, a jester with his bag of amusements, speaking nonsense. At worst I was a madwoman. What I could never hope to be was a lady. My extravagant gown, the paint and powder—I felt as if the mask were slipping, leaving me stripped bare, naked and defenceless as a babe.

My cousin must have read the plummeting of my spirits on my face, for his own expression softened, and he wrapped a supportive arm about my shoulders. "Oh, go on; you're fine. No one suspects a thing. But later I demand an audience with Miss Somerville. I'm never sure you're listening when you're like this."

"I am listening," I assured him. "Only don't alienate

Mr. Thornfax. He'll have plenty of other reasons to flee my side soon enough."

Archie clucked his tongue. "The sooner the better, in my opinion. Francis Thornfax is a regular pirate! D'you know he scuppered his own ship when they tried to seize his opium in Hong Kong?"

"I understood it was an accident," I said primly. Archie Mavety was always in possession of different information than the rest of the world, and he always interpreted the facts in the worst possible light—the better to sell his newspapers, he'd once confessed to me without a hint of shame. The more success he achieved as a reporter, the more I learned to take his wild tales of conspiracy and murder with a grain of salt.

"Well, 'tis no accident he's zeroed in on you, Leo. You look positively delectable tonight." Archie tweaked one of my curls so that it sprang back against my neck. "Is your sister's plan to have Thornfax propose to you or to swallow you whole? Look there, how the man glares at me for commandeering you!"

I made a point of *not* looking over at Mr. Thornfax. "Stop your pestering, Archibald. You should learn to be happy even when you don't happen to be the centre of attention."

"Careful! That's the Lady Hastings, not Mrs. Dewhurst," Archie laughed.

"Oh, d-d-damn," I stuttered, and blushed scarlet. He was right. In chiding my cousin, and perhaps in remembering my fond history with him, Mimic had shifted to the regal tones of Aunt Emmaline. I shook my head and dug my nails into my palms, desperate to silence myself.

"Anyhow, I'll give you your point: Thornfax takes up too much space in the room for my liking." Archie sighed and patted my shoulder. "'Tisn't fair that any man should be that dashing *and* that rich! Here he comes," he warned, nodding toward Mr. Thornfax with a good imitation of friendliness.

By the time Archie left me alone with my suitor again, I'd recovered from Mimic's lapse.

"'Tis stuffy in here, don't you find?" said Mr. Thornfax. His hand was warm upon my elbow. "Mightn't we escape to fresher air? Your sister suggests the plum court would be pleasant on a mild evening like this."

Never too soon to throw us together, is it, Christa? I thought. Still I had to admire Mr. Thornfax's poise in taking up my sister's unsubtle hints without betraying any awareness of her overeagerness.

The courtyard between the main house and Daniel's consulting rooms was dominated by a solitary, ancient plum tree. The sheltered site had encouraged the tree to an unnatural stature. Tonight its budding branches screened out the moon, throwing a dense thatch of shadow across the cobbles. The yellow square that marked the surgery window seemed very far away, and none of the party noises reached us this far past the kitchens. It was indeed a mild night, but I shivered anyhow at the sudden darkness and silence.

Mr. Thornfax slipped out of his coat and placed it over my shoulders. I breathed his scent of leather and tobacco, and from under my lashes allowed myself to admire the sculptural hollows between his jaw and the white wing-collar of his shirt.

"I hope I have not made you uncomfortable with my directness concerning your difficulties with speech," he said.

I shook my head. It was all the staring and whispering that made me uncomfortable, all the sympathetic patting of my hand and the exaggerated kindness of tone that made me feel like a leper or an especially slow schoolchild. Mr. Thornfax's directness was an unprecedented relief.

"I called on the Lady Hastings last week to discuss the matter. I know it was rash"—he looked at me sidelong, ducking his head in a charming gesture of apology that made me smile—"but I understood from Dr. Dewhurst that I'd need to meet with the countess's approval in any case, if I'm to have a chance at your hand."

"N-now that *is* d-direct," I said. Joy fluttered like a flag within me at this forthright statement of his intentions.

I saw Mr. Thornfax pause, noting how I had stuttered, how my voice had changed—for it was my own voice now, lower and less strident than Christabel's. Then he continued as if nothing had happened. "If I am direct 'tis nothing compared to your aunt. She was rather short with me, I thought."

I bit my lip. Aunt Emmaline had an irritating habit of telling people precisely what was on her mind. And unlike my sister the countess was in no great hurry to see me married. She had herself been married at sixteen and widowed at twenty-five. I'd heard her say she wished she'd had a chance to know herself before knowing a husband. But Aunt Emma knew that my situation was exceptionally difficult, and she'd promised Christabel she wouldn't stand in the way of a marriage if the man was suitable. "What did she s-say?" I managed.

"She was of the opinion that there was no point in her bothering to become further acquainted with me until you were sure of me."

"Unt-til I was sure of you," I repeated. Was that a smile tugging at the corners of Mr. Thornfax's mouth? Was he laughing at me? It was too dark to be certain.

"Yes. She was quite clear about it. I was bold enough to inquire how such a condition could be ascertained, and she suggested I ask you directly."

I felt very warm. Was he about to make a proposal?

"Are you?" he said, and touched my hand.

"W-what?"

"Sure of me." He was definitely smiling now. I could hear it in his voice.

Of course I am sure! I wanted to shout. What could Aunt Emma possibly have been thinking? *Only* look *at the man*, I wanted to tell her. Francis Thornfax was the delivering angel I'd longed for, the shining knight come at last to my rescue. I'd hardly dared hope that Daniel might be right—that Mr. Thornfax might not mind my deficiencies, that he might be immune to society's disapproval. And now that I'd heard, from the man himself, this confirmation of his interest in me? The darkness barred me from a clear view of his beautiful face, those guileless blue eyes, and that full, shapely smile— and I was grateful for the darkness. I felt I might say anything, do anything!

"I presume the Lady Hastings had in mind your feelings," he spurred me gently. "Would you share them with me?"

"I … I f-feel—" I stopped. *Happy* was not precisely the word Mr. Thornfax would expect, nor was *hopeful* quite right.

He was asking what I felt about him, toward him, as a person. It occurred to me that I'd never honestly considered what I thought of Mr. Thornfax as a person. I'd been too preoccupied with not frightening him away.

I saw Mr. Thornfax hesitate and draw back from me, squaring his shoulders in case my answer wasn't what he was hoping. I might disappoint him yet, I thought, panic seizing me.

"Surely you've heard the old proverb," Mimic improvised, raising my face to his. "A man might know the possibility of a woman but never her sum." They were my aunt Emma's words, but I had uttered them in the husky, sensual voice of the actress who played Salomé last June at the Royal Theatre.

A sudden, bright light from the surgery lit Mr. Thornfax's confused expression before the thwack of the door closing threw us back into darkness. A beat of silence followed. Then a solid weight slammed into my side and knocked me clear off my feet.

Mr. Thornfax swore in surprise. He managed to catch me round the waist only just in time to stop my fall.

Tom Rampling stumbled at the impact too, and he grabbed my arm, hopping awkwardly to steady himself. "I'm so sorry, sir! I am—" Hatless, barefoot, with his shirt cuffs rolled past his elbows, he broke off and stared when he saw it was me he'd run down. "Milady. Oh, no! You should go inside at once!"

"What's the m-matter?" I asked him.

He gasped, "The doctor!" Then he wheeled and continued at a full run toward the house.

"Rampling!" Mr. Thornfax shouted after him but got no response. "Are you injured, Miss Somerville? That was a poor apology from the boy indeed. I shall speak to him about it."

"No, p-p-please don't." I caught myself: Why should I defend Tom Rampling? "One of Dr. D-Dewhurst's patients, no doubt, is in need of m-medical attention."

Mr. Thornfax picked up his coat, which had been knocked to the ground, and smoothed it back over my shoulders. "Your brother-in-law keeps a great many of his patients here about the house, doesn't he?" he said. He led me deeper into the tree's shadowy wreath. Lifting my hand and turning it palm up, he traced my bare forearm with his fingers. "And you, Miss Somerville? Are you one of his experimental subjects? Have you too benefited from his findings?"

"I d-don't know what you m-mean." Mr. Thornfax's touch was gentle as could be, his tone teasing, yet I quaked with uncertainty and sudden, unaccountable shame. When I first came to Hastings House, Daniel had suggested a daily dose of morphine for my stammering. My aunt had overruled him, citing the various opiate treatments I'd already undergone, without good results, as a child. But I sensed that morphine therapy was not exactly the "findings" Mr. Thornfax meant.

He held my chin and tipped my face up to his. I could not make out the expression in his eyes. "No, I see that you don't know what I mean." He turned my hand over again and touched his lips to my gloved knuckles. "I am glad of it. I want you kept out"—another swift, light kiss—"kept pure. I made that clear to him."

The black net of plum branches expanded overhead, and it seemed to my confused senses that it threatened to ensnare us. I pressed a hand to the tree trunk for support, but its surface pulsed and tilted under my touch. Evidently I had not recovered from Tom's collision with me.

"... not five minutes after you left, sir. I swear to you, I tried everything in my power to revive her. You should not have left her!" Tom's words from just beyond the shadows were breathless, frantic.

"Lower your voice, boy!" my brother-in-law huffed, trying to keep pace. Light poured into the courtyard once again from the surgery door flung open. Just beyond the threshold someone—a girl—lay unmoving on the floor.

Mr. Thornfax and I hurried across the yard to see what was wrong.

Kneeling over the fallen girl, Daniel took his stethoscope from Tom and pressed it to her chest. I ducked inside the door and saw that it was Hattie lying there, her face white as chalk, her legs splayed under her skirts.

After a minute of tense silence Daniel shook his head.

Startled by a sudden, high-pitched wail I looked up to see the small boy from the courtyard cowering behind the spiral staircase. Tom's woollen cap was perched backward over the boy's forehead, and his wan face was streaked with tears.

"Be quiet, Will," Daniel told him, but the wailing only got louder. "Take him upstairs, Rampling; he'll raise the neighbourhood." Daniel turned and saw us in the doorway. "Oh, good, Thornfax. Here—help me move the body."

Mr. Thornfax stepped past me to assist the doctor. He took hold of Hattie's wrists, and Daniel grasped her ankles.

"Sorry, mum! I'm so sorry!" Hattie's voice—or rather, Mimic's voice, speaking as Hattie—rang out, freezing Tom on the stairs and cutting off young Will mid-sob. "It's just as I'm so poorly, I haven't near the strength to stand!"

All heads swivelled my way. Mr. Thornfax dropped Hattie's arms and shot to my side. I watched Tom start back down the stairs, too, his knuckles white on the railing and his eyes fixed on me.

Mimic warmed to the role, infusing a weary, regretful note into Hattie's voice: "I don't want another dose, I swear it to you. But as soon as I'm past the hour I gets so sick!"

"Miss Somerville, what ails you?" Mr. Thornfax looked from me to Daniel. "Is this one of her fits, Dewhurst?"

I tried not to look down at Hattie again, but I couldn't help myself. In death the girl's face had become almost pretty, the features softening and the lashes of the closed eyes sweeping a delicate shadow above each cheekbone. *The peace that passeth all understanding be upon you.* My father's weekly blessing from the pulpit was perverse given the cold tiled floor and the indignity of Hattie's sprawled position. I bit my lips but could not stop talking. "Have mercy, mum!" Mimic-as-Hattie moaned. "Only hold me here till Tom arrives. I promised him. He's 'elping me."

Tom stood before me, and I was startled to see tears on his ashen cheeks. "Forgive me, Hattie," he quavered. "It was my fault, not yours!" His hands came up to clasp my shoulders.

Dr. Dewhurst spun him round by the arm. "Be quiet, Thomas. For pity's sake, that's not your dead girl!"

"It's Hattie haunting her, sir. I'm sure of it!"

"Nonsense. Miss Somerville mimics those she hears in this life, not in the next. Leonora, leave it off at once! Go on now. Go up to bed at once."

"Dear Tom," I said. "My dear, dear Tom." Then I turned and fled for the house.

I heard Tom shout my name, and his muffled footfalls on the stones behind me, and my brother-in-law calling him back. I didn't stop running until I'd reached my bedroom and barred the door.

SIX

So there it is, my secret, my scandal: Mad Miss Mimic. The name is apt enough, for it comes on me like a madness at times, so that I say things I don't truly understand, or would never say if I could stop myself. But here is another secret, even more scandalous: Mimic is my secret joy. She emerges like a bubble bursting in the head, a glimmering behind the eyes. She floats up from the belly to the tongue. She is a latch opening in my heart. The words pour out of me freely without the slightest thought or effort. The shame comes only afterward—when I realize whom I have hurt or frightened, who has been shocked or disgusted by my performance. Who will never look at me the same way again.

My sister may have hoped to cure me of Mimic or to banish her forever, but the truth is that she has been a part of me as long as I can remember, and I truly don't believe she can be stopped. I have been aping the voices of other people from my earliest struggles with speech. My aunt Emmaline claims to be the first person to have noticed my capacity for imitation, one day at Kew Gardens about a year before my mother died of the scarlet fever. I was only four years old and already a stutterer. As Aunt Emma tells the tale, I was sitting on a bench beside her eating an ice lolly. We were watching two little German girls in matching white hoopskirts chase a black rooster round and round the lawn. I was far too shy to join in their game, but I imitated their gay laughter and the foreign words they were using to call the bird. The moment my aunt asked me to repeat the performance I reverted to my own faltering, broken speech—but after that, Aunt Emma says, she listened carefully and marked the moments when my tongue would suddenly break free in someone else's voice.

I began elocution lessons at the age of five, once it became clear the stuttering was more than a passing phase. Over the following years numerous tutors were hired, various methods were employed, and one experimental therapy after another was tested and discarded. Stern, scholarly diction-men with their monocles and alphabet charts. Flamboyant singing instructors with their scales and metronomes. Scientists with their phonographic reels and electrical-pulse devices. Mimic would emerge whenever I was most pressed and badgered by these practitioners, and once she had revealed herself nothing could deter them from trying to draw her out again and again.

How did I achieve such accurate impersonations of other voices, even voices of persons much older than myself and even, occasionally, of the opposite sex? What trick of my memory could produce a near-perfect reproduction of statements whose meaning I didn't even comprehend? And—most fascinating of all to my doctors, therapists, and coaches— why were my imitations free of the stammer that plagued my everyday speech? Scientific curiosity brought many an expert to my father's door, and many of them offered to treat me for free. But curiosity also tempted several of them past the bounds of their usual methods. It was during this period that I was dosed with various experimental medicines, including opium and morphine preparations. I spent whole days in and out of sleep, raving, terrified by fever dreams. My father, busy with his sermons and parish visits, was slow to notice how I suffered.

By seven I was having nightmares even when I wasn't drugged, and was often found sleepwalking far from my bed. During these episodes Mimic took free rein of my tongue—much to the distress of our servants, some of whom assumed, as Tom Rampling had done, that I was haunted. Christabel's beloved governess Rachel left our household after I wandered up to her garret one night and terrorized her with a particularly vivid and drawn-out impression of the livery boy who'd fallen from the carriage-house roof earlier that week and broken his leg. It was about that time that my sister fixed on the name "Mimic" for this precocious but unmanageable aspect of my condition. Mimic came to stand for everything Christabel hated most about me: the public embarrassment, the disruption of peaceful routine, and most of all, the unequal demand on Father's attention.

Christa was relieved when I began to spend longer and longer periods with Aunt Emmaline at her estate at Kew, a forty-five-mile journey from Holybourne. It was discovered that my nighttime disturbances waned when I stayed at Kew, that my appetite and colour improved, and that in general I was happier and quieter. My father supposed it was mothering I craved, and I knew this conclusion saddened him and made him mourn the loss of his wife all over again. I confess I never corrected him, though he was wrong. I couldn't risk his calling me home permanently if he were to discover that it wasn't the lack of a female role model that afflicted me.

The truth was much simpler: my aunt Emma banned all the medicines and therapies. Perhaps even more important was that she left Mimic alone. Oh, she found my impressions amusing enough—she would laugh, or lean forward in fascination and egg Mimic on with questions and conversation—but she didn't much care when and where Mimic would manifest, and she didn't mind my stuttering either. She always said that she was more interested in *what* I had to say than in *how* I said it.

When I heard that Hattie's body would be buried in the potter's field behind Saint John's School in Hampstead, I had Bess search the wardrobes for the black dress I wore to Father's funeral. That morning I entered the breakfast room and laid my black straw bonnet on the sideboard. My sister glanced up at me and promptly overturned the bowl of boiled eggs. "Are you deliberately trying to be ridiculous, Leonora?" she sputtered.

I snatched up two of the eggs before they cleared the table's edge. Then I squared my shoulders and took my seat, nodding what I hoped was a nonchalant good morning to Daniel.

"We shall *not* be attending the funeral of a tweeny maid!" shrilled Christa. "'Tis bad enough Dr. Dewhurst insists on arranging it all himself instead of leaving it for Beadall."

"'Tisn't a funeral, in any case," said my brother-in-law. "The parson will pray, perhaps, if he's not too far into his cups already. And we'll be lucky if the gravediggers show up in all this weather."

"You heard him, Leo," my sister said. "And anyhow, haven't you played out your share of spectacle recently enough? Do go and take off that costume at once."

I hung my head at Christa's reference to the card party. These last few days at Hastings had been torture. Concealing our maid's death from the party guests was hard enough on my sister, who'd had to retire earlier than she would have liked and turn down several invitations for the next day, when Daniel needed things quiet to make his arrangements. Worse still was Christabel's conclusion, after Daniel had told her everything, that I must have scared Mr. Thornfax off for good. She'd received a note of thanks from him, of course, but it was brief and businesslike enough to convince her he meant to pursue no further contact with us. There was no mention in the note of my name. "No doubt," Christa had said, "he couldn't see a way to touch on the subject without sounding impolite."

I appealed now to Daniel: "Please. I saw her d-dead. I must see her at rest."

Christabel snorted and then squawked in outrage as Daniel shrugged his assent.

"It won't be comfortable," he warned. "The rain has made a disaster of the roads. And do bring your own umbrella. There isn't room for Bess in the carriage."

In fact there was scarcely room in the carriage for anyone once Beadall finished loading the six enormous baskets Daniel had ordered our cook to prepare for the schoolchildren of

Saint John's. I wedged myself between the containers with a hand on each stack to hold it steady. My brother-in-law heaved himself up onto the seat opposite me, scattering raindrops into my lap.

I looked up from tucking my skirts to see Tom Rampling in the door. He hovered, one foot in and one foot out, clearly surprised to see me. "Shall I ride up top, Doctor?" he said.

"Nonsense, you'd be soaked through. Squeeze in here beside me."

The sight of Tom's slim frame pressed shoulder to shoulder with Daniel's girth might have been amusing, if I'd been able to lift my eyes from the floor. But my cheeks were burning with the memory of my last parting from Tom.

"Are you well, Miss Somerville?" he said politely, when we were under way.

That deep, calm voice of his, still as a forest pool! He'd sounded so frantic and undone in the surgery, confronted with my performance. I had fled. Mimic had stolen the voice of a dead girl, a girl Tom Rampling had obviously cared for, and then I had run away without explanation or apology.

"I—I am—" My tongue seized. I swallowed and tried again, but the words would not come. I glanced up: Tom's solemn grey eyes were steady on mine but guarded—wary, no doubt, of further hysterics from me. Defeated, I sighed and resumed my scrutiny of the floor.

To ease my discomfort Daniel addressed Tom on the subject of a patient they planned to visit later that evening, a man who had been badly bitten by a dog. Tom was to swab carbolic acid on all the furniture, even the bedposts, Daniel told him, in hopes of preventing infection.

"I'll have to be subtle about it," Tom said, "or risk offending old Mrs. Cobb. She fancies herself the finest house-keeper in Cheapside."

The change in subject had loosened my throat. Fearful of missing my chance I interrupted their conversation: "I am sorry a-b-bout Hattie. And for my b-b-b"—I changed tack, abandoning *behaviour*—"my foolish w-words."

"'Twas the shock," Daniel stated before Tom could reply. "Say no more of it, Miss Somerville."

And so I said no more, and they returned to their medical matters as the carriage left the streets of Paddington and St. John's Wood and began to jolt and splash its way over the pitted roads of Hampstead. I could hear that Tom Rampling was intelligent and curious, with a ready understanding of the scientific terminology my brother-in-law had taught him. Except for Tom's working-class speech—a burr on certain consonants, a flatness to the vowels—the two men sounded more like colleagues than master and assistant. At times I felt Tom's eyes on me, but each time I braved a glance he looked away.

The steady drizzle made our shared space damp and close. I smelled the pipe tobacco in my brother-in-law's pocket, the still-warm bread in the basket beside me, and also a soap-fresh scent that I thought might be Tom's. I felt my lids growing heavy, my head drooping on the arm I'd braced against the baskets.

I woke when the carriage stopped at the low brick building on Frognall Rise that housed the two classrooms of the Saint John's Parish School for Indigent Children. Daniel had begun doctoring the school's pupils several years ago, just after the

Education Act was passed and Saint John's, like all of the city's ragged schools, was suddenly filled to bursting with filthy, malnourished street children. Hattie had attended the school for a brief time before her illness forced her to stay at Hastings House, close to Daniel's surgery for her treatment, and she began to work for us as a maid.

Tom reached beside me and passed the baskets out to the caretaker. Two skinny boys squinted through the rain for a closer look into the carriage and burst into giggles when I leaned forward and waved to them. With Tom's assistance they carried the baskets into the school. A black-robed man with wild white eyebrows and a crimson nose returned with Tom and collapsed onto the seat beside me before we could be introduced. Daniel grimaced at me in sympathy as the smell of gin overpowered the carriage.

We turned about and drove on until the road dwindled to a pair of wet ribbons in the grass. The parson grumbled loudly and tirelessly about his many duties at the school, and being asked to oblige the fanciful requests of certain gentlemen from town, and what might the muddy conditions do to his new boots. At last we stopped at a rail fence where two men in oilskins leaned against a cart with their shovels propped beside them. They were eating apples, and when Daniel greeted them they tossed the cores in soaring arcs swallowed by the rain.

My hair had escaped its pins as I slept, and I felt it clinging to my neck as Daniel handed me down onto the soggy turf. I angled my umbrella until it shielded me from the bold stares of the gravediggers. We made a rather ragtag party straggling across the field, wading through sodden yellow straw and skirting cowpats and dead thistles. Spring had barely touched this land. The sparse new shoots lay flat under the heavy pewter sky. Here and there were planted makeshift crosses, some painted white, some no more than two twigs tied with twine.

My brother-in-law steered the rector, Tom was engaged with the shovelmen, and so I found myself lagging behind alone, reluctant to approach the dark hole and the plain wooden box beside it. By the time I drew level with the grave-side I was shivering, though more with nerves than with the damp.

The parson's oration was even briefer than Daniel had warned me it would be. A few inaudible lines mumbled from the prayer book, and, "May the Lord smile upon this lass in death as He never did in her poor, short life and give her His peace. Amen." He clapped his hands once, swung about, and staggered back toward the carriage.

The rest of us looked at one another, somewhat at a loss for what to do next. My brother-in-law nodded to the gravediggers, who took up the coffin straps and, on a count of three, swung the box down into the hole. The wood thumped dully as the first great shovelfuls of mud were dropped upon it.

"Stop! Please, wait," Tom said. He pulled his satchel from his shoulder and took out a battered straw hat with a posy of dried flowers. Crouching in the muck he turned the bonnet between his hands a moment and then dropped it gently into the grave.

As the men went back to work I stared into the hole where Hattie's body would be covered over forever. The steep walls of earth would buckle and slide soon enough in this rain, even if the grave weren't being filled in by human hands. This sullen, hungry muck held the mothers who had birthed us. It had swallowed our beloved fathers' bones. If I lived to a hundred, still this muck would someday claim my body, too. My throat went raw at the thought, and my chest was vised in an icy grip. I shivered harder and sniffled, feeling small and adrift in this ocean of unfeeling grass.

"Why are you here, milady?" Tom was next to me, his voice quiet in my ear. I lifted my umbrella to offer him shelter but he stepped back, out of its circle. "Did you know Hattie very well?"

I looked up at him, his delicate face smooth and severe as marble, his eyes the same dark, leaden grey as the sky behind him. Rainwater coursed down the spirals of his hair and dripped onto his cheekbones. Tom knew that Hattie and I couldn't have been friends. I sensed an accusation and felt ashamed without knowing why.

"Are you not curious, at all, about how she died?" he continued.

I frowned. "I had not c-considered—"

"No, of course you hadn't." His expression suddenly darkened into the same disdain I'd seen in the parlour that day when Hattie had collapsed.

"Are you angry?"

"Yes!" he snapped. "Yes," he repeated more softly, when Daniel's head lifted from his conversation with the grave-diggers. "The girl's death was needless and cruel, and I'm angry that you should pretend to have known her, when you know nothing."

I stared at him. "I know n-n-nothing of m-m—" I could not manage *medicine*, but I persisted. "I'm no d-doctor. Of course I do not know."

Tom's lips made a straight line.

"Why don't you t-tell me, then," I said.

He stared out across the field.

"Tell me."

He sucked in a breath, blew out the air in a rush, and shook his head. "Forgive me, Miss Somerville. Your words, when Hattie died … they made me wonder if you did know, somehow. But it isn't my place to chide you, and it isn't yours to know the business of Dr. Dewhurst.

"Only, milady"—he ducked his head to see me more clearly in the umbrella's shadow, and an almost desperate note entered his voice—"why come, in all this horrid weather, to this sorry excuse for a funeral?"

My parents died, I wanted to say. *I know how it feels to lose someone.* And I wanted to tell him that death demands that we stop and think. It asks us to stop, and to look at one another, and to think about what we are doing. Death doesn't let us carry on as if nothing has changed.

I watched the water drip from the tip of his nose, from his earlobes. He looked so wretched and forlorn that I wanted to hold my umbrella over him whether he should like it or not.

It dawned on me that I didn't know anything at all about Tom Rampling. Not even who his parents were, or if they were still alive. How had he come to Hastings? And where did he go at the end of each day when his work at the surgery was done? Tom was right: I knew nothing. And I found that, yes, I was curious—very curious indeed.

Even if I could have found a way to ask, though, I had no time; Daniel was ready to go home. He took my arm and passed my umbrella to Tom, holding his own, larger one over me as we crossed back to the carriage. The ride was awkward and heavy with unspoken questions. Tom was seated next to me this time, but he pressed himself so close to his side of the carriage that even Daniel could have fit between us. He spoke only to the doctor and only when Daniel asked him a direct question. I couldn't see a way to return to our graveside conversation. I couldn't even turn to look straight at Tom. Finally I unsnapped the rain cover and busied myself with gazing out the window, ignoring the fact that my dress grew soggier by the minute. This time it was my brother-in-law who eventually slept, his chins spilling onto his chest, his clasped hands over his belly rising and falling with his snores. And still Tom Rampling stayed silent.

SEVEN

*H*astings House was always deadly sombre in between social occasions, with icy stone floors and damp, smoky rooms due to the tricky fireplaces and unreliable gas supply. The incessant rain had encouraged moss on the drive, and all day water chuckled noisily through the eaves.

Kept indoors the Dewhurst children grew irritable, and when their nurse took to bed with a cold they began to plague the rest of the household with their tantrums and whining. "They give me such headaches," Christabel moaned, and she declared her sitting room off limits to anyone underage.

In an effort to make up for displeasing my sister at the card party I took it upon myself to entertain my nephews. I asked Bess to hang a sheet for shadow puppets. Bertie— named Albert for my father but given the nickname almost at birth—kept dodging around the sheet to see what I was doing, so the game became flapping our arms to make baby Alexander giggle at the wild shapes. Next we played with Bertie's trains. His "jumpit car" was his favourite engine, a tin windup toy with a habit of leaping off its track and somersaulting through the air, sending both boys into fits of laughter. Curious about the malfunction I turned the toy over and found that it had been modified with gears and a set of tiny springs.

"Tom fixed it," Bertie told me. "It got stuck, so Tom fixed it better than ever."

When Alexander started to yawn I turned him over to Bess, found Bertie a sweater, and brought the boy downstairs in an effort to keep things quiet for the others. The cook had gone out, so I took the opportunity to make a cup of chocolate for my nephew. We perched on stools at the big work table with the copper pots hanging over our heads and watched the kitchen maid, her arms coated in flour to the elbows, roll out dough for pork pies. We watched her, that is, and she watched me—Sally had the same furtive, fascinated face all the servants at Hastings House wore in my presence, like a visitor to Bedlam waiting for the inmates to riot. Whatever might Mad Miss Mimic do next? What glimmer of insanity might I reveal to her, that she could tell about it later for the amusement of the servants' table?

I kept silent and bore the scrutiny as best I could, for Bertie's sake. His shoulders barely cleared the table, but for a three-year-old he looked very proud and grown-up in his sailor suit, spreading jam on his biscuit with the little knife I gave him and drinking his chocolate from an adult-sized teacup.

At last I convinced him to come away, and we set to exploring the hallways round the storerooms and servants' quarters. Bertie found a hat by the side door that had fallen from a hook on the wall. "Put on it," he commanded me, reaching for it with his fat little arms. I plunked it onto his head and laughed at the way it hid his eyes, but he tore it off again and stomped his foot. "Put on it, Leo!" he shouted.

"Shh, don't b-boss," I said, and I took the hat. Its swooping, unfashionable shape looked familiar—it was Mrs. Fayerweather's, from our card party. The old lady must have left it behind by mistake, and the relentless rains had discouraged any of her servants from coming to claim it.

"Please put on it, Leo?" said Bertie, sweet as treacle.

So I donned the ridiculous bonnet and struck a haughty pose for him. "N-now then," I began—and Mimic stepped in, chirping hoarsely in perfect memory of Mrs. Fayerweather's voice: "Now then, young man, what lessons shall we learn today?"

Bertie's eyes widened. "Rhymes!" he said.

"Shall we learn a rhyme? Very well, then." I paced the hall, striking my heels against the stones. "Are you ready, Master Albert?"

"Yes, Lady!" Bertie stood at attention.

"I shall recite it first in full, and then you shall repeat it until you are fluent," I ordered.

> Learn well your grammar,
> And never stammer,
> Write well and neatly,
> And sing most sweetly.

Line by line we repeated Lewis Carroll's droll little lesson until Bertie was marching behind me, up and down the chilly hallways, shouting the lines without a single mistake:

Drink tea, not coffee;
Never eat toffy.
Eat bread with butter.
Once more, don't stutter.

This was my favourite of the poems Aunt Emma had taught me as a child at Kew, especially after she told me that Mr. Carroll, who also wrote my favourite book, *Alice's Adventures in Wonderland*, had wished for a career in the church but been held back by his severe stammer.

"'Drink tea, not coffee! Never eat toffy! Eat bread with butter!'" we chanted. I don't care if Sally should hear it, I thought, or Mrs. Nussey, or any of them. Mimic's voice sang out of my throat like a rowdy aria, defiant in the face of the silences and stares of Hastings House.

Rounding a corner I nearly collided with a broadly grinning Tom Rampling.

"'Once more, don't stutter!'" Bertie's momentum drove his little body full-force into the backs of my knees, and Tom grabbed my arms to steady me. Flushing, I tipped Mrs. Fayerweather's hat into my hands.

"Please," Tom said, "don't stop on my account. Only, why mayn't I eat toffee?"

Bertie squeezed between us. "Halloa, Tom!"

"Hello, Master Albert. Fine day, isn't it?"

Bertie shook his head so vigorously that his hair stood up like milkweed fluff. "'Tisn't. 'Tis raining manimals."

I was mystified, but Tom understood him at once: "Animals. Like cats and dogs, do you mean?"

"Yes!" Bertie beamed up at him.

"Well. I'd better make use of this, then." Tom took an umbrella from the hook. He bent to retrieve a crate of apothecary bottles and a spool of copper wire from the floor and tucked them under his arm. "Good day, Miss Somerville."

My voice—Mimic's, Mrs. Fayerweather's—had fled. But the amusement lighting those grey eyes and the warmth under his words flooded me not with embarrassment but relief. Tom Rampling did not despise me! Well, he may think me very silly, I amended. But he didn't bear me a grudge, at least. I supposed I was still conscience-stricken over Mimic's use of Hattie, or it would not matter so much what Tom Rampling thought.

"Good day, Tom!" Bertie yelled out the door as the slim figure was swallowed by the rain.

When the weather finally cleared the next day, and Bess mentioned she had errands near Covent Garden, I leapt at the opportunity to escape the prison of Hastings House. My sister fretted at me about the Black Glove—hadn't it been two weeks since the last attack, and wouldn't the criminal gang decide that today was a fine day to bomb the markets— but Christa was going out too, to High Street with her lady friends, so she could hardly refuse me the same pleasure.

Each time Bess entered a shop I stayed outside under the awning or just beside the door and watched the lively bustle of workaday London. Oh, the city was a foul, noisy place! We'd travelled only ten minutes by carriage from the handsome streets surrounding Hastings, only a couple of dozen blocks, but we'd entered a different universe. Here the clatter of hooves and wooden wheels forced everyone to shout his business. The rain had turned all the horse muck to soup, so that clouds of flies gathered at the curbs. The red-jacketed boys dodging among traffic with pan and brush could not keep up with the filth and were coated in it to the thighs.

But the sun was shining, raising a steam of vapours from the damp buildings. A barrel-organ player had drawn a crowd. He had a green parrot tied to a perch, and when he turned the handle and the machine wheezed its tune, the bird flapped its wings and shrieked.

There are things I cannot say in any voice, not even with Mimic's help. A blue dream of sky. White clouds like lace being tatted at one end and unravelled at the other. The clouds called out to the birds on the sills, and with whistles of rapture they took flight, hundreds and thousands of black wings hurled skyward. They flocked over the rooftops, now a fine, long line, now full as billowing sails. *Freedom! Freedom!* their cries promised, and for a moment I almost felt I could leap up into their midst with my skirts supporting me like a kite.

A well-dressed young couple stopped to hear the hurdy-gurdy, and I watched as the gentleman, laughing, used his walking stick to scrape something from the heel of his lady's boot. Cabbage, I guessed, for wilted and rotten cabbages dotted the street where a produce cart had tipped. The lady, not much older than I, balanced against her husband with a gloved hand spread on his chest.

Freedom and protection! The two great gifts that only a husband of good standing could bring. Over these past days I'd tried not to dwell on my failure with Mr. Thornfax. In my weekly letter to my aunt Emma I hadn't even mentioned it, though normally I hid nothing from her. Too good to be true, I told myself over and over, like a charm against undue disappointment. He was too good to be true. And I'd done my best to ignore the inner voice that added, *You mean too good for you.*

Now, though, I could not resist imagining Mr. Thornfax here on the street with me—tall, golden-haired, smiling. Perhaps he'd wear a beaver-lined overcoat like the gentleman across the street. When I closed my eyes to add detail to the daydream, however, I saw only Mr. Thornfax's look of puzzlement at Mimic's behaviour at the sight of poor Hattie lying on the floor. He hadn't been frightened and upset with me, like Tom Rampling—but then, he had never known Hattie while she was alive, so Hattie's voice from my mouth would have been not eerie, but only bizarre. Mad Miss Mimic.

I'd been able to discover very little about the girl's death. A few days after her funeral I'd braved my brother-in-law's study, but Daniel had offered no real answers. "Best not to dwell on our failures, little sister," was all he would say.

"W-as it the fault of T-Tom Rampling, as he said on the night Hattie d-died?" I'd persisted.

Daniel shook his head. "To men of science, there can be no question of fault. Rampling is a good boy, and very clever in his way, but I'm afraid he has impractical notions. 'Progress depends on practicality,' I always need remind him. To assign fault only muddles the matter."

The gentleman at the barrel organ was patting his jacket pockets and searching the curb. His young wife lifted her skirts to assist him. He turned about him with an accusing air, then took her arm and moved rapidly off.

As I watched, another gentleman on my side of the street, about to climb into a carriage seat, suddenly jumped back with a shout.

"Thief! Hi!" he called to his driver, who leapt down and ran in pursuit of a small boy. I glimpsed bare, mud-splashed legs and a woollen cap. As the child dodged across the street I saw that it was the young boy from Daniel's surgery, the one who had wailed so loudly and had to be dragged upstairs by Tom Rampling when Hattie died—Will, his name was. The shock of recognition and the oddness of the coincidence spurred me to leave my post and step into the street for a better look.

Caught by the collar, young Will had the presence of mind to drop the stolen pocket watch, and as the driver bent to retrieve it, he delivered the man a sharp kick to the shin and twisted free of his grip. With a series of curses the driver gave up and went to return the watch to his master. Will wove and darted this way and that among the shuffle of fruit stands and sidewalk-sellers. I managed to keep him in sight by walking fast and staying a distance back so as not to alert him to my presence. I sidestepped garbage and horse-piles, twisting to avoid the parasols and packages of shoppers, keeping always before my eyes the little brown cap and the flash of bare white knees.

Will turned down James Street, cut across an alley, rounded two sharp corners, and scampered the length of a row of cattle stalls. He must have declared himself beyond danger then, for he dropped to a slow trot. I was growing very warm in my embroidered jacket and shoved my bonnet back from my head. My shoes were not meant for such an escapade; twice I nearly turned an ankle on the slippery cobbles.

The streets narrowed and, in places, were nearly blocked where window shutters stood open. The clamour of the market gave way to the crying of babies and the baying of dogs. Coal smoke and the stench of sewage choked the air. We went down a stone staircase and crossed a courtyard with high, mudded walls, stables, and a dovecote. Will turned into a narrower alley still. If I entered after him, it would be obvious I was chasing him.

"Will! D-do stop!" I called. "I m-must speak with you!"

The boy paused and turned. I knew he recognized me by the way he tilted his head, frightened but also curious. He'd heard me use Hattie's voice, after all. I closed the distance and went to one knee before him so that our faces were level. Dirt streaked his cheeks, and his sandy hair fell into his eyes. I resisted the urge to tuck it under his cap.

With dismay I spied in Will's pocket the round impression of another gentleman's watch. During the chase I'd nearly convinced myself that the theft was the impulsive mischief of a wild boy. He'd been standing very still but now, following my eyes to the evidence of his crime, he gave a little quiver, as might a rabbit cornered in the garden. "They's for Tom, mum, I swear to you!" he said, so quickly that it was a moment before I understood.

"Why does T-Tom need p-pocket-watches?"

"I can't say, mum. If Tom's nicked he'll be sent to Aus-tray-lia!" Will's eyes grew round as he invoked the name of that terrifying country.

"If you're c-caught it will go b-badly for you as well," I reminded him.

He drew himself up in a ragged approximation of pride. "I'm never caught!" he declared.

Until that moment I'd been driven by nothing but a kind of urgent curiosity. Now I was overcome with confusion and doubt. Tom Rampling wasn't a thief. He seemed so dutiful, so serious, always. And I'd seen his gentleness with children; he would never trade on the naïve bravado of a child for such a base and cowardly purpose. Would he?

Young Will took advantage of my hesitation and darted farther down the alley, vanishing through a narrow archway.

I followed, wondering whether the boy was meeting Tom directly. Past the arch the alley dropped downhill. Boards were laid over runnels of oozing mud, and I had to go gingerly, steadying my balance against the brick wall. Farther down the slope the way was blocked by an overturned wagon. I realized there was nowhere Will could have gone but through a curtained doorway I had already passed on my right.

I turned back just as a girl emerged from behind the curtain. Her soiled bodice revealed much of her bosom, and her hair hung in coils over her heavily rouged cheeks. She leered at me through scarlet-painted lips. "You lost, mum?"

"I … I w-was at Covent G-Garden," I said, stupidly. "I'm l-looking for young W-Will."

"Ain' no 'young Will' here, mum," she said. "Not when he comes home all inna fright, nohow. I'm his sister. You's speakin' to me, not him."

"He s-stays at Hastings House, with Dr. D-Dewhurst," I tried to explain.

The girl's blue eyes widened. "Is it you, the one Tom tells about? The stumbletongue girl? Is you, ain' it?"

I coloured in confusion.

She put her hands on her hips. "Tom Rampling. My sweetheart," she enunciated, as if explaining to a small, stupid child. "He works for Dew'urst, too. He tol' us all about you. How they keep you penned up in that big house, an' treat you hard. You ain' altogether as pretty a thing as he likes to tell it, mind."

She was interrupted by a low snarl, and a toothy snout emerged beside her as a massive dog advanced, growling, toward me. I backed hastily against the opposite wall.

"Oh, don' mind him, there. Rufus! Drop off it!" the painted girl yelled, spurring the hound to intersperse his growls with wheezing barks and ferocious snaps of his jaws.

A shout echoed within the house, and the girl called into the darkness over her shoulder. "Aye, Mrs. Clampitt! Here's a lady after our Will!"

Sweeping aside the curtain, an aged parody of the younger woman emerged into the alley. She wore grey ringlets, and her rouged mouth made a thin circle of red around gapped and blackened teeth. Shrivelled breasts were propped and puckered into a semblance of cleavage, with a yellowed lace kerchief spilling from between them.

"What's here?" Mrs. Clampitt said. "Ah, Daisy, you've found a lost lamb!" She threw her arms wide, revealing a dark stain on each armpit of her gown. "And what a pretty, nervous thing. White as snow, this one! What soft fleece."

"She's the one as Tom tol' us," said Daisy, sounding rather sullen about it now.

I slid a few inches along the bricks, the rough surface catching at my jacket. The dog stalked me, stiff-legged, snarling. Saliva pooled between his front feet.

Mrs. Clampitt advanced, too. "Don't be skittish, lass; there's a good girl. Rufus can smell fear. Dogs, you know, can't help but take an interest in a lamb. You best come in now. Come and rest your poor feet. Godssakes, and just look at those shoes for walking!"

"D-does M-Mr. Rampling live here?" I said.

Mrs. Clampitt took my arm. "That boy is family to us, even since he's gone up in the world. After his poor mamma died in that jail 'twas me took him in, you know. Him and Daisy here grew up like twins, they did. You come in now, and I'll tell you it all."

Daisy drew aside the curtain, and I stared into the dank interior. A man with a red face and a crooked nose sat with a glass and bottle on the table in front of him; beyond him I could see nothing but shadows. Fear bloomed in my belly. I knew I could not enter that dark space.

I took another step sideways along the wall and cowered behind my arms as the dog lunged forward. I heard a thud and a whine. I peeped out to see Rufus slink beneath Mrs. Clampitt's skirt.

Beside me stood a whip-thin man with lank hair and drooping whiskers. Where he had come from I could not say. The man carried a stick, which he swept in an arc to show me how he'd struck the dog.

"Now, Mr. Sears, this here's our guest," said Mrs. Clampitt. "It's Dr. Dewhurst's sister-in-law, ain't that right, lass?"

"'Tain't no guest o' yours," the man sneered. He took hold of my arm, leaning close to my face, and I closed my eyes against his fetid breath on my cheek. "Dewhurst's kin, izzit? I wonder what 'e'd say to us 'avin' her. I wonder, wouldn't 'e offer us 'is services at a greatly reduced price, if we was to inform 'im?"

I crossed my arms and gripped my elbows to curb my trembling. "P-please, l-let me g-go."

"You daft man." Mrs. Clampitt clucked, sounding more amused than angered by his scheming. "Kidnapping won't pay for your morbid cravings. That doctor's got us all over his barrel, and well you know it!"

"Aye, but maybe we'll send 'im a token, at least. Give us your purse, love," he said, and snatched my reticule from my hand.

"Please, I have n-nothing."

This produced giggles from Daisy and Mrs. Clampitt. "Oh, my poor lamb," the woman crooned. "But you have so much! Your lovely pelisse, for one."

"And that bonnet," added Mr. Sears. "Share with us, and we'll let you be quick on your way."

I shook my head more vigorously. The dog had commenced barking again, this time in excitement. More girls were pouring through the doorway now, each painted and costumed like Daisy.

"Would ye need 'elp?" Mr. Sears suggested, reaching for my hair. I shook him off and yanked on the ribbons to release my bonnet into his hands. Then, terrified beyond reason and stupidly eager to believe his lie about letting me go, I shrugged out of my jacket and tossed it to Mrs. Clampitt.

Mr. Sears drew a sharp breath. "Them's pearl buttons on that dress!" And with a twist of his filthy fingers he plucked one from my waist.

One of the girls darted forward and made a snatch at a button. She received a blow from Mr. Sears's stick. Mrs. Clampitt slapped him hard in retaliation—and then I was crowded all round by grasping, tearing hands. Lace, buttons, and hairpins were torn away, and I couldn't breathe for the panic pressing in my chest.

"Her shoes!"

I was shoved into the bricks, my shoulder scraping the rough surface as I fell. My forehead hit the downspout, and my vision wavered and dimmed.

I opened my mouth and screamed, and did not—found that I could not—stop.

EIGHT

*I*t was more than a scream. Mimic had called up the most harrowing human sound I knew. The crest of it was sheer fright and desperation, but it gained momentum from something much darker than my own emotions of the moment. It told of something much more dire than the theft of a silk jacket and a few buttons, and it went on and on. And on.

Mimic's sound rose and fell and rose again like a riptide. The screaming blasted the soot-stained walls and foamed up to the wan slice of sky above us. It lapped against my own skin, raising the small hairs on my neck and chilling me to my core.

My attackers drew back as if physically buffeted. One of the smaller girls fell into panicked tears, and Mr. Sears's fingers scrabbled for purchase against the bricks like he was being dragged by an undertow.

And then Tom Rampling was there, saying my name and glaring round at the faces now peeking timidly from behind shutters and around corners. "You might have stepped in!"

he shouted at the red-faced man who stood, now, in the curtained doorway. "Don't you know who she is?"

The man crossed his arms and grinned. "Don't much care," he retorted, "but she makes a good fuss, don't she?"

"*He* will care, when you tell him," Tom said. Gently he drew together the torn edges of my bodice. Gently he clasped an arm round my shoulders and led me, stumbling and swaying, from the alley.

"Milady," he murmured, "there now, milady," and I realized the scream had stopped but had left behind a kind of panting moan that must have been almost as alarming to Tom's ears. I forced myself to be quiet, fighting the tight, agonizing pressure in my throat.

Tom shepherded me several blocks in this stumbling fashion, until I had to stop and lean forward, hands on my knees, to ease the dizziness.

"I'm s-sorry," I said, and the word became a sob.

"No," he said. "No, no need." He looked at me, and his fingers brushed my cheeks as if he might save the tears before they fell. Then he patted my hand and said, in a deliberately light tone, "I should call you Lady Luck. I've never heard of Mr. Sears's gang falling back once they've snared someone in their alley. I should think your name will be famous in Seven Dials for years to come."

I couldn't quite smile. Seven Dials was part of the St. Giles Rookery, one of London's most notoriously dangerous neighbourhoods. It had been beyond foolish of me to wander this way alone. "If I am lucky it is only b-because you c-came upon me. I thank you for your r-rescue."

Tom shook his head. "I wouldn't have been able to call

them off without your … your voice." He hesitated. "It wasn't by luck I found you, either. The boy, Will, snuck out the back way and fetched me. He said you'd followed him into the Dials, and I thought I had better come see you safe."

I remembered then why I'd been pursuing the little boy in the first place. My rescuer was not, perhaps, the gentle hero he pretended. He might instead be the basest kind of criminal: a pocket-picker who got innocent children to do his vile work. And that painted girl—Daisy—had called him her sweetheart. Another wave of faintness swept over me.

Tom touched the sore spot on my forehead, and I winced. "You've had a shock atop injury," he said. "You need a rest. Something hot to drink. Please, let me take you to my grandmother's rooms. She lives not far from here."

I thought of refusing, but I could not see how I would last long enough to make it all the way back to Hastings House on foot. And some part of me still refused to believe Tom guilty, or still trusted him despite the possibility of guilt. Whatever he is, I reasoned foggily, he isn't dangerous. At least not to me.

Ten minutes later I found myself seated on a threadbare sofa in a tiny sitting room, sipping warm cider, nibbling a biscuit, and being introduced to Tom's grandmother, Mrs. Alcott. The old woman's grey braid snaked over her shoulder and struck my lap as she leaned to cup my face in her hands. She was nearly blind, Tom had told me, and her clouded eyes were sunk deep into her leathery cheeks. "She's pretty, is she not? Tom, is hers a pretty face?" Her voice was girlish and kind.

"Yes," Tom said quietly. "Yes, very pretty." I couldn't see him past Mrs. Alcott's body.

Her hands hovered at my head. "Her hair is quite wild for a lady."

I shuddered, recalling the stolen pins and the violent pulling.

"Tom, come put this to rights," Mrs. Alcott said, and Tom circled the sofa and, without ceremony, began to smooth my hair, combing it with his fingers and rearranging the remaining pins. He seemed oblivious to any strangeness in his attending me like Bess would. His touch was light as a caress, and I couldn't suppress a sigh.

"Clever fingers, that lad has got. Braids, twists as fast as you please!" Mrs. Alcott settled into a rocker by the window. "And, do you know"—she leaned forward conspiratorially—"he is also a first-rate lockpick and cutpurse!"

I blinked. It occurred to me that Mrs. Alcott's mind might not be wholly sound, and a quick glance at the way Tom bit his lip confirmed my suspicions.

"Show her your spoils, Tom!" she persisted.

"Grandmamma, I hardly think Miss Somerville—"

"Look to that table, my dear, just beside you."

I looked. Laid out across the table's surface was a gleaming array of miniature brass gears, wheels, and springs. And three or four gold watch cases.

Tom took a chair across from me. His usually pale cheeks were crimson, and his eyes were fixed on the floor.

Now you should speak, I silently begged him. *Now you should redeem yourself.*

Mrs. Alcott continued, unaware of her grandson's discomfort. "My Tom can fix anything, build anything from nothing. Look there! Built that one just last week, he did." She pointed at a small wooden box on the table.

"Grandmamma, really. Miss Somerville will think me a braggart. Or a lagabout."

"A braggabout!" Mrs. Alcott's laugh was heartier than her speaking voice. Despite the circumstances I felt my mouth twitch into a smile.

Tom's ears were still red, but he brought the box over to me and wound a tiny handle on its side. He clicked a switch, and I squeaked in surprise. A tune played, and a pair of glass birds with metal beaks whirled and tilted to tap out a tinkling rhythm on a copper plate.

Tom moved to switch it off again, but I stayed his hand. "A m-moment more," I begged, and held the box tight between my hands.

It was like light captured in a net of sparkling sound. It was like a kaleidoscope of colour behind my eyes. Though the melody was delicate as thrushsong, I was sure that Tom and I could not speak to each other and be heard. The birds' waltz was erratic, but I knew it obeyed the dance master of the clockworks beneath the plate. The innards of the box beat and whirred through my fingertips like a racing pulse.

Certain that the tiny room should be glowing, that the mildewed wallpaper and greying cushions should be washed clean and gilded with angelic light, I looked up and gave a shaky laugh.

Mrs. Alcott had fallen fast asleep in her chair.

Tom's gaze followed mine, and then we looked at each other. I felt another smile tug at my mouth and saw colour rise in his cheeks and an answering smile, shy and supremely vulnerable.

In that instant I wished more than anything that I could forgive Tom Rampling for being a thief. The music box was the most beautiful thing I'd ever seen. And this fine-boned man, whose sharp knee nudged into mine when he shifted on the cushion? He was beautiful, too. The curve of his pale cheekbone, the bluish vein at his temple, the fine, luminous skin—he appeared to me to be constructed of the same ethereal magic as his creation.

Tom was watching the music box in my lap as its music and movement wound down. "It is not what you think," he said, and inclined his head toward the table spread with watch parts. "I am not—"

"I saw Will d-do it," I interrupted, eager to stop him before he lied to me.

A muscle moved in Tom's jaw. "He never did it before today. I swear it to you. And I told him he must never do it again."

"These are all your own s-spoils, then."

"Yes, but—"

"Are they for Mrs. C-Clampitt? Do you b-bring them there?"

"No! Miss Somerville, it is not what you think," he repeated. "'Tis not simply a lark."

I turned the music box over and watched the tiny gears tick to a halt.

"I bought the parts for that one," he said quickly.

"Larks?" I said, turning the box upright again. "Is that what these b-birds are?" Then, with Mrs. Alcott's precise degree of fondness and mirth, Mimic said, "Braggabout!" and I laughed Mrs. Alcott's hearty laugh.

Tom replaced the music box on the table and perched again on the chair opposite me. "If you are not haunted, why do you do it?" he said. All signs of shyness and vulnerability were gone.

"I c-cannot help it." My cheeks were very hot. "It c-comes un-b-bidden, when I do not know w-what to say."

"Your screaming, that scared off Mr. Sears—"

I nodded. "That was Mimic too."

"Who?"

"My s-sister's name for it. 'Mimic.'"

"No. I meant who were you mimicking, when you were under attack?"

It was the first time someone other than my cousin Archie had asked me about Mimic's sources. In fact I was a bit ashamed at the misery Mimic had called up in the alleyway, at the way I'd traded on another person's woes to free myself. When I'd apologized and wept after he rescued me, my apology hadn't been wholly for Tom Rampling. I'd been sorry, rather, for using another person's sorrows in my own interest.

"Would you tell me?" There was no judgment or derision in Tom's face, only curiosity. So I told him, haltingly, of the summer my father had performed mass funeral services nearly every week. The cholera had taken so many, so quickly, that there wasn't time for elaborate rites. Christa and I had been shut up at the house for months for fear of infection, so I remembered mostly relief at being allowed to attend the service once the threat of infection had waned. Mrs. Cavendish, I learned later, had been one of the village's most stalwart nurses, caring for dozens of her ill and dying neighbours after her own family had all passed away. But at this funeral she'd flung herself from her pew into the aisle, crawled on all fours to the centre of the church, thrown back her greying head, and launched into a wailing scream that no amount of entreating and consoling by her friends could silence.

My father had waited calmly some moments through the interruption. Then he'd descended from the pulpit and approached the heartbroken woman, taken her in his arms, and, on his knees in the middle of the church, prayed over her. Even so the sound did not stop, and I remembered finally being taken from the chapel by my nurse and walking home amid a hushed and shuffling crowd benumbed by grief.

When I finished my story Tom smiled and shook his head.

"W-what is it?" I ventured.

"Mimic was your great friend and ally today." His voice warmed, dropped lower: "Miss Luck, I shall call you, with her at your command."

"I don't c-command her. There is n-no 'her.' Just m-me, and a tongue I cannot c-control." I swallowed and struggled to look away but failed. His smile crinkled the fine skin at the corners of his eyes and sparked the grey irises with warmth. Again I thought of the music box and its merry tune, and I wondered which was the real Tom Rampling: the sneak-thief or the savior? The solemn, stone-faced one or this one radiating happiness?

NINE

I expected uproar at Hastings House over my disappearance and my dishevelled state. But Tom brought
me round the back door and handed me to Bess directly,
telling her only in broad terms what had happened. The
maid was red-eyed, and she wiped away tears of relief as
she cleaned me up and whisked away my torn dress before
sending notice to my sister. I supposed it wouldn't reflect well
on Bess, either, that I had wandered away from her company
and fallen into danger.

When Christa did come to see me that evening she was
only mildly concerned about my late return. After listening
impatiently to my stammering excuses about my scraped
shoulder—I said nothing about being attacked or rescued
by Tom—she merely said to Bess, "Tell Mrs. Nussey we'll
have the dressmaker tomorrow to fix some lace to cover
that."

When Bess was dismissed I learned the reason for
Christa's distraction. "Leo, listen to this. Mr. Thornfax has
asked us to the opera on Saturday!"

"Us?"

"Well, Daniel has a prior engagement. But you and I will go with him—and, don't you know, he has a box, Leo!" I'd heard about Francis Thornfax's private box at the Royal Opera House several times already from my sister. I knew she'd been desperate for the invitation. "We shall be *seen.*" She sighed, draping herself across my bed.

I couldn't help but laugh. Christabel had once begged our aunt Emmaline for a private box at the opera—she'd even attempted to argue that such a thing would make the perfect wedding gift—but Aunt Emma had scoffed at the notion of "throwing good coins after vanity." The Lady Hastings loved opera and had taken us to *Faust* and *The Magic Flute* when we were younger, but she'd never understood my sister's yearning for society's attention and approval.

Emily came in carrying a tray with a small bottle and a glass of water.

"Oh, at last!" Christa sprang up from the bed to meet her at the door. She squirted a quick series of laudanum droplets into the water and drank back the draught in one gulp. "And next time," she scolded the maid, "do ensure it doesn't take you so long to find me."

She returned to my bed, flopped onto her belly, and propped her chin on her hands. "Do you know what Mr. Thornfax told Daniel the other day? He said that he found you 'utterly bewitching'!"

"D-does that mean he liked me after all?"

"It means that, somehow, your ridiculous theatrics at the party last week intrigued him. Or else he thought you pretty enough that he doesn't care how deranged you are."

"I'm not d-deranged," I protested, but it was such an old quarrel between us that my protest lacked conviction.

"Either way I consider it very good news indeed." She frowned at my muslin nightdress. "Where are your silks? The French lace? Leo, you *must* take responsibility for your own future!"

"Is Mr. Thornfax c-coming to my b-bedroom?"

"Don't be clever," she snapped. She gathered herself off my bed and flounced to the door. "And don't you go rambling about the city like that again, exhausting and injuring yourself. I intend to keep you quiet and safe until Thornfax takes you off my hands for good."

Saturday morning a note arrived for my sister from Mr. Thornfax. She squealed when she read it, and then made a game of not telling me what it contained or how she'd responded to it. I gave up guessing too quickly for her liking, though, so she followed me all round the house, jittery with suppressed excitement.

Finally I said, "Well? W-what is it? Will he pr-propose?"

"Silly Leo!" Christa tittered. "He asked the colour of your dress, that's all."

That evening, when Mr. Thornfax arrived and was ushered into the parlour, I was presented to him in a lavender gown whose bodice had been artfully altered to reveal less of my marred shoulder and more of my bosom. After the briefest of hellos Christa dragged all the servants out of the room with her. I'd envisioned a corsage or perhaps a lace shawl, so I was surprised when Mr. Thornfax handed me a flat silver box. A necklace! A heavy, ornate choker of amethysts and diamonds set in gold, fully two inches wide, with a carved jade medallion suspended from the centre. It was icy cold, and I gasped as he fastened it round my neck.

He whistled low and turned me to the mirror on the mantel. The jewels flashed in the gaslight and sent violet starbursts across my throat and chest.

I took a breath and turned to face Mr. Thornfax. "It's"—I skated around *beautiful*—"lovely. I thank you, s-sir."

He placed an elbow on the mantel. "Miss Somerville, I am truly sorry your servant girl died," he said. "But I must confess that I was grateful for the opportunity it gave me to see what you might do and say in unexpected circumstances."

Shame pricked over my skin. I'd hoped that Mimic's outburst at the surgery would not need talking about, but I'd forgotten Mr. Thornfax's direct manner.

"I've given the matter a great deal of thought. I realize now how much pressure you must have felt, all during that party, to *converse* with everyone. I realize how even I must have pressed you to speak, when you would rather have not."

I gaped at him. It was the first time in my memory that a man had attempted to see the thing from my point of view. My past suitors, in avoiding the subject altogether, had only grown more and more nervous about my dysfluency. Mr. Greenlove would talk incessantly in an attempt to fill in both our parts of the conversation. Poor Mr. Kelso would actually wince whenever I stuttered, which of course made the stuttering worse. After a while, with those men, the tension had built so high that the air between us fairly crackled with anticipation of Mimic's next appearance.

Mr. Thornfax, though, was entirely at his ease. Absorbed in the subject, he crossed one ankle over the other and rubbed his thumb absently along his jaw. "We will often need to appear in public together. That cannot be avoided," he said. "But I should like you somehow to feel safe, to be easy on my arm."

I could feel myself becoming easier with him even as he spoke. It was as if his charm and confidence were being transferred from his body to mine, encircling me like a cloak. I smiled at him.

"There, you see? Those eyes, that smile—that is all you need to share, Miss Somerville, and everyone you meet will be enchanted with you. You needn't speak at all. Not one word, unless you wish it." Mr. Thornfax turned me to the mirror again and adjusted the jade medallion in the hollow between my collarbones. His palms lingered on my shoulders as he set his chin playfully atop my head. He made a silly face at our reflection, and I laughed, but I'd also glimpsed a heated appreciation in his eyes that brought colour to my cheeks.

Christabel paled and gave a little shriek when she saw what I was wearing. "Oh! Sir, you are too good!"

"Thornfax, really," Daniel admonished with a smile. "You'll make my wife forever discontented with the baubles I can buy her."

The Dewhurst children, brought downstairs by Greta to be kissed, were instantly fond of Mr. Thornfax's gift, too: Bertie's eyes shone when I knelt to embrace him, and baby Alexander lunged for the necklace with both fists and screamed when Greta pried him away.

A heavy fog had descended over the city, and we did not see until we were halfway down the steps that Mr. Thornfax had brought his state carriage to convey us. This produced in my sister further squeals and flutterings. Mr. Thornfax excused himself a moment to speak with his driver, a round-shouldered man called Curtis.

We waited beside the carriage while Emily fetched the ivory fan my sister had forgotten upstairs. Daniel joined the men beside the horses' tossing heads, their voices competing with the jangling bridle bells. Apparently Daniel's prior engagement had been cancelled, for I heard him ask Mr. Thornfax whether he was certain he oughtn't to come along with us to the opera after all.

"'Tis a show of confidence in your business partner to entrust your wife to him," Mr. Thornfax responded.

Daniel said something I couldn't hear, and Mr. Thornfax shook his head. "No, I assure you. Not with Curtis at the ready." And he threw a playful punch at his driver, who ducked and stepped back, seeming rather embarrassed.

Curtis could have been Daniel's twin, I observed. They were identical in height and girth and had matching bald pates and ruddy, fleshy jowls. But if these were twins, they had been separated at birth and sent down very different paths. Curtis's hunched shoulders only accentuated the bulky, built-up muscles of his arms and back. The skin of his face was heavily pocked—ravaged by some childhood disease—and his nose was flattened to one side. I remembered overhearing Mr. Thornfax, on one of his early business visits to Hastings, telling Daniel that Curtis had once fought in the rings at Vauxhall. They'd joked that a boxer made the best carriage driver, because he'd leap down from the seat and wallop anyone blocking traffic.

Just as Christa's maid returned, Tom Rampling came round the side of the house. He pulled up short when he saw me and continued more slowly toward us, smoothing his vest and unrolling his sleeves to fasten the cuffs. I was grateful that Christa was occupied with Emily, because Tom stared openly at me, taking in my gown, my hair, my face. Worried he might say something about our previous encounter, I moved down along the carriage to head him off and made a pretense of checking my heel.

"Miss Luck." The soft voice sent an unexpected shiver through me, and I took a steadying breath before looking up at him. His grey gaze settled on Mr. Thornfax's gift at my throat. Tom scrubbed a hand across his mouth and looked away.

I drew my wrap self-consciously round my shoulders. How garish and ostentatious the necklace is, I suddenly thought. How he must despise me for wearing it. Then I wondered why, exactly, it should be despicable to wear a gift from a wealthy suitor. I released the wrap again and lifted my head a little higher, silently daring Tom to comment.

He shook his head, brows drawn. "You are transformed, milady. Hardly the ragged maid in need of rescue now."

"I was n-never ragged—" I began, but stopped when I remembered my torn dress and missing buttons. "All right, m-maybe I was, a little. You n-needn't worry a-b-bout me, you know." I had no idea what I meant by this last statement, but I wanted, with a sudden urgency, to reassure him.

"Mr. Rampling. Don't the Somerville ladies look lovely tonight?" Mr. Thornfax, rounding the corner of the carriage, gave Tom a clap on the shoulder. I noticed Tom flinch a little. He looked suddenly pale and plain next to the broad-shouldered gentleman with his golden mane and fine clothes.

Mr. Thornfax dropped his voice. "I understand I must thank you for seeing Miss Somerville safely out of danger."

"I—Sir, I did not …" Tom trailed off.

"You were painted in quite the gallant colours. I owe you a great debt for your part in guarding this lady's well-being, and her virtue." He took Tom's hand and shook it. "Above all, you know, I want Miss Somerville kept safe."

I kept my eyes on my shoes. I hadn't realized Mr. Thornfax knew anything about how I'd been attacked in the alleyway, didn't understand how he could know. He had shown me great consideration by not mentioning it in front of Daniel and Christabel.

My sister now walked up to us. Tom turned to include her and made a tight bow. "Mrs. Dewhurst. Miss Somerville."

I curtsied and bade Tom a polite good night, feeling the damp night rush in again against my skin as Mr. Thornfax handed me into the carriage. The maids helped settle our bustles and overskirts across the leather seats so the silk would not crease. Unexpectedly the men's voices rose in heated conversation outside, and I was startled to hear Tom's among them. "Opera," I heard him say, and I thought I caught "danger to the ladies."

Beside me Christa spoke over them, wondering what could possibly be causing such a delay, and what if we should be late. I felt like slapping her to make her quiet. I caught a sharp comment from Mr. Thornfax—"mind yourself," it might have been—and then Daniel's voice, low and soothing. A moment later Mr. Thornfax swung himself into the carriage beside Christabel and called to Curtis, and we were off.

"Was there an argument, sir?" my sister wondered.

Mr. Thornfax sat back and propped an elbow on the windowsill. "Your husband's boy is cleverer than is strictly necessary, I think. He would do all our jobs for us if we let him."

"Tom Rampling? How disagreeable of him! I've always said to Dr. Dewhurst 'tis unwise to bring that boy up so high. Daniel would teach Tom all his secrets if it meant he could sit in his easy chair and drink port wine." Christa reached across Mr. Thornfax to tweak the ruby cuff-clip at his wrist, setting it square. The gesture was more matronly than flirtatious; I could see she was delighted to be discussing her household with a man she hoped would join it, one day soon.

"Has he been very long in the doctor's employ?" Mr. Thornfax asked.

"Years and years—we'd only just gotten married. Dr. Dewhurst had him directly from Seven Dials, you know, all starved and slumduggered." Christa adopted a confiding whisper. "The police were after him for house-breaking and all sorts of things, but my husband declared such promise in the boy that he insisted on clearing all, setting all to rights, and bringing him home."

In all my time at Hastings I had never heard this history from either Christabel or Daniel. Fearful of betraying my agitation I held my hands tight in my lap and gazed out the carriage window into the fog.

Mr. Thornfax said, "Is Dewhurst always so soft, then?"

Christa clucked her tongue in fond exasperation. "Tom

was but the start of his madness for charity. 'Tis Tom brings all these souls to my husband's door, and not a one leaves again without some easement of pain and suffering."

Mr. Thornfax frowned. "I had assumed the doctor more ... strategic, in choosing orphans and paupers to test his medical treatments. Perhaps I shall speak with him."

Christabel talked without stop all the way to Covent Garden, with Mr. Thornfax supplying polite answers to her questions whenever she paused long enough to listen. My head spun with the effort to make sense of what I'd heard, both the disagreement outside the carriage and my sister's revelation. "It is not what you think," Tom had told me, of Will's crime and the dismantled watch parts in his grandmother's room. Yet Tom *was* a criminal—or at least he had been one when Daniel found him, according to my sister.

Mr. Thornfax offered us each an arm as we ascended the stairs of the white-columned opera house. The chattering crowd in the foyer parted for us like pigeons before galloping riders. Mr. Thornfax made dozens of introductions, his strong hand resting between my shoulder blades or at my waist each time he presented me. He remembered not only the names of all the ladies and gentlemen who approached us, but also a flattering fact or detail about each person to share with me in his or her presence, so that one by one he set them beaming with pleasure before he released their hands.

"Wherever did you find her, Thornfax?" a whiskered gentleman demanded.

"Is she not ravishing?" Mr. Thornfax purred.

"Roses and cream," the man agreed, pressing his lips to my glove and leaving a damp spot.

"Will there be an announcement?" asked an enormous lady, perspiring under her fox-fur stole.

"One only dares to hope," said Mr. Thornfax, provoking smiles all round and a long, delighted laugh from Christabel.

I decided it was a relief not to have to think of conversation, to be introduced and admired and praised without needing to be clever or coherent. Freed of any duty to speak I used my eyes, instead. The gilt-framed mirrors showed Mr. Thornfax and me from all angles, and I couldn't help but notice what a handsome couple we made. He stood a head taller than most of the crowd, and he'd paired his tailcoat with a smart midnight-blue waister in place of the more traditional white. My dress with its plunging décolletage was shapely through the bust and hips, gathered into a sumptuous froth of ruffles and folds at the back.

But it was the necklace that really drew all eyes to me. Regal, exotic, imperial—it lent a deeper bronze to my coiled hair and a paler pearl sheen to my skin. Warmed by my pulse it seemed to cast a glow all round my body.

A butler in a braid-trimmed velvet coat placed a flute of champagne in my hand, and from the corner of my eye I watched how my throat lengthened under the glittering choker as I swallowed the fizzing liquid.

Mr. Thornfax must have been watching, too, for his gaze grew intent, and he bent toward me. "You are absolutely splendid," he whispered. His warm breath on my ear sent a shiver across my skin.

I saw myself reflected not just in the mirrors but in the eyes of the other ladies—envious and admiring—and in the eyes of the men, hungry and restless. And Mimic, although she did not speak, began to play the role. Which role? I hardly knew—I would not have been able to describe it. I was not a flirt or a seductress, certainly not a world-weary courtesan. But neither was I an innocent, tongue-tied maid.

I blushed and smiled and pressed Mr. Thornfax's arm as I'd been doing since our entrance twenty minutes before. But Mimic now made small adjustments: my tongue darted out to moisten my lips, and my lips remained parted ever so slightly. My bosom swelled above my bodice when I breathed. Mr. Thornfax murmured a joke to me, and I gave a husky laugh that drew keen glances from several gentlemen nearby.

Mr. Thornfax led me over to an elderly man with a trim white beard and pince-nez glasses. "May I introduce my father," he said. "Mr. Charles Thornfax, the Lord Rosbury."

I gave my hand, and the old man took it stiffly but kept his eyes on his son. "Another bright ornament for your arm, I see," he said.

Mr. Thornfax cleared his throat. "This is Miss Leonora Somerville," he said. "I believe you are acquainted with her aunt, the Countess of Hastings."

A cold bark of laughter. "Emmaline doesn't know *you*, obviously, or this child wouldn't be anywhere near your reach."

After my cousin Archie's badgering of Mr. Thornfax at our party, I had listened at Hastings for snippets about the troubled relationship between father and son. Lord Rosbury's hard-won fortune in the cotton mills of the North. His late marriage, his heartbreak at his wife's death, his retreat into London politics while his young son grew up under the care of paid staff. His bitter outrage at Mr. Thornfax's refusal to take over management of the mills. As Daniel had explained it to Christa, "Six years as a seaman and Thornfax has quadrupled what his father made in a lifetime. But to the old man he'll only ever be a disappointment."

Now Lord Rosbury clucked his tongue and reached out to pat my hand where it rested in the crook of Mr. Thornfax's arm. "Enjoy him while you may, my dear. He'll run right off to sea again, soon enough."

Mr. Thornfax stiffened. A tremor of fury racked his muscles under my fingers.

Fearing violence, I angled my body between the two men. Mimic did not break her silence. But she did step forward, stand on tiptoe, and kiss the old man on the cheek, leaning into him and lingering to leave a soft sigh in his whiskers.

Caught off guard, Lord Rosbury had to steady himself against my shoulder, and a bright point of colour appeared in the centre of each sunken cheek. "Well, well," he muttered, looking at the floor. "The Lady Hastings's niece, indeed."

Mr. Thornfax wheeled me away without further comment, but his snort of suppressed mirth rang like applause in my ears.

We found Christa and climbed the stairs to the second balcony. Mr. Thornfax steered us across the gallery and through the curtained doorway into his private box. More champagne waited for us in a silver bucket, and lavish bouquets of tulips and narcissi fragranced the air. As soon as we were seated Christabel opened the strings of her reticule, fished out a tiny bottle, and added a splash of laudanum to her champagne glass.

"Are you ill?" I whispered to her.

"I shan't be, now," she replied, and lifted the glass to her lips.

We hardly had time to take out our little opera glasses before the curtain rose and the music began. Fortunately for my sister the auditorium lights were not lowered for perform- ances in London as, my aunt Emma had once informed me, was the modern practice in New York, and so Christa could continue to scan the crowd below us and in the galleries opposite once the show began.

I had never seen *La Sonnambula*, and of course I could not understand the Italian. The story, so far as I could glean from gesture and music alone, concerned a betrothed couple, their jealous ex-lovers, a long-lost son, and a phantom come to haunt the village. The young soprano playing the lead role was new to London, and her slim figure belied the warm, robust timbre of her voice. The soaring notes of her aria made my heart swell and my throat ache. I pressed my fingers over my lips, half-afraid Mimic would decide to sing along.

Mr. Thornfax's low voice at my ear broke into my absorp- tion. "A man might have worried that a mutemouth wife would appear simple or dull," he teased. "Have you any idea how perfect you are? I saw how you managed my father back there. The poor old man couldn't decide whether you were an empress or a glad-girl. I do believe you could play either role just as well, if I asked you."

It was a shocking thing to say. But Mr. Thornfax was only speaking the truth, as usual—and it was a truth Mimic had already guessed. I was playing neither an innocent nor a whore but someone exotic, someone unguessable. I was a mystery. Borne along by the voluptuous chords onstage, with half of London watching me and Mr. Thornfax's impetuous words still echoing in my head, I found myself stirring, growing ever warmer and more languid in my body. Was this Mimic's pleasure or mine? I couldn't tell.

At the interval there was more smiling and hand-pressing. We never made it out of our box; a parade of guests pressed in behind and beside and all round us. Christabel and I were introduced to scores of ladies and gentlemen, so many that I would never remember who was whom. It didn't matter. I was giddy with champagne, and Mimic was aglow in her role, and Mr. Thornfax was utterly enchanted by her, by me. He sat back in his seat, shaking his head and smiling in mock exasperation at the attention showered upon me. He touched my necklace's little clasp as if to check whether it was secure, and then he let his fingertip stroke the downy skin at my nape, laughing aloud when I gasped and shivered.

I have him now, I found myself thinking. 'Tis a triumph. A conquest. Right now he would give me anything I wanted.

Despite his attentions to me, Mr. Thornfax never for a moment overlooked my sister. "I daresay, Christabel, Dewhurst was a fool to let you come alone," he said. "The eyes of every bachelor and every unhappily married man are fixed on you."

Christa fluttered her fan at him. "Isn't he awful?" She giggled to the ladies next to her. "Isn't he cruel?" Her medicine had evidently warded off her headache. My sister was beside herself with delight.

Finally we settled into our seats once more, and a group of villagers took the stage to profess the tragic innocence of the soprano. Then their cries of alarm conveyed her sudden peril: the sleepwalking heroine was crossing a high bridge, her eyes closed and her voice dreamy and detached.

Up in Mr. Thornfax's box, thirst began to dry my tongue. Weariness crept over me despite the suspense onstage. Perhaps Mr. Thornfax would give me anything I wanted, I considered. But I hadn't the faintest idea what that might be. I glanced at his broad hand resting on his knee and caught myself comparing it to Tom Rampling's pale, quick-fingered hand. It made me feel disloyal, but then I could not decide whether the guilt was for Tom or for Mr. Thornfax. Self-consciousness knifed a gulf between Mimic, winning and pliant, and the shrinking, uncomfortable girl who hid within. I wondered, suddenly glum, whether the second half of the opera would go on as long as the first.

A shout drew our attention to the gallery opposite us. I thought I saw young Will darting behind an empty seat. It made no sense—a street boy at the opera!—but here came an usher hurrying after him. The man waved for help from another usher and, half-crouching in the aisle, gestured apologies as he scanned the rows for the boy. I spied Will again, a white face and a woollen cap ducking along the railings.

My first thought was that he must be searching for us, that there must be some emergency at home. Next I thought of Tom. Did he know that Will was here? My surprise and befuddlement at seeing the little boy so far from home, looking so small and so out of place in his frayed breeches and bare feet, drew me fully to standing.

Suddenly there was a great flash of blinding white light and a roar that shook the seats beneath us.

TEN

I remember how I kept looking over at the stage. I cannot recall how long it took the orchestra to stop playing—the music could not have been heard over the din in any case. The actors all tumbled forward like marionettes with cut strings, trying see out into the gallery. Maybe I was still feeling the after-effects of Mimic's wordless performance, or maybe it was the shock, but I remember how *wrong* it seemed to me that the show stopped and yet the curtain didn't come down. *Play on*, I remember thinking, *or else retire to the wings!* It was awful to see the players no longer controlling the show.

The show had shifted from stage to audience, only now the action was all too real. I was thrown sideways, and Mr. Thornfax caught me in his arms. Through the haze past his shoulder I saw a crack open in the opposite balcony's gilt façade. Screams chorused across the theatre as patrons felt the tremors and fled their seats. The crack gaped wider and vanished behind a cascade of plaster. I watched, mesmerized with terror, as the entire second-tier balcony lurched and tilted. People on that side began to shove each other and climb over the backs of seats. A lady's feathered hat somehow flew free of the melee and sailed, with a perverse sense of cheer, over the railing into the dust-choked space below.

Then a dreadful tearing sound filled my ears, and a section of seats broke entirely away. Mr. Thornfax disentangled himself from me and leaned forward for a clearer view. Beside me Christabel shrieked, "The Lord Rosbury!" and I, too, spied the frail form of Mr. Thornfax's father amid the scrambling throng on the balcony. I watched him reach up his arms, twiglike wrists extending from the sleeves, and grab on to a young man standing beside him. Lord Rosbury was half-lifted out of his seat as the man attempted to pull away. As the balcony tipped farther the two men tumbled sideways. They slid across the floor, slammed into the railing, and disappeared into the chaos below.

Something struck my leg. I turned to see Christa collapsed on the floor beside her seat. Mr. Thornfax rushed to the hall to catch an usher, and the two men half-carried my sister from the box. I snatched up our things and followed, keeping as close as I could through the panicked hive of the gallery.

All this time I searched and searched for a sight of young Will. I knew with horrified certainty that the blast had occurred directly where he'd been hidden. And yet my stubborn mind refused to grasp the fact of the boy's death. I kept telling myself, in all the fevered crush of movement and noise, that if I could only glimpse Will, if I could only find him here somewhere, then he would be safe. I craned to see over the swarm of dusty hats and dishevelled hair. My knees struck a marble bench and I stood atop it to scan the crowd. In my distraction I nearly lost Mr. Thornfax as he shouldered on ahead. I had to force myself to get down and push my way closer to him. In those first stunned moments I think I really believed I could conjure the little boy back to life.

Mr. Thornfax veered away from the crush of fleeing patrons and led us to a service door. Curtis, waiting outside with the carriage, jumped down to help him put Christabel across the seat.

"Care for your sister," Mr. Thornfax said, pressing my hand. "I must help here where I can." The orders he gave Curtis were drowned out by the sobs Christa unleashed as soon as she and I were alone.

It took everything I had to calm my sister's hysterics on the way home. She seemed not to mind Mimic's use of our old nurse Mrs. Dawson saying, "There, now. There, now," as I held her and stroked her hair. I could barely support her up the stairs of Hastings House, and the servants who rushed to take her from my embrace were so occupied with her care that they left me quite alone.

I stood for several minutes there in our dark foyer, light-headed and sick, struggling to breathe. Mr. Thornfax's necklace bit at my throat like a garrote. I wrestled with its clasps, and when I finally had the thing in my hand it seemed to weigh fifty pounds. I avoided my reflection in the hall mirror.

Daniel intercepted me on the stairs. "Are you all right?"

The world cracked open, I thought. *People fell to their deaths.* "Yes," I managed.

"Less rattled than poor Mrs. Dewhurst, I'll wager." He held my hands and turned me this way and that, checking for damage. His gaze lingered upon the jewelled chain wrapped round my fingers. He made no remark except to mumble, "He might at least have brought you home himself."

"The L-Lord Rosbury was there," I told him. "He ... h-his s-seat ..." It was impossible to put words to what I'd seen.

"Ah." My brother-in-law shook his head. "Of course, then, Mr. Thornfax would have needed to stay behind. A great loss for him."

"Young Will, t-too." My voice wobbled. "F-from your surgery."

Daniel frowned. "You've had a shock, Leonora. You were mistaken."

"But I s-saw—"

"No." He composed his face into a smile and put a hand on my back. "No one from Hastings House was there except you and Christabel."

Will was caught! A wild flare of hope. My brother-in-law must mean that Will was caught thieving and carted off before the blast, and Daniel punished him and sent him to bed, and he only wishes now to keep the matter quiet. But even as I thought it, the impossibility of it pressed against my skull. A thudding pain struck up behind my eyes and across the back of my head.

Daniel puffed a little as we climbed the stairs together. "And Leonora, I would caution you about being too soft with the street urchins I employ. 'Tis different here than in the country. Servants are not family, and these foundlings are not even proper servants." He patted my shoulder. "I shall have a nostrum sent up to your room, in case your sleep is troubled tonight."

Alone in my bed I lay for a long while in a kind of

shivering shock. I must have dozed off, because I started awake again at the sound of voices in the doorway.

"Miss Somerville," Tom said. The fine bones of his face seemed to shift and shrink in the flickering light of the oil lamp he held.

"I tried to stop him, miss!" Bess clutched her coat together over her nightdress, her mussed hair spilling from her cap. "He broke the lock on my door!"

"I didn't break it, Bess. You'll find it in perfect working order. What was I to do? You wouldn't want everyone roused by knocking."

A first-rate lockpick and thief. I sat up and struggled to free my legs from the coverlet. "B-bring my dressing gown," I told Bess.

"Miss, you mustn't receive him here!"

"Milady, only if you're well enough. Are you? They said—they told me you appeared unhurt—" Tom choked the words off.

Bess held the gown like a screen while I threaded my arms into the sleeves. Not knowing how else to proceed I pulled Tom into the hall and closed the bedroom door behind me, leaving Bess inside. "What is it?"

His hand hovered at my waist and then dropped, the knuckles clenched white against his thigh. "Miss Somerville, I must know. Did you see him? Young Will, the boy from Seven Dials."

Young Will. The evening's events rushed back upon me all in a blow.

Tom swallowed hard. "Did he … did you see if he got away?"

How did Tom know the boy had been at the opera house tonight? It took me a moment to find my voice. "He was s-standing right there, d-directly in the b-b—" I could not say *blast*, but no other words were possible, either, to describe the terrible roar of light and dust that had filled the gallery.

Tom sagged against the door. He gave a small, strangled moan. His face bore such a look of sorrowful regret that a sudden thought struck me cold with horror. Will had been wandering that crowd of opulence and finery on an errand of thievery. He'd been pocket-picking again for Tom Rampling.

"You were painted in quite the gallant colours."

Mr. Thornfax's smooth baritone jerked Tom to attention, straight as a poker against the wall. His head swivelled wildly. When he discovered we were still alone in the hallway, he gaped at me. "What?"

"You are cleverer than is strictly necessary, I think." I squeezed my eyes shut, trying to think, trying to banish Mimic.

"You've had a shock tonight, milady. I am glad you were not hurt, at least."

"You would do all our jobs for us, if we let you," said Mimic-as-Thornfax.

"It's all right. I'll fetch Bess for you." Tom reached for the door handle.

"You s-sent him," I choked out, in my own voice at last.

Tom's eyes widened.

"Will. He stole for you. P-pocket watches. You sent him!"

He reeled back as though I'd struck him. "No!"

"Then w-why do you look so g-guilty?" Tears blinded me and I scrubbed them angrily from my eyes.

"Because I failed him." He shook his head again, as if trying to dislodge something painful. "I failed him, and that amounts to the same thing." Before I could reply he wrenched away from me and tore down the stairs.

This time sleep would not arrive. The facts seemed dreadful to me. I could separate nothing clearly, save this: a little boy was dead. My brother-in-law was quite right, of course. Little boys died all the time in London—little girls, too—and were neither mourned nor remembered. The workhouses and paupers' asylums overflowed with children like Will, orphaned or abandoned by destitute parents. They survived only by begging and tramping. Or they gathered into gangs, living in makeshift criminal "families" with the likes of Mr. Sears and Mrs. Clampitt. Wherever they went, their little lives hung on a hair.

I had imagined, though, that Daniel was fond of the children he doctored. He asked our cook to boil the bones and other remnants of our meals into soup for them, and several of his little charges came nearly every day to eat in the scullery. I'd often helped him pack a basket of fresh fruit and jars of boiled beef for the poor and sick when he left for his rounds in the East End. He'd paid Will for running errands and Hattie for carrying coal and emptying chamber pots. Why would he have done that if he didn't care about their fate?

In the end, my head awhirl and my heart aching, I drank the laudanum preparation Bess had left beside my bed and sank into a deadened sleep.

ELEVEN

I slept extremely late, and when I came downstairs I saw my cousin Archibald Mavety in our front hall. Beadall was helping him on with his coat.

"Archie!" I called. I felt rather floaty and light. Quite peaceful and agreeable, and Archie was ravishing in his sky-blue jacket and striped trousers. "P-please, won't you stay for b-breakfast?"

He snorted. "You've missed it."

"Tea, then." My knee bumped the umbrella stand and I watched it wobble and fall.

"My, but the ladies of Hastings House are groggy this morning. Please tell me the good doctor hasn't got you up on the dope as well as your sister?" His tone was light, but he looked genuinely worried as we embraced.

I kissed his cheek and asked Beadall to have refreshments brought into the parlour.

We took our seats in the sunlit room, and a moment later Mrs. Nussey came with the tea. Beadall, behind her, carried an enormous arrangement of flowers in a crystal vase. "Arrived this morning from Mr. Thornfax," he said.

Archie gave a low whistle. I stared at the profusion of ruffled purple tulips, the blue hyacinths, the white hothouse lilies. The heavy scent filled the parlour, and my stomach turned as I remembered the decadence of the opera box. "Bring them up to Mrs. Dewhurst," I told Beadall. "Tell her he s-sent them for her."

The moment we were alone Archie lifted his freckled hands as if waiting for the heavens to fill them. "What the devil happened last night, Leo? I have the outline of it from the police, but I should like to hear your eyewitness account."

I told him. As he listened he took out his little book and marked down several notes. He seemed especially to like the part about Mr. Thornfax and the usher carrying Christabel to safety. I left out Tom Rampling's late-night visit to my room, of course, and the fact that young Will had almost certainly been killed in the blast.

But still Archie said, "I wonder which poor orphan was murdered this time."

"What d-do you mean?"

He rolled his eyes. "Don't you ever read my newspaper column? This is the fourth explosion in half as many months. The Black Glove is clever. They know there is no one harder to find or predict than a street child. No one is less likely to be enquired about, afterward."

Servants are not family, and these foundlings are not even proper servants. The memory of Daniel's words punched through the pleasantness I'd felt upon waking. "And they found one? A s-street child?"

"Yes, I had it straight from the chief inspector this morning: a boy in rags counted among the dead. The police understand 'tis the details make the story, you see."

The light, floaty feeling drained away entirely, leaving behind a fogginess that was one beat away from nausea. "Have … have they identified the d-dead?" I asked him.

"Not officially. Not yet." Archie looked at me sidelong. "Why?" Then his eyes widened and he lunged forward in his chair to give my knees a little shake. "Did you see someone go down in the blast? It wasn't a parliamentarian, was it?"

I blinked; I had still been thinking of Will. "The Lord Ros-b-bury," I said.

Archie snapped his fingers. "I've heard only rumours so far. So it's true?"

"He was there, y-yes."

"Good God." Archie leapt up and walked to the window. The sun lit his fine blond hair into a blinding halo. "Oh, this will make a roaring good story, Leo! Now I only need the note, and my triumph is complete."

"What n-note?"

"There always has to be a note. It's only a question of timing the thing properly so that I can get a lead story about the explosion and another, separate piece about the Black Glove's note. The timing is paramount with these things, you know. The timing and the details."

He was pacing a tight circuit on the rug now, and the movement made me queasy. I leaned back against the cushions. Dizziness tilted the room before my eyes, and I struggled to cut through the laudanum's lingering fog.

"You do know Thornfax inherits his title?" Archie said,

and sprawled into his chair again. "There's a whole story just in itself! The wastrel son returns from the East to seek his father's blessing." He clapped a hand to his breast. "But alas! 'Tis too late!"

I frowned. "What are you t-talking about?"

"Rosbury, you idiot." Archie grinned. "Your splendid suitor is now a lord."

"Mr. Mavety!" Daniel stood, red-faced, in the parlour door. "What in the devil's name are you doing still here?"

"I'm just leaving now, Doctor," Archie said, and made a face at me as Daniel put a hand on his collar and fairly yanked him from his chair.

When he was gone my brother-in-law rounded on me: "Did you say anything to him?"

"I t-told him the Lord Rosbury was in the g-gallery."

"I forbid you to speak with that man again."

"Archie is my cousin," I reminded him.

"He's a newspaperman! He has more concern for his career than for his family. Make no mistake, Leonora, he doesn't care for your good name, either. Scandal and hearsay—that is what he lives for."

Archie's sheer glee in the face of what had happened did seem rather insensitive. He seemed to reckon the catastrophe in words and sentences instead of lives lost. What was more, he seemed to know a great deal about the Black Glove. He knew so much that he could predict—could even brag about—the timing of the gang's letter claiming responsibility for the explosion. But then, I considered, Daniel was hiding something, too. If his anger at Archie pointed to anything, it was not the doctor's loyalty to his family but his reluctance to face facts.

A few days later the Lady Hastings called Mr. Thornfax and me to luncheon in Gordon Square. She wanted to offer her condolences as well as to congratulate him on his summons to Parliament, now that he was to assume his father's title and become the next Lord Rosbury. I suspected she also wanted confirmation of what I'd hinted at in the letter I'd hastily posted after the opera to reassure her of my safety: that a genuine mutual regard was developing between Mr. Thornfax and me. My aunt Emma knew me so well that she would be able to read my feelings on my face.

Bess accompanied me from Hastings House in Mr. Thornfax's carriage that Wednesday, but we dropped her for a visit with her brother, who worked as a steward in a home near Gordon Square. Mr. Thornfax used our few minutes alone to apologize for sending Christabel and me home so abruptly after the opera house violence and for not calling on us in the days that followed.

"N-not at all. Your p-poor father—" I tried to say.

"There was business to attend to, of course. The police, my father's household affairs, the notices to send. It's taken everything in my power just to ensure they'll release the body in time for the funeral on Saturday—" He caught himself, pressing his fingers to his forehead. "Forgive me, Miss Somerville. I don't mean to be so revolting about things."

"Not at all," I repeated.

"It isn't the funeral arrangements that I've found so exhausting, to tell you the truth," he said, and he leaned forward in the carriage to face me. "It is no secret to you, I'm sure, that my father and I were never great friends."

Forthright as always. I nodded uncertainly.

"'Tis a case of what the public needs to see, you understand."

"And w-what is that?"

"Grief, of course. Or the manful suppression of it." Mr. Thornfax sighed. "And, you know, I do feel sadness. I did not expect to feel anything, but the sadness is there. 'Tis not quite the right kind of sadness, though."

He looked so desolate just then that I reached out and touched his hand. "Why isn't it the right k-kind?"

Mr. Thornfax caught my hand in his and traced a finger across my palm. "Well, 'tis hardly manful. I feel like … well, I feel rather like a little boy again. Left all alone in the world."

"Like you f-felt when your m-mother died," I guessed.

"Yes." His blue eyes shot to mine.

I knew how it went. It had happened to me less than two years before. 'Twas Father who had died then, but I had found myself mourning Mother all over again. And I was only five years old when I lost her.

Mr. Thornfax tilted his head in invitation, and I leaned forward to bring my face to his. Very slowly, very softly, he brushed his cheek against mine. "We are both alone in the world, are we not, Leonora," he whispered.

"Y-yes. Only I am not lonely j-just now," I whispered back.

I felt his smile as a kiss against my cheek. After a moment

he sat back, slipped his hand from mine, and cleared his throat. "With your aunt, at least, I think we needn't pretend to be grieving. She was quite vocal about my father's shortcomings, last time we met."

And indeed I saw no pretense of grief between my aunt and Mr. Thornfax during our visit. As we pulled up in the carriage her butler was there waiting with an umbrella to shelter us from the steady drizzle. The sounds of the pianoforte filled the foyer as we doffed our coats and hats. When we were announced Aunt Emmaline rose from the piano bench and clasped our hands in greeting.

Until my father died I had never noticed how much his looks resembled those of his older sister. But every time I saw Aunt Emma after a short absence, I saw him in her: the long nose, the strong jaw, the kindly crinkles around the eyes. My aunt's keen brown eyes, though, were all her own. They regarded one straight-on, friendly but always appraising. I remembered a long-ago visitor to Kew remarking that to be *seen* by the Lady Hastings felt rather like being *seen through*.

Today she wore purple silk with a rust-orange striped overskirt. She and Mr. Thornfax exchanged pleasantries while I looked round at the familiar furnishings. It was odd to be greeted as a formal guest here. In the old days, whenever Aunt Emma had business in town, she would bring me with her from her country home in Kew to Gordon Square in London. In the old days, upon entering this room, I would have simply joined my aunt at the piano where she would plunk out a music-hall tune. She would sing to me in her rough contralto, and afterward we would dress for dinner in the most ridiculous of her Paris furs. Or she would read to me from Mr. Carroll and coax me to stumble through the parts of the White Rabbit, Alice, and the twins, while she played her favourite role: the Queen of Hearts.

Aunt Emma said how relieved she was that we hadn't been injured in the opera house disaster—nine souls dead, and thrice that number injured, she had read in the papers— and how dreadful for all London to be going round in a muddle of terror wondering when next the Black Glove would attack. She said how much she would miss Lord Rosbury, and then told us that the "dear old man" had disapproved most vehemently of her taking this house after the death of the Earl of Hastings.

"What was his complaint?" Mr. Thornfax said, adding, "Not that my father ever needed much grounds to launch a complaint."

"Oh, 'tis sited too close to the boarding halls of University College for his liking. He thought I should stay on in Hastings House and remarry as soon as I could. 'A lady in your position can't be too careful,' he was fond of reminding me."

"'Be careful,'" Mr. Thornfax echoed. "The very anthem of my childhood!"

My aunt gave a sympathetic nod. Then she rose and fetched a thick, slightly moth-eaten orange shawl from the back of a chair. This she wrapped snugly round my shoulders.

Mr. Thornfax had stood with her, clutching his teacup to stop it rattling in the saucer, and he smiled at me as he settled back in his seat. "The colour suits you, Miss Somerville, but I think perhaps in silk?"

I smiled back. Aunt Emma knew how much I loved this old shawl. By giving it to me she was acknowledging the awkwardness of this meeting for me, and thereby lessening that awkwardness considerably.

Now she laughed. "Look at my niece basking in your attention, Mr. Thornfax. Like the princess with her golden ball."

Mr. Thornfax cocked his head. "Wouldn't that make me the loathsome frog?"

"Ah, but a frog is a little dragon, you know. If one goes back far enough in legend, all the pond-dwellers are dragons."

Mr. Thornfax laughed, too. "You flatter me, my lady." He put down his teacup and picked up a little statuette of Harlequin. My aunt had been given it in her theatre days as thanks for one of her performances. She packed Harlequin in her case whenever she moved between Kew and town; he was her talisman, she said. I used to be allowed to play with him on the rug with my dolls. I felt an odd kind of jealousy, watching the man toy with him so casually.

Mr. Thornfax seemed very comfortable with my aunt. They spoke of his writ of summons to the House of Lords, and of Mr. Thornfax's plans for an endowment to the Royal Observatory at Greenwich in his father's name.

"Charles Thornfax wasn't one to gaze at the stars," my aunt remarked.

"No," agreed Mr. Thornfax, "but he was a great admirer of efficiency. I plan to promote the Greenwich Meridian, you see. Adopting a global standard for time will bring shipping and trade into better alignment. Not to mention the railways."

Aunt Emma seemed impressed. "A politician already," she said.

Luncheon was laid, and we moved to the dining room. I'd never properly dined with Mr. Thornfax before—Christa had kept me from the table when he'd come to visit Daniel at Hastings House—and I was struck by the effortless elegance of his table manners. Waving aside her servants, he held the countess's chair for her and served her wine from the crystal decanter. He offered us the choicest portions of the roast chicken and cabbage; he murmured his compliments to the cook the moment he'd tasted his meal.

Aunt Emma waited until we'd moved on to our custard and strawberries. Then she said, "I hear that Archibald Mavety is no longer welcome at Hastings House. Can you enlighten me in this matter, Mr. Thornfax?"

Mr. Thornfax touched his napkin to his mouth. "I believe he offended Dr. Dewhurst quite badly."

My aunt gave a delicate snort. "Daniel can be such a prig."

I stifled a smile to see that Mr. Thornfax looked slightly shocked.

"That man—that newspaper—has always been friendly to the Hastingses," she persisted. "What could Dr. Dewhurst possibly be worried about?"

"Friendship is one thing, Lady Hastings. Family is another. Especially when slander is in play."

"Slander?"

"The man is in such hot pursuit of the so-called Black Glove that he'd rather like to see the plot link up with the doctor's pharmaceutical efforts somehow," Mr. Thornfax said.

The countess drew herself up and smoothed her silver hair. She had a way of stacking herself like so many sacks of grain upon a chair. "Surely not! I could never believe such a thing of Daniel, could you?"

"I think 'tis likelier that young Mr. Mavety has invented the entire fiction, opium gang and all, to sell his newspapers."

"The Black Glove—a fiction? But then tell me, who is bombing our city?"

"There are many in London who stand to lose money if opium is banned. Any street-corner chemist can put together a good lightshow from the stuff on his shelves. And he might do it if he thinks it'll scare people into letting him keep mixing his laudanum for a farthing an ounce." Mr. Thornfax shrugged. "I shouldn't be surprised if there were a dozen Black Gloves across the city by now."

"But Archibald wouldn't deliberately falsify a story."

Mr. Thornfax raised his palms and smiled. "I am sorry. I know you are fond of the lad. And truthfully, I don't know all the details of his quarrel with Dr. Dewhurst."

Aunt Emma had been watching me from the corner of her eye and must have seen from my fidgeting that I knew something. When our visit was concluded and we were waiting for our coats, she begged Mr. Thornfax for a moment alone with her niece.

"Well? What did Archibald say to you?" she demanded when she'd closed the parlour door behind me.

"I d-don't—" I began, but she waved a hand to silence me. "Do let's hear it in his words; it's been too long since you did your cousin's voice."

Before I could object Mimic leapt in, evidently delighted at the invitation. I parroted Archie's comments about the orphans' deaths and his speculations about when the Black Glove's letter would arrive.

"But what does it mean? What has it to do with your brother-in-law?"

I shook my head.

She sighed. "Well, you mustn't worry yourself about it all. I am sure the opera house explosion was a terrible shock to you, my dear. But I believe you are in good hands with Francis Thornfax. I looked into his business affairs on your behalf, of course. He's just sold all but his smallest and newest ship, so he must mean what he says about supporting the ban on opium, even if importing the stuff is what secured him his fortune."

I sighed. "He is p-perfect."

Aunt Emma laughed. "Of course he is perfect. He shall be a lord!"

On our way home Mr. Thornfax wondered whether we might detour to the Embankment. "Since the weather has cleared I'd like to show you my new ship. We needn't even leave the carriage, if you prefer."

I sensed this was important to him. "M-might we go a-b-board?" I said, and he grinned, pleased, but shook his head. "We haven't a chaperone, Miss Somerville."

The streets narrowed and grew crowded as traffic was squeezed between the wharves and loading-cranes along the river. Mr. Thornfax nodded to our left. "That's my store-house there, on the ground floor." I craned my neck to read the words in white paint at the top of the tall building with its dozens of stacked windows: NICHOLSON'S WHARF. "Your brother-in-law's laboratory is housed inside, too, now that I won't be dealing with such large shipments.

"Ah, that *is* lucky—there's our boy Rampling." He thumped the carriage bonnet for Curtis to stop and hallooed out to Tom, who looked up from locking the warehouse door.

"Good day, Mr. Thornfax, Miss Somerville." Tom's black cap had been turned backward; when he finished making his bow he replaced it right, keeping his eyes on Mr. Thornfax.

"I wonder, Mr. Rampling—would you be willing to accompany us aboard my new clipper, docked just downriver? Miss Somerville has expressed her interest in a tour."

Tom's eyes flew to mine and away again. "Of course, milord."

"Climb in, then. Dewhurst trusts you. He'll take your word I kept the lady safe."

Tom climbed into the carriage beside Mr. Thornfax, filling the space with his clean, familiar scent, now tinged with salt air—a confusing contrast with Mr. Thornfax's aura of boot polish and tobacco. We drove past Billingsgate and along the tight avenue in front of the magisterial Custom House, bustling with sailors and militiamen, and Mr. Thornfax did not seem to notice the strain between his companions as he talked of his new ship's capabilities. He'd christened her *Heroine*, he told us, though they'd not yet had time to paint the name on the hull or finish the gilding on the figurehead. This trip to London was her maiden voyage; she'd been crafted to his precise specifications in Aberdeen. "She'll carry tea and wool with the best of the clippers, of course, but she'll also keep Dr. Dewhurst supplied more efficiently and discreetly than before. She will be faster and more seaworthy than any vessel in the Empire." Mr. Thornfax was beaming. "The *Heroine*'ll give even the *Cutty Sark* a run for her money, I'll wager!"

"W-w-will you r-race her, then?" I was self-conscious with Tom listening to our conversation, and my stutter became more pronounced.

"As soon as may be," Mr. Thornfax said. He shifted to the seat beside me. "Shall I teach you to sail, Miss Somerville?"

"Oh yes, p-please."

"You won't take her to sea!" Tom exclaimed.

"Whyever not?" Mr. Thornfax looked surprised at Tom's vehemence.

"She ... Miss Somerville would not be comfortable." Tom was very red in the face.

Mr. Thornfax spread his arm across the back of the seat, brushing my hair with his sleeve. "Of course Miss Somerville's comfort is paramount," he said. "But you know, Leonora, when we are married you needn't even leave Hastings House, if you like. I'll be often at sea, but I'll visit whenever I come ashore."

Now it was my turn to blush. His use of my Christian name, the mention of marriage—it was very unlike Mr. Thornfax to be so familiar with me in front of others. I realized at once that this casualness was pitched to unbalance Tom Rampling. A lesser man might have reprimanded Tom openly for his impertinence. Mr. Thornfax, with characteristic deftness, hadn't swayed from his friendly enthusiasm but had nonetheless managed to remind Tom of his place in relation to a lady and a future lord.

And judging by Tom's dark expression it had worked. "Forgive me, milord," he said. "But I understood that you'd sold your shipping business?"

Mr. Thornfax shrugged. "I can only be on one ship at a time, can't I? There!" He pointed at the river and shouted at Curtis to stop.

TWELVE

The *Heroine*, tall, trim, and gleaming, was tethered by a steep gangplank to the pier. Mr. Thornfax leapt from the carriage after Tom and, in his enthusiasm, strode directly down the dock, so that Tom had to come round and hand me down. The lapse of manners amused me—it was so rare to see something break through Mr. Thornfax's perfect civility. His love for his boat, like his sadness that morning in the carriage, made him more human in my eyes. I was falling deeper in love with Francis Thornfax by the hour today, it seemed.

I was still smiling when I took Tom's hand, but I stopped when I saw the fearsome scowl on his face. He noted my surprise and checked himself—a marble-pale politeness replaced the anger and scorn—but I'd gotten quite good at reading Tom Rampling's eyes. Right now they were all the roiling grey of a tempest. "W-what is it?" I said.

He shook his head, glanced at Curtis, and toed a gobbet of seaweed with his boot.

"You n-needn't be so s-surly with him, you know," I said.

"But you shall marry him."

It wasn't a question, exactly. Nor was Tom's tone derisive or angry. Yet I felt accused, and I bristled at the notion that Tom should accuse me of anything. "He has n-not asked for me, yet," I said, a touch stiffly.

He let out his breath. After a long moment he said, "You're not dressed for the Docks, milady. That's a chill wind." The stormy eyes had softened to concern, and there was pity there, too — he felt sorry for me.

Tom Rampling's pity was a good deal harder to take than his anger. I flounced past him, hurrying after Mr. Thornfax, who'd finally realized his mistake and turned back for me.

The gangplank arced and swayed in the wind. I clung to the ropes despite Mr. Thornfax's steadying arms on either side of me, and I fixed my eyes on the brass post above us, trying to ignore how my toes caught in the hem of my skirt. At last Mr. Thornfax grasped me round the waist and hoisted me up over the lip and onto the deck of the *Heroine*. He jumped down beside me and threw his arms wide. "My first visit aboard!" he crowed.

I laughed. "I'm honoured to sh-share in it, then."

"Yes," he said, and took my hand. "Come, Miss Somerville, let's explore."

When we crossed the polished deck, though, we found the midship house was locked. Mr. Thornfax looked round at Tom lingering at the top of the gangway. "What do you say, Mr. Rampling?"

Tom came over, and Mr. Thornfax stood back and waved him toward the brass keyhole. "I've no key, you see. They must have sent it direct to my office."

"I'm sorry, milord. What can I do?"

"Can you get us in without damaging the lock?"

Tom reddened.

"I do my research, Mr. Rampling. You hadn't been at work in my warehouse six hours before I had your whole history. Now what will you need to work your magic here? Wire? A blade?"

Tom could not look at us. He had to clear his throat to speak. "Neither, milord." Very reluctantly he took a little leather sleeve from his pocket and unrolled it to reveal a set of tiny iron picks. His ears were crimson as he bent over the lock, but he had the door open in a trice, and Mr. Thornfax whooped and thumped him on the shoulder.

"This is the whole trouble with England," said Mr. Thornfax, as he took the narrow steps down and reached back for my hand. "Our country is like an enormous fishbowl. Each man strives to swim faster than his countrymen, or to appear bigger and more colourful, but if you stop to notice you'll see we're all just swimming round and round in circles—keep with us, now, Mr. Rampling, and light that lantern so we can see the cabinet-work in the galley," he called.

We passed through the skylit mess room with its iron-footed table and filed through a narrow door along the corridor of sailors' berths. I pressed my skirts to my legs to stop them catching on the rows of hooks and handles. The galley was already outfitted with neatly hung copper pots, griddles, ladles, and kettles. Mr. Thornfax pointed out how the dishes were stowed behind special rails so they wouldn't jostle in rough seas.

Mr. Thornfax tried the door of the second deck house

and whooped again to find it unlocked. Inside the saloon he ran his hands lovingly over the surface of the mahogany dining table. Here the chairs were upholstered in leather, and the transom was fitted with a semicircular velvet sofa. After a few minutes of looking round the room, Mr. Thornfax returned to his theme: "What nobody ever tells us, growing up in England, is that the world is much wider than we realize. In fact it isn't a fishbowl at all. 'Tis an ocean!"

What was it my aunt had said at lunch? *In the right sort of legend every pond dweller might be a dragon.* Poor sad Tom Rampling with his lies and his bad conscience, I thought. No wonder he was surly. His life was lived in the murkiest depths of the pond, while Mr. Thornfax could range across the whole of the Empire.

As if his thoughts had run along the same lines as mine Mr. Thornfax put a kindly hand to Tom's shoulder. "Here is the truth about most men, Mr. Rampling. Most men—the vast numbers of men in England, the multitude of clerks and cobblers and doctors and fishmongers and, yes, the politicians, too—most never dare to stop swimming in little circles, no matter how easy it might be simply to break from the crowd and make for the open sea. Take yourself, now. You seem a clever lad. Cunning, even.

"But most men—they may be clever or cunning, they may dream their whole lives of better, broader prospects, but they cling, terrified, to what they know. And so they are forever doomed to a life of servitude, drudgery, and petty crime. Of lock-breaking, say."

He led us into the master cabin, dominated by a massive, velvet-covered bed piled with silk pillows. The three of us stood just inside the doorway, awestruck. Panels of bird's-eye maple were trimmed with satinwood and set with reliefs of teak, rosewood, ebony—there were more varieties of wood inlaid here than I could name. These were interspersed with panels of mirror and surmounted by enamelled cornices edged with gold. It was all so beautiful that I forgot what I was looking at until Tom coughed into his fist and mumbled that he thought perhaps we should continue our tour elsewhere, if his lord was amenable?

It was my marriage bed we were looking at, of course—or at least a bed in which I might someday find myself sleeping, now and again, with my husband when he was docked in London. The blush that rose to my cheeks was stoked warmer still when I looked up to find Mr. Thornfax watching me with an open question on his face: *What do you think?* My suitor looked almost anxious for my reaction, and I allowed my smile to answer him with equal openness: *'Tis more than I could have imagined.*

Tom cleared his throat again. "We should go." This time he didn't bother to hide the anger on his face. His hands were clenched fists at his sides.

Alarmed at this display of churlishness I glanced from him to Mr. Thornfax, but the taller man only laughed and nodded. "Of course. Of course, we shall go, Mr. Rampling." He waved him ahead and, except for pointing out a water closet and the library, allowed Tom to lead us at a brisk clip through the cabins and back onto the deck.

He made no sign of noticing Tom's sullen behaviour as we disembarked, and he kept up an affable commentary all through the ride back to Hastings House, where Tom had said he was expected in Dr. Dewhurst's surgery. But at the door, after Tom bade us a curt goodbye and was about to circle round the house, Mr. Thornfax stopped him gently by the arm. "As I was saying earlier, Mr. Rampling," he said, "England's prisons are filled nearly to bursting with ambitious and clever young men exactly like yourself."

Tom scraped his heel along the stones and looked off across the drive. "And what do you suggest, milord?" he said finally.

"Only that you put your various talents to better use. My man tells me that those nimble fingers of yours can build anything he asks of you, almost before he asks it. To speak the truth I suspect you're a good deal cleverer than he is. You could go far with me, Mr. Rampling. You really could."

"Thank you, milord." The low voice was wretched.

I exhaled, realizing I'd been holding my breath. Mr. Thornfax should have been stern with Tom—would have had every right to discipline him for his behaviour—and instead he was offering him the promise of advancement. I hoped Tom felt as wretched as he sounded. I hoped he was thoroughly ashamed of his bad temper.

THIRTEEN

*L*ord Rosbury's funeral service at St. Paul's Cathedral that Saturday was overseen by a cheerful sun high in a cloudless sky. Holding Daniel by the arm, Christa lingered on the steps to toy with her new ebony fan and wave about the little black envelope containing our invitation to the private reception to follow. "Operas and other amusements are one thing," she'd trilled when the card arrived, "but to have you publicly at his side at such a solemn, formal event! He will be introducing you to his whole family, Leonora!" A new mourning ensemble had been ordered for me at once, complete with lace and ruched satin overskirts.

"You ladies are a perfect match for the parade horses," Aunt Emmaline commented, steering us to our seats. "I think you must share a milliner."

I, too, had noticed the similarity between our bonnets' trimmings and the arrangement of black bows and ostrich feathers decorating the horses' bridles. The politician's crotchety conservatism was forgiven now that he was gone. It seemed all London had arrived to pay tribute, arrayed in a morbid splendour of which, my aunt remarked, Lord Rosbury himself would certainly have disapproved.

Mr. Thornfax was seated at the front of the church with his family. I examined the back of his head—the trimmed blond hair, the stiff white collar above the black suit. Next to him was a thin woman with stooped shoulders. "His spinster cousin," Christa informed me in a loud whisper, drawing a glare from our aunt.

The domed cathedral was hushed and cool after the excitement outside. Sir Christopher Wren's ingenious architecture ensured that sound would carry across the pews no matter how soft-spoken the cleric, and this one read in crisp diction and in ringing tones. There was a boys' choir in red robes, and a trumpeter, and a scholar down from Oxford who read from Milton's *Lycidas*.

This is how death is beaten, I mused, gazing up at the jewel-toned window where Saint John the Divine raised his hands to the four horsemen. Death may come to claim our individual lives, but it cannot do away with art and beauty and wealth so abundant. This is how we build our immortality.

The funeral cortège through the city streets was hemmed in on all sides by spectators. Everyone doffed his hat and fell silent as we drove by, for custom dictated it bad luck not to watch the hearse disappear. And then, too, London of late had been racked with anxiety about the Black Glove. Scanning the plain, scrubbed faces in the crowd, the Sunday-best clothing, and the carefully shined shoes, I wondered how many wives must be afraid when their husbands went to work in the morning, how many parents must fret when their children skipped off to play outside. Perhaps it wasn't the Lord Rosbury they had come to mourn, exactly. Perhaps we were all gripped by the feeling that at any moment the axe could fall.

The funeral procession was not headed to a cemetery at all. Despite his entitlement to a plot in Highgate, Lord Rosbury had stipulated in his will that his body be transported north to be laid next to his wife's, once the London formalities were concluded. Also in accord with the will, the funerary reception was being held at the deceased's own house in Sloane Street. Mr. Thornfax had already had half the rooms cleared of furniture—"Horrible, dank clutter everywhere!" I'd heard him complain to Daniel—and planned to sell the property as soon as he could. It was an imposing house, with a narrow front door and many pairs of arched windows like eyes glaring over the road. Inside it was dim and smelled of vinegar despite the vases everywhere brimming with lilies and white roses.

Mr. Thornfax's few London relations appeared pleased enough to make my acquaintance but, beyond that, not particularly interested in conversation. He put me by his side for a tour of the room—"Come along, please, and redeem me in their eyes," he said—but the trio of aged aunts merely nodded dimly at his introduction, and the spinster cousin clutched her prayer book and kept her eyes on the floor. Mr. Thornfax rolled his eyes when I asked him if there was anyone to whom I should especially pay my respects. "We shall never see any of these people again, if I have a say in it," he said, and winked at me as he added, "and I do."

Still, he was attentive and gracious to everyone in the room. "Oh, but you have the look of your father!" said a sorrowing old man who'd once been Lord Rosbury's solicitor. Mr. Thornfax grasped the man's hand with both of his own and declared that he was most honoured by the compliment. The old ladies cooed and flocked around him and called him a poor, poor boy, and Mr. Thornfax ducked his head and dashed tears from his eyes. Parliamentary men tried to take him aside and convince him to take up his father's stance against the opium ban, and he would tell them, "No politics today, sirs. Today is my father's day."

Being on Mr. Thornfax's arm in public was like finding a bubble of sweeter, more breathable air in the pall of gloom. Wherever he went he drew round himself a circle of charm. And in that circle, I found, there were no prying questions, no cruel opinions, no patronizing words of advice. No one so much as looked askance at me. Every time Mr. Thornfax introduced me he would touch my collar or my nape with one smooth fingertip, and once people saw what I was to him 'twas enough: I was beloved, too, and therefore utterly, instantly immune from social scrutiny. On Mr. Thornfax's arm in public I could breathe.

Christabel by contrast grew more and more agitated as the event wore on. She drank glass after glass of brandy. She kept telling the guests how she'd witnessed the Lord Rosbury fall from the balcony, even after Aunt Emmaline took her aside to say we ought to remember him in life not in death.

"Did you bring nothing for me at all?" she said to Dr. Dewhurst, more than once, and, "Have you sent word? Will it be delivered soon?" She darted to the window repeatedly and kept fiddling with her fan until she knocked a lady's punch glass from her hand. My own drink was spilt when she tugged my arm violently and exclaimed, "Oh, look, Leonora darling. What a surprise: it's your dear nephews come to pay their condolences to Mr. Thornfax!"

Exchanging looks of alarm Daniel and I followed her to the drive, where Greta was attempting to coax a very reluctant Bertie and Alexander from the carriage. It was well past the boys' dinnertime and naptime, and one look at Bertie's flushed cheeks and scowling brow told me he was hungry and overtired.

Christa reached her arms out to him. "Albert, there's my sweet boy. Come and meet Mr. Thornfax's aunties!"

"Stay wid Tom." Bertie pouted, and hung on to the carriage door with both hands.

"Silly boy. What are you—?"

Tom Rampling emerged from the carriage beside Bertie and stepped onto the gravel with Alexander's arms clamped tightly round his neck. The baby's silk suit was even more rumpled than his brother's, and he buried his pink face in Tom's shoulder.

"Ah, excellent, Mr. Rampling," Daniel said. "I had hoped you would receive my message on such short notice. Hitched a ride with the whole Dewhurst clan, have you?"

"Greta! Take them away from that man at once," Christabel hissed.

"Stay wid Tom!" Bertie sat on Tom's shoe and wrapped his limbs around Tom's leg like a chimpanzee. Out of habit Tom lifted his foot a bit, and Bertie erupted in a wild fit of giggles. His little straw hat popped off and rolled under the carriage.

"My dear, whyever have you had Greta bring the children

here?" Daniel wondered. "You know they're far too young for this sort of gathering. It's not at all appropriate."

"Nonsense, Dr. Dewhurst." Christa made her voice bright. "We must show them what sweet babies the Somerville women can produce!"

My face flamed, and I glanced back to ensure that Mr. Thornfax and his family hadn't seen us all dash outside. Then I caught Tom's expression—a mix of horror and amusement, cloaked a second too late—and my humiliation increased.

Greta attempted to pry Alexander from Tom's neck and was rewarded with an ear-splitting wail. "Sorry, mum," she said. "It's only they're so fond of Tom, you see."

"Dr. Dewhurst. Take your sons in hand!" Christa ordered.

"I don't see what I can—"

"I won't have them touched by that … that *criminal*," she spat, and stamped her foot.

Daniel took her by the elbow. "My dear, you are becoming overwrought."

"He's a friend to whores and cutthroats! You told me yourself."

The doctor coloured. "I said no such thing."

"Yes, you did," Christa shrilled, raising her voice over Alexander's squalling. "'Tom Rampling has too keen a conscience for wastrels and fallen girls,' you said." She narrowed her eyes venomously at Tom. "It is my belief you have fallen in with an opium gang. What do you say to that, Mr. Rampling?"

Tom's face was hewn stone, his eyes steel grey. Only his red ears betrayed his embarrassment. He put the screaming, flailing baby into Greta's arms and bent down to murmur to

Bertie. In a moment the boy released Tom's leg, only to climb mulishly back into the carriage.

"Now look what he's done!" Christabel was in tears.

"Mrs. Dewhurst, here is your remedy," Tom said, and handed her a blue glass vial from his pocket.

"Daniel, 'tis time to take your family home." Aunt Emmaline's low voice somehow cut through the din of Alexander's tantrum. Behind her a small group of onlookers had gathered in the doorway. "Miss Somerville and I will follow you in my chaise."

As usual the countess's tone brooked no dissent. My sister sniffled and looked at her shoes, and Daniel nodded at the butler to retrieve their coats.

When Christa, Greta, and the boys had been loaded into the carriage, Daniel turned Tom aside. "I am sorry for all this fuss, Rampling," I heard him say. "Thank you for coming to my wife's rescue, even if she cannot appreciate it just now. I believe Curtis waits in the mews to convey you to the laboratory. Mr. Thornfax keeps insisting that you're just the man for these urgent duties of his, so I shan't begrudge you the time away."

Aunt Emma steered me back inside and turned the guests' questions aside with a vague comment about the difficulties of finding good nursemaids for babies nowadays.

Later, as we drove back to Hastings House in her carriage, my aunt said, "Is your sister entirely happy, do you think?"

I shook my head no. In fact over the past week I'd come to realize that Archie's insinuation about "dope" and the ladies of Hastings was well founded: Christabel imbibed a heavy daily dosage of laudanum. I had begun to notice that she was going to bed early every night despite napping two hours or more every afternoon. When she wasn't groggy she was agitated, perceiving dangers and enemies everywhere. The "remedy" Tom had brought her at the doctor's bidding today was almost certainly laudanum, too.

"Do you think Dr. Dewhurst is a good man?" Aunt Emmaline continued. "Does he love poor Christabel, I mean? I can't help but feel she may have been hasty in marrying him after all that sorry business back at Holybourne."

By *sorry business* my aunt meant George Clayton. We seldom spoke Mr. Clayton's name; certainly, neither of us would ever speak it in Christa's presence for fear of stirring old hurts. After all, it had been the Lady Hastings who'd driven that handsome young suitor from our house five years ago when it was revealed he was trying to win Christa's money rather than her heart. And it was me—or rather, Mimic—who had revealed it, after overhearing Mr. Clayton in conversation with his dissolute London friends. At twelve I had understood only dimly what it all meant. Aunt Emma had needed to explain to me the danger of a fortune hunter to a young woman destined to inherit.

"From now on I shall take it upon myself to investigate any young man visiting Holybourne," Aunt Emma had decided. "'Tis my money that makes you and Christabel targets for rogues like Clayton, so 'tis my duty to ensure you make good marriages."

That same September Christabel had met Daniel Dewhurst—plump, balding, twelve years her senior—and begged to be allowed to marry him at once. Aunt Emmaline had found Dr. Dewhurst's finances mediocre but his prospects in medicine promising and his character solidly affable. She'd given her blessing upon the match, along with her permission—and a sufficient allowance—for the newlyweds to set up residence at Hastings House. By Michaelmas that year my sister was married and gone, and I was left alone with my ailing father at Holybourne.

But Daniel *was* fond of his young wife, I thought. In these past eighteen months with them at Hastings I had never seen him impatient or short with her. He smiled at her, and stroked her hair, and told her she was beautiful nearly every day. "I believe D-Daniel l-loves her," I told Aunt Emma.

She nodded. "And the new Lord Rosbury? Shall he care for you properly, do you think?"

"I hope he t-takes me away to sea!" I said.

Aunt Emma laughed. "I'm sure he would, my dear, if you asked him!"

Until the words left my lips I'd had no idea exactly how desperate I was to leave Hastings House. But the thought of Mr. Thornfax marrying me and then leaving me behind while he went sea-voyaging seemed a dreadful prospect, suddenly. It wasn't only Hastings's dank halls and Christa's erratic moods. It was the whole business of Tom Rampling. Tom, with his pale skin and dark, unruly curls. Tom, with his gentle, clever fingers unselfconsciously smoothing my hair. Tom, who could pick a lock—or a pocket, presumably—as easily as breathing. Tom, who had never exactly lied to me, had never denied his responsibility for the death of young Will. Whether he was good or bad—or worse, that he might

somehow be good *and* bad at the same time—Tom Rampling
had become such a puzzle for me that I felt it would be best
to go far away from him.

Mr. Thornfax, at least, was always direct with me, was
always exactly himself. How I admired his forthrightness!
Perhaps I should simply be direct with him in return, and tell
him I wanted a life with him at sea. If he insisted that it wasn't
safe, or that a ship was no place for a lady, I would find a way
to convince him otherwise. I smiled inwardly at the memory
of his warm hand at my nape today, his clear blue gaze upon
my face. I could talk to Mr. Thornfax despite my stammer,
despite Mimic's intrusions, even, and he would listen to me.
Of that much I could be sure.

My aunt, as usual, seemed to read my unspoken feelings
on my face. She reached over, drew me into a sturdy embrace,
and said, "Above all, Leonora, you must know your own mind.
Only take care to discover all the facts before you make it up!"

As we pulled through the gates of Hastings, Aunt Emma
sighed and said she always forgot how grand a house it was.
"It was never my home, not really," she mused. "I was too
young when I married the count and became its mistress. I
never got over my intimidation of the place."

"The Countess of Hastings, intimidated? N-never!"
She laughed.

"It isn't my home, either," I reminded her.

Aunt Emma kissed me and said, by way of a goodbye,
"You'll make your own home soon enough, my dear. Perhaps
even a floating one!"

The London Examiner

APRIL 8TH, 1872

New Hon. Lord Rosbury: "We Will Not Be Intimidated"

ARCHIBALD MAVETY, SPECIAL REPORTER

⊱⊰─◦─⊱⊰

NEARLY ONE THOUSAND mourners gathered on Saturday at St. Paul's to bid farewell to Charles Thornfax, the late Lord Rosbury, tragically killed in the explosion at Covent Garden that claimed the lives of almost a dozen men and women.

This reporter overheard amongst the ladies and gentlemen in attendance much speculation as to the reasons for the opera house blast. Faulty gas lines were mentioned, and the negligence or ignorance of the theatre manager, Mr. Elson, was a prolific theme for comment. In the interests of expunging the mark on this poor man's name, let me now reveal what I have discovered as to the continuing investigation of the case. Police have confirmed that a note delivered to poor Mr. Elson the next day does indeed match the others and was written in the hand of the same person or persons responsible for previous attacks: the criminal organization calling itself the Black Glove.

When asked whether the increase in violence will deter Parliament from passing the anti-opium bill this session, the deceased's son, Francis Thornfax, our new Lord Rosbury, stated, "My father's tragic death proves that he was wrong to oppose the ban on opium. The profits won by importing the poppy are nothing compared to the costs we have suffered—are continuing to suffer! England needs public stability and peace, and despite the best efforts of our police these gangs of criminals will continue to flourish in this city until their livelihood—the trade and sale of opium—has been stamped out for good. The ban must pass! We will not be intimidated." But the question remains: Will the Black Glove and its rival gangs be stymied by the opium ban as Parliament seems to believe? And if the bill threatens these thugs and miscreants, must we expect an increase in violence over the next two months leading up to the vote?

FOURTEEN

As the days passed into weeks, thoughts of the bombings and of opium-trade politics and of poor Hattie's fate kept whirling round my head. I found that I could not keep my mind on ladies' lunches and card games. I would open a novel and see only the smoke and dust rising in the opera gallery. I would hear Bertie laugh and think for a moment that it was young Will chased by Tom across the yard. Even when I was with Mr. Thornfax—when we walked in the park, when we dined with Christa and Daniel, when we danced at a ball, when we visited Parliament and he introduced me to some of his new friends there—part of my mind was always preoccupied by fear of the Black Glove. At night I woke again and again with dreams of people falling to their deaths. To ease my nerves I would lie in my bed and imagine the tinkling of a music box, the delicate tapping of crystal birds.

One afternoon in late April, nearly three weeks after Lord Rosbury's funeral, I screwed up my courage and crossed the plum court. My breath came shorter as I approached Daniel's surgery, and I hesitated at the door.

Partly it was the still-raw memory of poor Hattie lying on the tiles just inside. But I had other memories of doctors' offices—no less harrowing for being older than the recollection of Hattie's death. Sterile, comfortless rooms where I waited and tried not to look at the walls with their frightening diagrams of cross-sectioned larynxes, of incisions to the tongue, of metal bracers suspended across the roof of the mouth and soldered to the teeth. One of my most frequent and lasting nightmares stemmed from the memory of standing against such a wall in such an office—as though I were just another illustration!—as Mr. Brinsmead, Surgical and Mechanical Dentist, pressed a wooden utensil into the back of my throat whilst I wept and struggled to say the alphabet around its intrusion. On that occasion Mimic had had enough. Spitting out the instrument I'd shrieked and cursed and hurled at the poor man every vile word Mimic had absorbed a few weeks before when I saw a horse-thief arrested in Holybourne village.

Today I was planning to ask my brother-in-law about the exact nature of Tom Rampling's misdeeds and why Mr. Thornfax might be taking such an interest in his skills. But it was not the doctor I saw when I stepped into the surgery. It was the girl from the Seven Dials alley, reclining on a pallet under a calico blanket.

"I'm s-sorry," I stammered. Half expecting Mr. Sears and his stick, I turned to flee.

"Miss Somerville, stay!" she said. A naked arm was thrust at me, and she nearly tumbled from the bed.

I closed the door and stood with my back against it. "Daisy, isn't it?"

"Yes, mum."

"What are you d-doing here?"

"Resting, mum. Doctor's orders."

"Are you a"—*patient* stopped my tongue—"is Dr. D-Dewhurst t-treating you?"

Daisy sighed, nodded, and let her head loll back on the pillow as if to demonstrate how in need of treatment she was. She did look dreadfully ill, I thought. Ghost-white without her face paint, and more bruised and withered through the neck and chest even than one month ago.

I thought of how she'd tried to protect young Will when I'd asked after him in the alley. She'd claimed to be his sister, in fact. I cast about for a tactful way to offer my condolences on her loss.

But Daisy anticipated me. Still gazing at the ceiling she drawled, "Me brother's dead, mum."

"I am s-sorry," I said, but she didn't seem to hear.

"It's me own fault. It should ha' been me that went. It was me as they asked to do it." She sniffled and wiped her nose with her filthy neckerchief.

"Who asked you? And to d-do what?" I wondered, but Daisy sighed again and, eyelids fluttering, seemed to slip into a sort of doze.

I ventured closer and winced at the pungent odours that rose from the bed. Black crescents ringed Daisy's fingernails; her hair, skin, and clothes alike were coated with yellowish grime. This girl was near my own age, but a life in London's dark and shelterless streets had bent and wasted her. I was jolted with a sudden sense of how easily, how arbitrarily, our situations might have been reversed. After all, I'd once been a patient of the poppy flower, too—maybe not of Dr. Dewhurst's new derivative of morphine, but certainly of more dilute versions of the drug. My memories of dozing and of dreaming poppy-dreams were still vivid enough. Only the move to Kew and my aunt's distaste for such treatments had saved me from what might have been a life confined to my bed. How thin, really, was the luck that saw me coddled and fed while this girl drudged and starved.

A small table nearby held several delicate glass tubes, each tipped with a pointed copper cap. I picked one up and held it to the light. Its inner surface was stained with a dark, resinous residue. A glass rod ran through the tube, flanged at one end and stoppered with a disc of India rubber at the other. A silver pin protruded through the copper cap. Drawing the rod from the tube and replacing it produced a puff of air from the needle; upon closer inspection it proved to be hollow.

"I wouldn't touch that."

Daisy's slurred words startled me. I nearly dropped the tube.

"Dr. Dewhurs'll get fearsome angry. Built those hisself, he did. Or rather, Tom builds 'em. Works of art, the doctor calls 'em."

"W-what is it?"

"A syringe. For me medicine. Sticks here in me arum." She extended her wrist to display a cluster of wine-coloured punctures inside her elbow.

My throat pinched shut. My brother-in-law had spoken of drugs being introduced under the skin for more direct absorption, but I had never imagined such a device for the purpose or such brutal effects of its use. I struggled to remember why

I'd come to the surgery. "Daisy. What did T-Tom Rampling have to do with Will's d-death?"

She sat up. "'Tweren't his fault, as I tol' him. Lauk, but he sunk in melancholy, bless his soul!" She gave a vacant smile. "I tol' him I'd marry him, if he'd only bring away a supply of me medicine with us."

"And w-what did he say to that?"

"He said he'd have me in a blink, acourse, only I needs get well first." Daisy placed a hand to her hollow cheek. "Tom is the best man I ever known, mum."

Naturally, I thought, Tom Rampling was a saint—in a universe of housebreakers and whores. With a sour taste on my tongue I bid Daisy a curt goodbye.

She lunged forward and took hold of my skirt. "Only I'm so afeared, mum!"

"Why?"

"Sure, it'll be me who goes next time."

Next time? It took me a moment to understand what she meant. I'd been so absorbed in the shock and horror of the opera house attack that I hadn't considered a "next time." "B-but why?" I asked her. "Why would you go at all?"

Daisy shrugged. "Can't get me medicine, elsewise."

"From Dr. D-Dewhurst?"

"It's too dear to hand round free. Mr. Watts says we has to work to pay our portion."

"And who is Mr. W-Watts?"

Another shrug. "The man what'll give us the blast stuff. My Tom, though. He says he'll fashion the lightning cap hisself, special. He'll keep me safe." The girl actually sounded proud.

Here was confirmation, then. Tom Rampling had helped to set the explosion that had killed young Will. Poor old Lord Rosbury, all those innocent people dead—it was Tom's doing.

Bile rose in my gullet. My thoughts raced and tumbled together. I had to tell someone at once, warn someone! My brother-in-law, perhaps—he knew that his assistant had a criminal past, but he couldn't know that Tom was a murderer! Could he? Or Archie. Maybe my cousin would know what to do. Aunt Emmaline! I should go directly to my aunt— but immediately I pictured her sitting straight in her chair, arching one eyebrow at me and questioning whether I was sure I truly had all the facts at my disposal.

I stared at the dark circles under Daisy's eyes, the hollows above her collarbones. One thought pushed out ahead of the jumble in my mind: they deserved each other, Tom Rampling and his Daisy.

"D-does your medicine cure you, do you think?" I asked her.

"Oh yes, mum." A dreamy look was in her eyes. "It feels like floating. Soft and sweet, like."

"Like laudanum?"

"No, mum. Laudanum just turns your head. Even morphine ain't the same, times I tried it. Dr. Dewhurst's doses make you fly and fly, forever."

Two mornings later I still hadn't decided what I should do. My indecision was unforgivable, I knew—my silence might be responsible for more innocent deaths, if Daisy was sent out to set an explosive as she feared she would be. Yet my thoughts were clouded with doubt upon doubt, and eventually I understood what it was I was waiting for. Tom Rampling hadn't been at Hastings since my encounter with Daisy, and I needed to see him to know for sure. Whether Tom would confirm or deny my accusations I didn't know, but I felt I needed to see the truth on his face, to hear it in his words, before I could act.

That morning I was fetching something from my bedchamber when I heard a noise below my open window. At the breakfast table I'd recognized Mr. Thornfax's handwriting on an envelope, but the note had been addressed to Daniel, not to me. Now I spied the man himself striding across the plum court to the surgery. The new Lord Rosbury was out of his funeral darks but wore a black arm band over his suit and a black felt bowler. He carried a silver-tipped walking stick, which he twirled like a baton as he walked. Regally handsome, he looked like he might own the whole world, and I shivered behind the curtain with all the furtive pleasure of a voyeur. This must be what a title does to a man, I thought. Lengthens his stride and sharpens the ring of his boots against the stones. And what would the title do to me, I wondered, once I became the Lady Rosbury?

The walking stick swung forward and struck the surgery door. "Dewhurst! What's keeping you?" Mr. Thornfax called.

The door creaked open. My brother-in-law appeared in smock and gloves. "Had I better meet you at the warehouse?"

"No, I'll wait, but make haste," said Mr. Thornfax. "Watts says the duty officer never sleeps past ten."

"Why should you care about that? Until your ban passes in the House your cargo is still perfectly legal."

Mr. Thornfax jabbed the stick at him. "That, my friend, is why you'd never make it in politics. Trust a scientist to take the letter of the law over its spirit!"

Daniel crossed his arms. "Bollocks. You're only concerned with appearances, Lord Rosbury. And anyhow I thought your new ship was inspection-proof."

A lady doesn't eavesdrop, I chided myself. But I couldn't tear myself from the window.

"I defy any wharf-hound to discover my *Heroine*'s secrets!" Mr. Thornfax declared. "That little clipper will bring me more profit than my old fleet entire, once the ban is in place."

"How do you mean?" said Daniel.

"Nothing raises prices like a law."

Dr. Dewhurst laughed. "Well said, Francis. Well said! I should sorely like to see *that* statement quoted in the newspapers."

"But you know there's no concealment in the warehouse itself, and before the *Heroine* is launched we've got to clear the last of your raw materials out of the way."

"All right, I'll make haste. Come in, then, and—"

Their conversation was cut off by the slam of the surgery door.

My fingers ached: I saw my knuckles clenched white around the window frame. My pulse throbbed in my throat. Smuggling, and the manufacture of Dr. Dewhurst's drug. That much I had understood from their exchange, at least. But Mr. Thornfax had also mentioned the name "Watts"— and I remembered that name from my conversation with Daisy in the surgery.

My aunt Emmaline's advice rang in my mind again:

Discover all the facts before you make up your mind. Tossing my book onto the bed I crossed to the wardrobe and shoved aside my dresses. I found a long over-jacket and shawl I had not worn often. From the dresser I collected gloves, a translucent silk scarf, and a small purse full of coins. Carrying my sturdiest boots I stole through the kitchens to the side door. From the hook I scooped Mrs. Fayerweather's forgotten bonnet, offering a silent apology in the unlikely case the old woman would finally remember to send for it today and find it missing.

I wrote a hasty note to Bess, telling her that I was going alone to call on neighbours down the road and would not be back for lunch. In the mews behind the house I began to run, suddenly afraid that I'd taken too long in dressing and would miss them altogether. But round the corner I saw Curtis still waiting by Mr. Thornfax's carriage, scuffing at the cobbles and emitting great huffs of smoke from his pipe. As soon as his back was turned I dashed past the front gate into Gloucester Street. I draped the scarf over Mrs. Fayerweather's bonnet, covering my face and tucking the edges into my collar as a lady might do when caught in a dust storm. Then, for the first time in all my seventeen years of life, I raised my hand and waved for a cab.

The driver of the two-horse brougham that pulled over to the curb leaned down to examine me. Before he could peer too close through my scarf I reached a coin up to him.

"Nicholson's Wharf!" Wearing Mrs. Fayerweather's hat on my head, I suppose I shouldn't have been surprised that Mimic would announce herself in the old woman's throaty chirrup.

The cabbie harrumphed but made no objection, so I

scrambled inside. I'd hailed the brougham rather than one of the cheaper, more popular hansom cabs because this style of carriage was more closed-in and private. Breathing deeply through my scarf the aromas of damp wool and tobacco from the seat cushions I felt, suddenly, quite cozy and safe. What a daft notion, that a young lady of good reputation should feel safe riding unaccompanied in a cab! Christa would have me pilloried, I thought, and I had to press my gloved fingers against my mouth to stop my laughter so the cabbie wouldn't hear it and think me utterly mad.

I spent most of the twenty-minute ride debating whether to order the driver to turn round and bring me home again. I scarcely had time to formulate a plan before we'd reached Upper Thames Street and I was assaulted by the stench of the river. Seabirds wheeled in the air overhead, their raucous screams echoed by the barking of the dogs who'd evidently just chased them off a feast of fish innards on the wharf. Taking a deep breath I stopped the driver and abandoned the temporary shelter of my cab.

The scent of fried eels and fish pies reminded me of distant childhood vacations at Brighton, but the air was decidedly less festive here. Beyond the traffic-choked London Bridge lay a dense, impassable forest of masts and sails. A beribboned touring steamer churned upriver, but its passengers were huddled under the canopy to escape the wind. It was low tide. The pilings wore long stockings of green slime. Ragged children in bare feet and grass hats scavenged the banks.

I scuttled along the quayside shopfronts and kiosks. Though I was in disguise my disguise was made up of finery, and finery was an unfamiliar sight to the hard-faced docksmen and foreign vendors whose cacophony of dialects thronged round me. I was aware of their curious glances, and at every moment I expected to be confronted by the leering smile of a Mrs. Clampitt or the grasping hands of her girls. When I spied a tea shop within sight of the Nicholson's Wharf building, I entered at once and fell into a seat by the lace-curtained window.

It was only a few minutes until the Thornfax carriage pulled up alongside the warehouse. Curtis leapt down, slid the great door aside, and led the horses forward until the carriage disappeared inside the building.

Only after I'd sipped half my tea, scalding myself several times in the process, and had spread out a newssheet in front of me to denote solitary absorption did I cease my trembling, frenetic actions and permit myself to think about what I was doing.

Know your own mind. I stared through the smudged glass as billowing clouds rolled across the sky and the sun shot them through with green, grey, and gold. Skiffs and barges inched past one another, the crewmen shouting and gesturing across the water. I'd heard that boys sometimes dared one another, when traffic was high, to cross the whole river's breadth by leaping from deck to deck. Also that they sometimes fell into the troughs between the vessels and were crushed before anyone noticed.

This recollection seemed suddenly, urgently relevant to my present situation. If I leapt, would I fall and be crushed? I had no intention of ship-hopping of course. But the move I was considering was no less perilous. *Discover all the facts, before you make up your mind.*

"Now then," I addressed myself, whispering behind my scarf. The resolve that had pushed me to abandon my bedchamber this morning now took on a clearer shape. I wanted to discover the facts. I wanted to do what was right. But most of all I wanted to be less afraid. Wearing a hat belonging to another woman was frightening. The act of stepping out on my own, of sitting alone in a public tea room, was frightening. Trespassing on the business activities of my suitor, not to mention those of my own brother-in-law, was unimaginably frightening. And discovering—well, I was too terrified even to imagine what I might discover in my search.

There was only one woman in my acquaintance who wasn't governed, even in some small measure, by fear: the Countess of Hastings. My aunt Emmaline went everywhere alone and did not mind if society labelled her mannish and unsociable. She had played Cleopatra at the Adelphi Theatre. She lived in Gordon Square, an area most of her generation considered too dangerous, because she preferred, as she put it, to "dodge the prying eyes." She carried a needle-thin silver dagger in the handle of her parasol, and as a child I once witnessed her brandish it at a cutpurse who'd sidled too close beside us on the trolley. Even on that occasion Aunt Emma had been utterly unafraid. When the thug had slunk away she'd simply slid the weapon back into its hiding place, tapped the handle snug against her boot, and murmured, "Don't tell your father, my dear."

The carriage emerged from the warehouse again with Curtis walking at the horses' heads. He leapt into his seat and turned the rig into the street. I could see the silhouette of

Daniel's hat and thought I caught the glint of Mr. Thornfax's jewelled cuff-clips where his arm rested on the sill.

I was frightened, yes—but, after all, fright had not stopped me from acting thus far. Leaving a coin on the table I tugged my shawl close about me and exited the shop.

Curtis had slid the heavy warehouse door closed but left it unlocked. The iron runners screeched against my weight and stuck fast. I flattened the brim of the hat to my cheeks to squeeze through the gap. Inside it was dim, cavernous, and fragrant with fresh timber and pitch. Before my eyes adjusted I mistook the flutter of pigeons in the rafters for bats, and I backed myself clumsily into the horse stall.

Breathe, I commanded myself. The rough slats of the wall caught the fabric of my glove as I felt my way deeper into the building. I stared down each menacing shape until it resolved into something I recognized: a stack of wooden pallets, a coil of mooring-rope, a pile of cork floats encrusted with barnacles, an enormous mast-lamp. The light improved as I neared a door thrown open to the water. Nicholson's dock was only a few dozen paces away, and I was greeted by the jaunty prow of Mr. Thornfax's new clipper wharfed nearby, now with her freshly painted moniker: *Heroine*. Wary of lingering sailors I skirted the rectangle of sunlight cast on the floor.

A fainter sliver of light drew me to the far end of the warehouse, where I found an ordinary wall panel without frame or handle, invisibly hinged and standing slightly ajar. Beyond it was a narrow room striped with sunlight from a high window. Motes of dust floated above the polished leather surface of a writing desk. Mr. Thornfax's office, I assumed, and I hastened to try the desk drawers, which were all locked. A pen-stand and blotter, several ledgers, a crystal decanter of brandy, two glasses, a cigar box—I felt a sudden frustration at the display. How could I find anything without any idea what I was looking for?

The muted clink of glassware brought me to shocked attention. Someone was in the room with me!—no, in a room adjacent to this one, through a doorway I'd failed to notice at the far end of the office. I tore the hat and scarf from my head, deciding on the spot to explain my presence to Mr. Thornfax as an innocent prank by an infatuated young girl.

But it was not Mr. Thornfax I saw when I inched forward and peeped round the partition. It was Tom Rampling.

FIFTEEN

*T*om stood with his back to me lifting a spherical flask up to the window. The sunlight licked indigo flames through his hair and limned the long muscles of his back through the translucent linen of his shirt. Round and round he swirled the cloudy liquid in the flask, held it still to note how it settled, then swirled it again. He set the vessel into a frame and reached beside him to a gas-jet burner spouting a yellow flame. Bending to steady an elbow on the counter he set to work in deft, delicate movements, soldering a copper wire round the lip of another, slimmer vial.

As I hung there watching him at his tasks, my fear edged into sheer fascination. I was looking at Tom, and he was utterly oblivious to my gaze upon him. Shirt buttons open, sleeves rolled past his elbows for work, his body was caressed by light. Filled with light. He tilted his head a little, and I watched how the light poured through his ear, making it a glowing whorl of red and gold. For the second time that day a voyeuristic thrill raised the fine hairs on my arms.

At last I blinked and tore my gaze away. I forced myself

to take advantage of Tom's absorption to examine the rest of the room—my brother-in-law's laboratory, I surmised. Apothecary jars lining the glass shelves refracted light against the tiled counter, a watery mosaic of blues, ambers, greens. There were dozens of racked pipettes with tan rubber bulbs, and an assortment of ceramic dishes stained with resin. On the wall nearest me hung several papers filled with mathematical calculations and chemical formulae. One page displayed a complicated diagram: a flame, a glass bulb like the one Tom had set down, a snaking tube, and a hollow reed sharpened to a point.

Tom straightened from his work.

I said, "What is it you do for him, precisely?"

He spun round, open-mouthed.

"Do you manufacture the drug that is killing your own beloved Daisy?" Mimic was again using Mrs. Fayerweather's voice, but Tom was too surprised to notice.

"Did—did he bring you here?" he whispered. "Thornfax?"

"Of course not." I couldn't prevent a note of pride from creeping in. "I followed him and Dr. Dewhurst."

Tom looked aghast. "Milady, you cannot be here. If he finds you—"

"What will he do, Mr. Rampling? Will he let my brother-in-law prescribe me a course of his deadly medicine? Or will he let you send me forth into a deadly explosion?" I had not realized until this moment just how very angry I was with Tom Rampling. My fury overtook any lingering shyness I felt at intruding on him, and I closed the distance between us so fast that he stumbled back against the counter.

I snatched up the copper-ringed vial. "And what is this?"

He shook his head and reached to retrieve it. "It will be a syringe, milady. The doctor—"

I flung the tube onto the counter with all my strength. It shattered with a satisfactory pop, scattering fragments in all directions.

There was real fear in Tom's eyes now. "Listen to me. Mr. Thornfax is not the mild gentleman you believe him. He mustn't find you discovering him in this way!"

"Perhaps it is you I mean to discover," I retorted. Reaching past him I lifted a black notebook from the counter, tipped the shards from its cover, and riffled through its pages. Daniel's spidery script laid out long columns of patients' names, dates, dosages. *Harriett Cooper (Hattie)*, I read, on a page dated from the night of her death. *Potency adjustment. Over-dosage.*

"Hold me here, Tom," said Mimic, using Hattie's voice, "so's I dun't go to him."

"Oh no, milady. Please don't," Tom whispered.

In my anger I'd cornered him against the counter, and even as he leaned away, Tom's body was only inches from mine. We'd been in this position once before—after Hattie's collapse in the parlour, when Tom had tried to bar my exit from the room. Then I had felt surprise and embarrassment, the self-consciousness of my own position as a lady and his as a servant. This time my anger overrode everything else. This time my every pore awakened to Tom's closeness, and my rage cartwheeled into a kind of wild, surging excitement. One of my hands leapt from the book to circle the white column of his throat. I felt his larynx jump under my thumb and I pressed into it, hard.

"Did you inject her?" The words seared my tongue.

"No," he rasped. "I swear it!" His shock at my assault had him gaping and wide-eyed. His fingers covered mine, trying to loosen my grip.

Mimic switched into Daisy's stupefied drawl: "Tom Rampling. My sweet'art. He said he'd take me away in a heartbeat!"

Tom pried my fingers from his neck, and the book fell to the floor between us as he twisted both my wrists behind me, turning me and pinning me to the counter. "Stop," he said.

I struggled, panting half in pain and half in exultation. "He'll keep me safe. Tom is the best man I ever known, mum."

Tom's body pressed tight to mine as he tried to hold me still. I felt his low, agonized groan reverberate through his chest against my jaw. "Stop, stop, stop," he begged.

"The doctor's doses make ye fly and fly, forever!" I took a shuddering breath, and then another, deeper one. After a few moments I let myself relax into Tom's embrace.

He released me at once, dropping my wrists and stepping back to make a foot of space between us. While it did little to dispel the tension and upset that charged the air, at least it permitted my heart to slow its crazed thumping inside my ribs.

Tom bent to pick up the doctor's book and set it on the counter. Slowly, cautiously, he reached for my hand where it hung, trembling, at my side. Two of his fingertips slid beneath the rim of my glove. "You have me wrong, milady. I am not your enemy, nor the enemy of those poor, wretched girls whose voices you mimic. I have tried—I have been trying, with all my power—to save their lives. To *prevent* more deaths."

His gaze had been fixed on my arm. Now he lifted his

eyes to meet mine. Clear and grey, fringed all round with curling lashes. The heat from his touch on my bruised wrist went straight up through my chest and down my spine.

I shook him off. "How have you t-tried? I m-must know it all, Tom!" Desperation hoarsened my voice. I wanted so badly to believe him that I could scarcely breathe.

"I swear I will explain it all. Only please, let me take you home now," he said.

The heavy tread of footsteps sent us lurching apart.

"That's Thornfax returned!" Tom gasped. Covering my mouth and grasping me by the back of my neck he wheeled me so fiercely round the end of the counter that I was too flustered to mention my plan of greeting Mr. Thornfax openly until it was too late, and we were crouched tight together behind the open door of a tall cabinet.

"Cozy quarters for a lord," came a nasal male voice from next door.

Mr. Thornfax's smooth chuckle came in answer. "I am nothing if not a patient man, Mr. Watts. And if you will be patient but a moment longer, I'll have you directly on your way."

I pulled Tom's hand from my mouth and whispered, "I won't c-call out."

"It's Mimic I fear will holler," he replied. He smelled of cedar and woodsmoke and clean cotton. And something else—I recognized the warm, male scent of Tom Rampling's own skin from the times we'd shared a carriage, from sitting close to him that day in his grandmother's room. I straightened my shoulders, grasping for some of the dignity I'd tossed aside moments earlier, but the movement only brought my side more snugly against his. I heard the sharp intake of Tom's breath and felt perversely gratified that our closeness affected him, too.

"There," said Mr. Thornfax. The desk chair scraped the floor. "Two o'clock Thursday, to the station master's own hand. I won't learn you've passed it off to a clerk. You'll do the job for which I'm paying you."

"Why forewarn 'em like this every time? I mean, if you'll tolerate my askin'—"

"I won't tolerate it, in fact," Mr. Thornfax cut in. "Mind you don't leave a fingerprint on the envelope, either. They say each man's is unique unto him, like a signature." I heard the tidy snap of his pocket watch, then: "Rampling?" Footsteps came striding our way. "That little bastard had better not have scarpered off without locking the door."

"I'm here, Lord Rosbury." Tom sprang out from our hiding place just as the men rounded the doorway. I could see, through the seam of the cabinet door, that Mr. Thornfax's man Watts was sunburnt, with a crushed nose and a twisted, sneering mouth. With a shock I recognized him from the alley, from the day I'd been tailing poor young Will. Mr. Watts had been the man at the table inside Mrs. Clampitt's hovel. The man who, when I was attacked, had merely stood there in the doorway smiling at my "fuss." If he was Mr. Thornfax's employee, it would explain how my suitor had known about my being attacked.

"What happened here?" Mr. Thornfax said, frowning at the disarray on the counter.

"Nothing, milord," Tom hastened to assure him. "A dropped syringe."

Mr. Thornfax picked up the round flask and lifted it, as Tom had done, to the window. "Amazing, isn't it? Add one chemical, boil another chemical away, and morphine quintuples its potency and value."

"That simple, is it?" said Watts.

Mr. Thornfax laughed. "Well, no. If it were that simple, I'd do it myself." He replaced the flask and turned to Tom. "Tell us about this dreadful whore of yours. Daisy, is it? Does she have enough sense left in her head to follow our instructions?"

"Daisy is ill, milord."

"Morphomania. They all suffer that, of course. How else should they keep coming back to us?"

"'Tis worse than the normal craving for morphine, milord. Undosed she is feverish and faint. Dosed she sleeps or talks nonsense." Tom's voice shook a little. "I think she may mistake the direction, or collapse in transit."

Mr. Thornfax leaned forward and cuffed him hard across the mouth. Swiftly he smoothed back the curls that had fallen into Tom's eyes at the blow. He pinched Tom's chin to pull him closer, and when Tom tried to pull away Mr. Thornfax clapped his other hand to the base of his skull and gripped harder, holding him caught there, so that Tom's jaw and cheek whitened under the bruising fingertips. At the same time Mr. Thornfax thrust his lips next to Tom's ear and said, "There now," and "Shh-shh," in mock-soothing tones that spurred Watts into nasty laughter.

I wanted to avert my eyes but found I could not—I couldn't even breathe. The change in Mr. Thornfax's bearing and demeanour rendered him nearly unrecognizable. It was as if a mask had suddenly been torn away. The relaxed, good-natured gaze to which I was accustomed was flashing with hateful resentment, and his voice was a hiss. His easy gait and open, confident stance had become coiled and predatory as a striking snake.

He eased his grip on Tom now, and stood back to regard him scornfully, fists on hips. "Well, what do you suggest, Master Rampling, as Daisy's champion? Shall you go along with her and lay your coat over the street for her to tread upon?"

Tom's hand came up to his face and dropped again. He squared his stance, breathed deep. "I'll go in her stead, milord. Gladly I will."

Another sharp, open-handed blow, and more laughter. I cringed and pressed my palm to my own mouth as blood sprang to Tom's lips.

Still Tom stood quiet, holding himself tightly in check, looking at the floor. I watched his fist clench at his side and then deliberately relax.

Mr. Thornfax's voice was cold: "You would go in her stead. And risk damage to that pretty face of yours, my boy? I should say you've a better future in Daisy's profession than she has." He touched a finger to Tom's injured mouth and smeared the blood like rouge across Tom's lips. Then he showed off his handiwork to Watts, who sniggered in approval of Tom's prettiness.

"Only mind you don't start sampling Dr. Dewhurst's medicine," Mr. Thornfax advised Tom. "It seems to do dreadful things to one's appearance." He wiped his bloodied finger on Tom's shirt, took out his riding gloves, and smoothed them over his hands. Then the two men withdrew and, as their steps retreated, I heard Mr. Thornfax say, "The desperate and perishing classes, Watts. Now there's a romance to weep over!"

Tom wiped the blood from his face. His ears were scarlet with insult and humiliation, and I inched back from my peephole, hoping he wouldn't know I'd watched him being beaten.

Or perhaps I hoped he wouldn't see what I was feeling. The practiced nonchalance with which Mr. Thornfax had hurt Tom shook me in a way that no impassioned display of temper might have done. The new Lord Rosbury was indeed perfect. A perfect monster.

And underneath my shock at witnessing Mr. Thornfax's true face there was another feeling, something much more secret and shameful to me. I had first sensed it two days ago in the surgery with Daisy, like a needle burrowing under my skin, and now I had to admit that it had fanned my anger at Tom, too.

The shameful thing had stabbed at me again as Mr. Thornfax taunted Tom about Daisy, twisting deeper still when Tom offered to go in her place. Now it was lodged like a knife in my chest. I took a ragged breath, swallowing the tears that rose in my throat.

Tom Rampling loved Daisy, else he would not have offered to die for her. And I—here was the secret I could no longer conceal from myself—I loved Tom Rampling, else I would not mind how he felt about another girl.

SIXTEEN

I crawled from my hiding spot and stood up, smoothing the dust off my skirts. I punched Mrs. Fayerweather's hat where I'd crushed its crown. "We had b-better go home," I said.

Tom avoided my eyes as studiously as I avoided his. "Let me be certain they've gone, first." He swept the broken glass and wire into a basin. He buttoned his collar where the reddened bands across his white throat still accused me like a martyr's wounds. He took his coat and cap from the hook and ducked ahead of me through the office and into the warehouse. "All right," he called, and after he'd secured the secret door I followed him through the dark space and into the street.

Tom led me at a near-run round the back of the building, weaving around scattered timber ends and soggy mounds of sawdust. On the boardwalk he reached for my hand. From the careful way he peered along each wharf before crossing the sunlit passageways, I knew that he hadn't had to exit the laboratory in this way before. It was my presence making him furtive, I realized. I was the criminal who must be hid. I was the one who had ventured where she should not go.

A gull perched atop a mast, gilded by the sinking sun. It raised its wings and crouched but did not fly. Laughter bubbled in my chest at the sight, and I suppressed it so that Tom would not worry I was becoming hysterical.

I had leapt. Like the riverboys, I'd leapt from one deck and landed on another: a surface that heaved and rolled but, to my great surprise and relief, had not pitched me off. Where I balanced now, though, was a world askew. Oh, it was still peopled by beer-sellers and fishwives and scavenging children, but all these poor souls went about their business in perfect ignorance. They did not know what I knew. How could they? They had not leapt as I had. They couldn't possibly see how disordered the world had become, how its most basic elements had been shuffled and scattered and turned on end.

Who was trustworthy and noble, who was a grasping, cold-blooded liar—the categories of human character spun and exploded within me like a Catherine wheel. They flashed behind my eyes, glittering and indistinct, as Tom and I emerged from a long alley into the strong sunlight of Adelaide Place. They brushed my skin like cats' tongues and made me shiver, even though I was warm and winded from the walk.

No one else saw what I saw. Not the baker in his flour-covered smock emptying crumbs for the pigeons from a sack, not the tall woman walking a pair of bulldogs on braided leather leashes. Even Tom—who dropped my hand now and kept a proper distance but tilted his chin to peer sidelong at me through his curls—even he might not see, exactly, how good and evil had swapped places and upended the world.

I should not ride in a cab unchaperoned with Tom Rampling. But then, I thought, I should not be walking with him unchaperoned, either. I knew one thing only: my beliefs about Tom had been flung from orbit along with everything else, and I needed to know where they—where he—might land. So I raised my arm to the first approaching brougham driver, opened the door, and pushed Tom up the step, scrambling in beside him before he could make protest.

Inside the cab, though, the padded seats, the shuttered dimness, and the air furred with the many smells of its passengers conspired to rob me of all inspiration. What could I possibly say to him? I felt suddenly weak, as dazed as Alice grown too big for the rabbit hole. And the enclosed space was alive, too, with Tom's presence next to me and the recent memory of our physical struggle. I sat with my hands pressed between my knees, struggling to gain governance of myself. I searched in vain for words to break the awkwardness, aware of a powerful yearning to touch and not to talk.

In the end it was Tom who broke the silence. "You must despise me."

I half-turned to him, taken off my guard by the dull misery in his voice. His hands lay like fallen birds in his lap.

"Cowering like a dog before your lord. Letting him use me so wretchedly."

"You are mistaken. It is not you I d-despise."

He glanced at me and away again, frowning, waiting.

He cannot see how the world is new, I thought. I remembered how I'd let Mr. Thornfax caress my neck and whisper to me at the opera, and my stomach lurched. "Flattered. B-blinded. How could I be so s-stupid? I could not s-see him for what he is."

"Thornfax took great pains not to be seen by you." Tom rubbed at a smear on the window.

"We must tell the p-police," I said.

"Tell them what?" Tom said. "That the Lord Rosbury slapped an assistant? No, I do know what you mean"—he waved a hand in apology for his sharpness—"I've puzzled over it from every angle, believe me. But there's no case against the man. Not yet. The police would never touch a man like Thornfax without real proof.

"I've needed to let him use me like this." Tom shot me a quick glance, shame mantling his face again. "I've let him believe in my eagerness to do anything he asks. I need his belief in my loyalty, you see, in order to know his plans."

Now it was my turn to frown and wait.

Tom took a heavy gold watch from his pocket. "Do you recognize this?"

I read the engraving. "Mr. Thornfax's! H-how—?"

"A man beating his dog doesn't mind his pocket," he said, a touch ruefully. He opened the case and, digging a fingernail into the seam, removed the watch face to expose the works. "I will build this into the detonation mechanism for the explosive Daisy must ignite."

"The lightning cap," I said, remembering Daisy's boasting in the surgery.

"Yes. If it operates the way I am hoping, it will delay the blast long enough for her to come away safely—long enough for an alarm to be raised, for an evacuation to occur.

"I'm not proud of the thievery, milady. But only the most expensive timepieces contain the necessary components for my device." This time the look he cast me revealed a glint of mischief. "I confess there will be a certain satisfaction in sabotaging Thornfax with his own timepiece."

He pointed out various gears and springs in an attempt to explain how the watch could be modified into a timer, but I was inattentive to the science, being overwhelmed with the relief of confirming what I'd already hoped beyond hope, what I'd known for certain, I think, the moment Mr. Thornfax had struck him in the lab: Tom Rampling was working at cross-purposes to his employers.

Tom's enthusiasm for his invention faded, however, when he recalled what had gone wrong for poor young Will at the opera house: "I hadn't got Watts to trust me enough yet to tell me the exact timing of the planned attack, or even the location. And then Daisy had taken a heavier dose than usual and was too sleepy to obey orders, so Watts grabbed Will and forced him to do it in her place. He … I must make the device simpler to manage. Will must have panicked and forgotten how to set the delay."

I recalled the argument between Tom and Mr. Thornfax at the carriage on the night of the opera blast, and Tom's devastation at the news that Will had died.

Gently he shook off the consoling hand I placed over his. "No, milady, I know what you will say. But the boy's death is my responsibility. As will be Daisy's, if I fail again.

"I introduced many of these poor souls to Dr. Dewhurst. I recruited patients for him everywhere before I knew how dangerous his cure is, how powerful are the morbid cravings it induces." He scrubbed a hand savagely across his eyes. "'Nervous disturbances,' he treats! As if every orphan in this city doesn't suffer from nervous disturbance!"

"W-why does he do it?" I said. My brother-in-law did not strike me as capable of deliberate inhumanity or murder for its own sake.

Tom shrugged. "There's a fortune to be made in the patent, he says, and the application for such a patent requires clinical trials."

"But if the d-drug is so addictive—"

"It will sell all the faster."

I considered this. Daniel Dewhurst was master of Hastings House but not in possession of the funds needed to maintain it. The Dewhursts were almost entirely dependent upon my aunt Emma. It was shocking but not wholly surprising to hear that Daniel might be pursuing this lucrative patent even at the cost of human lives. Perhaps he'd first initiated the friendship with Mr. Thornfax as a way of funding his researches, and only recently had the two been conspiring to smuggle the opium if it became illegal in England.

Tom anticipated my next question. "I do not understand exactly how Thornfax's violent schemes are enmeshed with the doctor's work. The Lord Rosbury has all the money a man could want, but he craves power. I've heard him boast that he'll have Parliament performing his tricks like trained monkeys."

I shuddered at such arrogance, and at the thought that I might not have become aware of it until it was too late. Did

Mr. Thornfax command the Black Glove, then? *Was* there a Black Glove aside from Mr. Thornfax, his man Watts, and the poor urchins they coerced into doing their bidding?

Tom cleared his throat. "I am sorry, milady. I should not speak so to you of your—of him."

"No. I am n-not—I am …" I fell silent. Absurd as it seemed, I was grateful for the events of the past few hours. Not just to Tom, for telling me the truth and for proving himself to be as kind and conscientious as I'd first believed him. I was grateful simply for having acted, for having striven and succeeded in some small way. And above all I was grateful because I realized that at some point, hiding in that laboratory, I had stopped being afraid.

Near to choking with my inability to express any of this to Tom, I plucked Mr. Thornfax's watch from his hand, snapped it shut, and held it in my fist. "Do you love Daisy?" I blurted.

Tom blinked. His brow creased. His mouth opened, closed again, and quirked with some private irony. He reached to retrieve the watch from me and withdrew his hand when I wouldn't release it. Then he reached again to let his fingers close over mine. "How could I love Daisy?" he said, soft as a sigh. "Miss Luck. With you in the world, how could I?"

I opened my palm to relinquish the watch. Instead of taking it he pinched my glove by the cuff and deftly peeled it from my hand, turning it inside out and trapping the watch within it. I laughed and made a lunge for the glove, but he pulled it away and stuffed it into his pocket.

I was breathless and off balance, my face suddenly poised very close to Tom's. He smoothed my hair to one side, the same fleeting, unthinking gesture as the first time he'd touched me, in the parlour so many weeks ago. I felt his warm breath against my lips and closed my eyes against a corresponding rush of heat in my belly. "P-please," I said, and Tom misunderstood and leaned away, removing his hand from my hair.

So I kissed him. It was nothing but a fumbling brush of my lips against his, but it drew from him a rough gasp of pleasure. He gathered me into his arms. His lips came down on mine and parted them, and I tasted the salt of his blood and the sweetness of his tongue. Our kisses after that were heedless of his bruises, heedless of anything except the sensations flaring between us like a match to a fuse.

There are things I simply cannot say. I heard myself moan, a low, sensual sound that was my own, not Mimic's—and yet it sounded wholly foreign to me. I tore my other glove from my hand and let my fingers revel in the silky luxury of Tom's hair, the rasp of skin at his jaw. Trails of fire followed his lips along my throat.

Tom buried his face against my neck, his hands encircling my ribs as if he were taking the measure of my heart. "Oh, Miss Luck," he breathed between kisses. "Oh, love. Oh, my love."

Losing ourselves in this way we were fortunate that the cab chanced to cross a stretch of broken road that jolted us nearly from our seats. I laughed aloud at our disarray, but then I glanced out and saw that we had already crossed Orchard Street and were nearing Portman. I shouted for the driver to stop and hastened to reassemble Mrs. Fayerweather's hat and my scarf-veil.

"I am—" Tom cleared his throat. "I must beg your pardon, Miss Somerville."

I looked at him. He sat rigid against the far wall of the cab. "N-no," I said.

"I should not—I ought to have greater mastery of myself." Tom's voice was laced with real self-disgust.

"P-please, Tom. I do n-not—"

He took the watch from inside my stolen glove and tossed the glove into my lap. Through clenched teeth he said, "I will understand if you report my impropriety to Dr. Dewhurst. Or I will tell him myself, if you wish it. I will accept the consequences."

"No. N-no, n-n-no—Thomas Rampling, that is quite enough! We shall part here as allies and conspirators, or we shan't part at all." Was that my aunt Emmaline's voice or someone else's Mimic had found? I was too desperate to bother trying to identify it. I leaned over, took hold of Tom's shirt with both hands, and shook him. "I have seen too much today, learned too many awful things, to let you go now and think we might not be friends. I couldn't bear it."

"Milady—"

I interrupted him: "It isn't only—it is that it might be dangerous, if anyone should know." Tom shook his head as if to disavow cowardice, but I rushed on: "Not only dangerous for you, but for me, too. I believe Lord Rosbury is capable of real violence if he should know."

Tom stilled, looking stricken. "Of course," he said, nodding. "Of course you are right."

"C-call me Leonora." Mimic had done her bit, apparently, and had gone on her way. "S-so I know we are friends. P-please, Tom."

"Leonora."

"Leo," I amended.

"Leo." Tom smiled in spite of himself.

I climbed out of the cab and paid the driver. Tom followed me out, and then we hesitated there together on the street. "Be c-careful," I told him shakily.

"You too, Miss Luck."

Neither of us wanted to be the first to turn away. But I might be seen, and my disguise might not hold, so it was I who shook free at last. I walked the short distance home without feeling the ground under my feet, without feeling anything at all but the memory of Tom's soft breath on my skin and his warm lips over mine.

SEVENTEEN

*I*n the cab Tom had told me he'd learned that the Black Glove's next move was planned for Thursday, the second of May. That was only five days hence. Mr. Thornfax had not revealed where the explosive would be set, but his mention to Watts of a station master made us suppose it would be a train derailment. Twice that week Mr. Thornfax called on me, and both times I pleaded illness, exaggerating the symptoms of the minor cold I'd picked up at the Docks so that Christa and the servants would believe me. I couldn't stand the thought of seeing him. I couldn't even stand the flowers he sent. I told Bess they made my sniffles worse so that she would take them away from my room.

I looked for Tom every day, but I didn't dare to seek him out for fear of arousing suspicions and disturbing him in his work on the timing device. I found plenty of excuses to be outside in hopes of seeing him. I played at marbles with Bertie on the drive, ignoring Mrs. Nussey's comments about dust on my skirts. I cajoled Christabel into coming out with me for walks, hoping the fresh air would counteract her druggish state but not wholly minding it when she simply lolled on the bench nearest the gates, as this allowed me to keep a covert lookout for Tom. I even resorted to carrying the tea to my brother-in-law in his consulting rooms, though I could scarcely look Daniel in the face after what I'd learned of his ambitions. Of Daisy, also, there was no sign.

When the first of May had come and gone without a word I felt myself becoming frantic. The constant, anxious anticipation left me with a headache and a sour stomach, but going to bed early did not help me sleep.

In desperation I got up again, gathered paper and pen, and composed a letter to the Lady Hastings. I gave her every particular of the past week's events, taking care to separate my suspicions and fears from the facts I had managed to discover. Setting the case to paper should have calmed me. Instead it exposed a stark truth: I had no proof. I could argue as elegantly as I wanted for a conspiracy of violence between Daniel and Mr. Thornfax, but without proof it amounted to the hysterical ramblings of a deranged young girl. Mad Miss Mimic, as ever.

Still, the next morning I braved the sheeting rain to meet the post-chaise at the gate. Beadall trudged beside me in his greatcoat and overshoes, casting me sidelong glances of ill-concealed irritation. I knew he liked to light his pipe as he waited for the driver and that he couldn't feel free to do so in my presence. I knew that holding the umbrella for me was uncomfortable with the household packages crammed under his other arm. I knew, too, that he was hurt by my apparent lack of trust in his competency: he'd seen my letter to Aunt Emma in my lap as I struggled with the boot-hook and said,

"No need to go out in the muck, Miss Somerville, especially if you're feeling poorly. I'm happy to add that one to the stack."

The letter had spent the night beneath my pillow. In the long, wakeful hours and the frightful dreams between those hours, it had become a poisoned dagger aimed at those who loved me. The accusations contained within, true or not, seemed so hateful that I'd cringed guiltily through breakfast and could not meet the Dewhursts' eyes. I trusted Beadall of course, but my anxiety was such that I could no sooner have put the letter into the butler's hand than march into my brother-in-law's study and read it aloud to him.

Past the gate the rain lashed the road into a river of mud. A blurred movement across the intersection drew my attention; squinting through the torrent I could just make out a small figure hunched beneath a tree in Portman Square. The post-chaise arrived, and as Beadall handed up the packages I felt a tugging on my skirt. A boy with chapped cheeks and filthy, dripping hair held out a note addressed to me. I took it, and he dashed away again before I could find a coin for him in my purse.

I gave the coin instead to the postman, along with the letter to Aunt Emma. Then, risking further rudeness, I had Beadall wait there with the umbrella while I opened the boy's note.

From Tom Rampling, two short sentences: *Daisy brings with her my work. It will go well today.*

With pounding pulse I tore the paper into bits and stuffed it into my pocket. Walking back to the house I wove and stumbled over the stones until Beadall took my arm under his. Inside I thanked him, mumbled something about a headache, and groped my way to my bedroom, where relief and fear worked together to dispatch me into the deepest sleep I'd achieved in many days.

I woke in the early afternoon. Bess had brought my lunch on a tray, and I satisfied her as to my health when I got up and ate everything on the plate. She brought me another bouquet from Mr. Thornfax, saying, "Look, Miss Somerville, just the loveliest note!"—and the poor girl seemed a bit crestfallen when I cut her off before she could read it to me. I told her I needed fresh air and should like to take a walk at once, alone, before the rain began again.

This time Mrs. Fayerweather's hat took me to Fleet Street and the offices of *The London Examiner*. If the past few days had taught me anything, it was that acting must be infinitely better than waiting. And if there was any news, no one would hear it sooner than my cousin Archie Mavety. I stepped down almost jauntily from the omnibus, shooing away the alms-beggars and bootblacks with ringing reproaches. It was becoming easier and easier to play the old woman. Mimic had begun blending Mrs. Fayerweather's with other remembered elderly voices. The cobbles shone in the weak sun and, except for the sooty creeks sluicing down the gutters carrying leaves and bits of trash, the city looked scrubbed and innocent as a child after bath time.

When I asked for him at the desk I was informed that Mr. Mavety was "out netting a whale of a story." So I found a tea shop much like the one at the Docks and took up my vigil by the window. It was not long before Archie climbed out of a cab, and I hurried to intercept him.

"What on earth are you doing behind that veil?" he asked, laughing, when I said hello.

It was the first time I'd seen my cousin since discovering the truth about Mr. Thornfax. Looking at his dear, freckled face I felt ashamed for suspecting him of fabricating the Black Glove stories. His instincts had been right in questioning Daniel about his medical patients and in thinking Mr. Thornfax too reckless and dangerous for me. In fact Archie had no idea just how right he was.

"I've borrowed the costume," Mimic answered him, still as Mrs. Fayerweather. "But let's not linger over that today. I am curious about the news you've been off to gather, Cousin."

"Well, your timing couldn't be better. They've bombed a rail train this time!"

My breath escaped in a rush.

Archie was climbing the stairs. I clutched up my skirts to keep pace with him. "Four people killed," he said. "Awful shame."

Four people? Nausea rose in my gut. *Four* lives snuffed out. And yet, the number was far lower than it might have been.

Archie confirmed this: "The train had just unloaded its passengers at Charing Cross. Fifteen minutes earlier and it would have been a right bloodbath. I'm certain it was a cock-up on the part of the Black Glove." He chuckled. "Gangster heads will roll tonight!"

My cousin's face was flushed, his hair was badly mussed, his coat was torn at the hem, and his neck was smeared with soot. All in all I'd never seen him so happy. He shoved open the door and had nearly rushed through it before he remembered to hold it for me.

"However can you confirm the Black Glove's involvement? Surely you can't print such a supposition without proof."

Archie sniggered and shook his head at my old-lady voice. "Oh, my Lady Leo. Oh ye of little faith." He nodded a hasty greeting to the desk boy and led me through a corridor to the copy room. Slamming his satchel to the floor and shooing another boy from his chair, he found a clean leaf of paper, whipped out a pencil, and began, with great speed and confidence, to write.

As the page filled with his untidy scrawl Archie informed me that he'd seen, with his own eyes, the note claiming responsibility for the blast. "Can you believe the Black Glove actually uses custom-designed stationery? An elegant black border and the outline of a miniature black glove at the letterhead! Even I thought it a touch overdramatic."

The station master, upon receiving the letter, had sent word to *The Examiner* even before calling for the police or the fire brigade. Archie viewed this as a triumph of the free press: "It's the public being terrorized by these gangs, so it's sensible to inform the public as soon as possible." He squinted up at my face to gauge my expression. "All right, I confess it also makes me feel terribly important! Old Mr. Gage asked for me personally. He'd read all my columns and told me he thought 'twas Mavety best equipped to 'andle the evidence, and make sommat sense of it,' as he put it.

"'Course, the police saw me about to copy the Black Glove's letter into my notebook and damn near tore the thing in their haste to take custody of it. Ruffians and thugs, all of them—" Archie gave a loud whistle, dropped his pencil, and, with a flourish, handed the leaf of paper to an old man who'd scurried to his side. "But it doesn't matter. There's enough in this story already to goggle the eyes of every Londoner with a penny to spend!"

I tweaked my cousin's sleeve. "Who were the unfortunate souls murdered in this blast? Won't you want to identify them in your report, or was there too much disfigurement for that?"

"No disfigurement at all. The exploded carriage was entirely empty, apparently. 'Tis a mystery how the charge was set without killing at least the bomb courier. The derailment overturned two cars, though, and the engine room caught fire. Two coal stokers, one porter"—Archie ticked the victims off on his fingers—"and a retired clerk with a ticket to Brighton. Remarkable how low the toll is, really."

So Daisy had survived! Tom's timer had done its work. Relief mingled with my lingering sickness over the deaths. I watched as the old man bent over Archie's copy and his stained fingers began to move like a piano player's over the wooden type boxes. With a rhythmic click of lead against lead he scooped the letters into his composing stick and stacked them into neat rows in the galley-frame. *Bloodied kerchief*, I read in the mirror-image script, and *laid in the mortuary to await inquest*. The tray was snatched away for proofing before I could decipher any more.

Here at least was a group of people who knew what to do with a violent catastrophe. How I envied my cousin! His freedom to visit the scene of disaster and to leave again with greater resolve and energy than before. His ability to harness chaos and fear, to channel them into the order of words and sentences.

"Sixteen thousand copies an hour!" Archie boasted. "I'd offer you a tour of the pressroom, but my story's already late, and I'm loath to show my face down there. In fact"—he threw an arm about my shoulders and steered me toward the door—"I think it wiser to see you home before you're entirely lost in the fray. 'Twill be dinnertime shortly, and I'm well aware how Mrs. Nussey hates asking your cook to reheat a potato."

The great clock was indeed striking the supper hour as I entered Hastings House. Daniel met me at the door with a black glare at Archie, who waved back at him from the cab. My brother-in-law motioned me into his study. He wore his dinner jacket, but his cuffs and tie were unfastened. Perhaps he simply wants help with them, I thought wildly. I bundled Mrs. Fayerweather's hat inside my coat and laid it on the console; I knew Beadall would probably find it and wonder, but I hoped he would simply hang it back where I'd found it.

It seemed, however, that Beadall had appointed himself my conscience and reported my doings of this morning to the doctor.

"I told you that you weren't to see that bloody-minded newsman again," Daniel thundered. But then, without preamble: "From whom did you receive a note this morning?"

I flushed. My mind whirled with a thousand poor excuses.

The black silk of his tie swung from Daniel's fingers and twined through them. "Bess says you've been coming and going constantly this week."

In all the years of Mimic's interference, for all the times she'd stolen another person's words and made them her own, she'd never deliberately invented a mistruth. And now, when I would have welcomed any outburst as a blessed distraction, she abandoned me completely.

I jumped as Daniel slammed a palm onto his desk. "Leonora. I *will* be satisfied in this!"

I took a breath. "The L-Lord Rosbury," I said.

"What?"

His surprise emboldened me. "He l-likes to write to me. I was em-b-barrassed, should anyone r-read it."

My brother-in-law swallowed, hesitating. "Have you been meeting with him? Unchaperoned?"

I shook my head. Then, seeing the intense relief on his face, I reconsidered. "But he has asked m-me to m-meet him."

"When?"

I blushed again, this time with the audacity of the lie I was weaving. "Well, t-today. But he did n-not come as p-promised."

Daniel bit his lip. Mr. Thornfax would have been at the rail station today, I imagined, or nearby at least, overseeing the attack. But it wouldn't be beyond him, would it, to organize a tryst with me as an alibi, even if it cost me my reputation. I prayed Daniel would not take it upon himself to ask Mr. Thornfax about it outright.

"I asked my c-cousin to fetch me home," I pressed. Painting Archie as the hero of my virtue was easy compared to accusing Mr. Thornfax of attempted seduction. I watched my brother-in-law's troubled face, wondering whether he was concerned for me or purely for the Somerville name.

He turned away from me and stepped to the window. I heard him mutter, "What does he think he—? He would have every one of us at his whim."

"P-pardon?"

Daniel had made a loop of the necktie and was stroking it as if for comfort. He cleared his throat. "I said, he should not involve you in an intrigue."

That was not exactly what he had said, but I thought it best to leave the matter there, and my brother-in-law did not chide me further about my conduct. "Make haste now," was all he said, and waved me upstairs to dress for dinner.

That evening, hours after Christa had retired to bed, I heard Mr. Thornfax's voice in the hall and crept to the stairs to listen.

"Should we not be celebrating? A human life has been spared, after all." Daniel's voice was low, placating.

"Loose ends are no cause for celebration!" Mr. Thornfax hissed back at him. "That girl can give every detail, every particular. She knew your face already, and Watts's. And now that Curtis has brought her to me, she knows mine as well."

"Come now, Thornfax. I hardly think the word of a wastrel *fille de joie* will stand against yours in a court of law."

"What do you call it? An 'over-dosage,' isn't it?"

There was a shocked silence. Then Daniel whispered, "Daisy is no threat to us. She'll come back to me freely, by noon tomorrow at the outside, in need of another treatment."

"She is not free. She will not be freed, and I wouldn't trust you to take care of her in any case."

I recognized the flinty edge in Mr. Thornfax's voice from the warehouse, and a chill swept through me. Part of me had wanted to deny what I'd heard and seen in the laboratory, despite everything Tom had told me. I still couldn't really reconcile Mr. Thornfax's easy, open manners with his scheming, or the blue-eyed, golden-haired goodness of his looks with the evidence of an evil heart. Part of me still wanted to pretend I'd imagined it all.

"Someone modified that explosive to delay its ignition," he was saying to Daniel.

"Modified? Surely you don't think—"

"Your sympathy for your patients could incriminate you, Doctor."

"A fluke! It must have been a fluke, Thornfax, an accident."

"Give me the damned dose, or I shall improvise with strychnine. Either way they'll know the syringe was of your manufacture. Which would you prefer?"

Silence.

Then Mr. Thornfax's boots thudded across the floor as Daniel led him through the house and across the court to his surgery.

EIGHTEEN

I watched from my bedroom window. It was only a minute or two until Mr. Thornfax took his leave. His hair flared gold in the doorway before darkness swallowed him.

For a long time afterward, in the wan light of the surgery, the shadowy figure of my brother-in-law paced back and forth. Twice he opened the door and leaned out, hands bracing the door frame and chest heaving as if he battled some ineluctable force of resistance, as if to follow Mr. Thornfax would require him to slingshot his body out through the resisting air. Both times he retreated.

Gazing down upon this private struggle I felt a moment of cold disgust for my brother in law. His dressing gown had come untied and his belly strained grossly under his nightshirt. The bare white legs underneath were spindly and knob-kneed; it seemed impossible they didn't collapse under all the weight they supported. The jowly face, the little, blinking eyes, the bald pate shining in the lamplight— weak, cowardly man! Selfish, gluttonous, grasping man, who even now, extinguishing the lights, waddling back to the house, probably told himself it didn't matter, it was out of his hands, there was nothing he could do to save Daisy. Who probably consoled himself—I heard the shuffling steps of his house slippers on the stairs, the click of his bedchamber door—that at least he'd made Daisy's exit from the world a little more comfortable by killing her with the medicine she loved so much.

I caught myself. How was I any different from Daniel? I too had stayed silent and allowed innocent people to die. Somehow I'd allowed myself to be consoled by Tom's efforts to minimize the damage. I had let myself believe, somehow, that the train wreck would result in no deaths at all. Instead four more people had lost their lives because of my silence.

I should have gone down to confront Daniel tonight directly after Mr. Thornfax left. I should have tried to spur his conscience into action. I should go this minute, I thought, and beg him to follow after Mr. Thornfax and stop him, or at least to go to the police! But if he asked me how I knew of Daisy's involvement in the train wreck, I would not know how to answer without giving away Tom. My conscience and my caution warred within me long after I lay down in my bed.

I could not sleep—could not even bring myself to blow out the candle. I felt numbed through, and my bones ached as if it were my own body wasted by the opiate fever. I kept imagining Daisy's thin, bruised arms, her sunken eyes stricken with terror.

I tried to stop these visions. It would not help Daisy for me to frighten myself picturing her fate. But now that I knew who Mr. Thornfax truly was, what monstrous pleasure he derived from exerting force over others, I could not help it. Daisy shut up in the dark. Daisy beaten—taunted and beaten, or worse—when she could not answer questions to Mr. Thornfax's satisfaction. Daisy heartened by the sight of a syringe in Mr. Thornfax's hand. Daisy soaring on the wings of the drug, blissful even as she knew she was flying into death.

I woke to a wet cloth scrubbing my face and found myself gagging on a mouthful of tooth powder. "Get up!" Bess ordered, with uncharacteristic shrillness. "Oh, why must you be difficult to rouse on this, of all days?"

I spat into the bowl she shoved under my chin. "W-what is it?"

"Mrs. Dewhurst says it must be the white muslin, but we've had no chance for starch or iron." Bess levered me to my feet and practically tore my nightdress off my shoulders. "And she told him you've been up here reading all morning long! As if you're some sort of layabout!"

I reached for Bess's hands, but she turned away from me and began yanking open and slamming the drawers of my bureau. Clean undergarments flew through the air and fell to my feet; a hail of gloves, handkerchiefs, and stockings pelted the bed. "Rosewater!" she wailed, lifting the empty bottle, and fled the room.

I dressed as fast as I could, shaking the sleep from my limbs. "W-what is it?" I tried again, as Christabel's maid bustled in through the door.

Emily held aloft my white walking-dress. "She didn't tell

you? Here, lift your arms. I'm to do your hair, Mrs. Dewhurst says, as I'm faster."

"Emily, p-please."

My head emerged through the neck of the gown, and she beamed at me. "There now! 'Something to go with your necklace,' he says. Well, my mistress guessed the white, and here's proof again: my mistress is never wrong."

Little Bertie burst into my chamber. He was red-faced and giggling, sporting a paper eye patch and brandishing a wooden sword. His mission of mutiny was confirmed by Greta, also red-faced, saying she'd only turned her back for a moment and off he'd gone. A dog was yapping somewhere downstairs, and I heard the shouts of the servants trying to quieten it. Chaos seemed to rule the day at Hastings House.

I grabbed Emily's wrist as she laid ready my hairpins. "T-tell me what is g-going on!"

"Mr. Thornfax—I mean the Lord Rosbury—has asked Dr. Dewhurst for your hand, Miss Somerville, and the doctor has told him yes!"

"Well, of course he said yes," chimed Bess, back again with the scent. "'Twas hardly a question. You're going to dine at Whitehall in celebration. The Lord Rosbury had it all planned in advance!"

I fell into the chair. My face in the mirror was ashen.

Emily lowered the hairbrush. "Miss Somerville, are you well? Your tea'll be up in a minute. 'Tis a shock before your breakfast, I'll warrant. Though 'tis mid-afternoon." She tutted.

Not thirty minutes later I was seated in Mr. Thornfax's carriage opposite Daniel and Christabel. My brother-in-law looked as exhausted as I felt, his eyelids puffed and the usual ruddiness gone from his cheeks. Christa by contrast fidgeted on her seat and prattled brightly about the fine weather and the gloss on the horses' coats and oh, what a fine joke not to tell us in advance about the party!

Mr. Thornfax had been standing beside the carriage to receive me as I was rushed from the front door, but I had turned my face away and thrown myself onto the seat without pause. Now, sitting next to me in a dove-grey suit, holding his matching grey top hat on his knees, he took my hand. He inclined his head to the black ribbon at my waist and said he appreciated my thoughtfulness in honouring his father. I nodded, still without looking at him. I'd tied on the ribbon in a kind of stupor, ignoring Bess's comment that it was violet I wanted to match my necklace and that I needn't wear mourning for my fiancé's relation—it struck me only now that I'd worn it not for the late Lord Rosbury at all, but for Daisy.

Daisy. Thinking her name brought a cold weight to my chest and a throbbing kernel of pain to the base of my skull. Did Tom know about her yet? Perhaps he didn't even know. I was glad I hadn't attempted the tea or the biscuits Bess had begged me to eat.

We disembarked at the Royal Banqueting House at Whitehall, where Christabel, as she was handed down, nearly sprawled onto the curb and had to be righted by Curtis.

Daniel put his wife on one arm and took me with the other. He bent to speak into my ear. "He will make good, you'll see. I knew his intentions for you were pure."

I gaped at him. No matter what sort of friendship these men shared, no matter what sort of deal they'd arranged—no matter how badly the Dewhursts wanted to see me settled—surely after last night Daniel must know I couldn't marry Mr. Thornfax! Disgust rose in me afresh. I had not imagined my brother-in-law to be as spineless—or as callous—as this.

Mr. Thornfax led us directly through the red-carpeted lobby into the colossal ballroom. A dozen large circular tables were crowded with guests. As we were announced, the guests pushed back their chairs and showered us with applause.

"My friends," Mr. Thornfax shouted, throwing up his hands. "Thank you for coming!" So all these were his friends. Our friends. Most I did not recognize—parliamentarians, from their dress, judges and lords, solicitors and their wives. They took my hand, and the ladies kissed me, and one or two told me how much they had always admired my aunt, the Countess of Hastings, and were sorry not to see her here.

I found myself forgetting each name as soon as it was given me, each face as soon as I turned away. I was not expected to speak, of course, but I found I could hardly think, either. The nights of lost sleep, last night's horror, Daniel's blithe betrayal—I was drowning under it. Above all: *Daisy, Daisy, Daisy*. I was drowning in her name. I moved as though under water, seeing indistinctly through the murk, my limbs dragging. I thought of the pond at Holybourne. If you put your feet down, the mud would hold your ankles fast. It was seething with leeches, and thrashing about would only make it worse.

"C-Christa, where is our aunt Emma?" I asked my sister, the first time I got her alone. I had never needed anyone like I needed my aunt at this moment.

"Silly. You know how she hates parties," Christabel

said. Her glass of champagne was still half-full, but she was slurring her words—already drunk, or laudanum-doped. Possibly both.

Our table was next to a low stage where a string quartet played Mozart. There was champagne, and trays came round with miniature custards and pineapple-cream ices. I drank, and I gazed up at Rubens's paintings on the ceiling. Rippling flesh, billowing robes, bristling weaponry. The figures seemed to break free of the plaster and paint, embracing or attacking one another randomly and without constraint.

Christabel had gone to chat with a lady two tables over. Now she teetered toward us, unbalanced, and caught herself on Mr. Thornfax's shoulder. She was rewarded with general laughter, and Mr. Thornfax and Daniel leapt to assist her to her seat.

More champagne arrived—toast after toast to the blessed couple. I drank. Mr. Thornfax angled his chair next to mine and raked his eyes over my figure. "You know, I always forget how young you are. Those jewels of mine on your neck look practically obscene."

I could not look at him. I couldn't stand to look at him: jovial, golden-haired, blamelessly handsome. Even worse would be to detect signs of tiredness after his labours last night. I could not bear that.

A man introduced to us as "Mr. Taunt, the famous portrait-photographer" unloaded a camera from a handcart while his assistant balanced the tripod. We were asked to stand, and our chairs were adjusted further. We were seated nearly hip to hip, with the light from the window strong on our faces. Young men appeared in overalls, too, with palettes and brushes. "They shall make a photograph now, but I want an oil painting as well," Mr. Thornfax explained. "They'll be taking sketches and colour samples."

We held ourselves immobile while Mr. Taunt developed his image. I kept feeling Mr. Thornfax's necklace tighten around my throat. I kept reaching up to tug at it, and poor Mr. Taunt had to begin again, and Mr. Thornfax finally caught both my hands in his and held them there.

"I saw a ladybird on my window this morning," I heard my sister say. "That means money, you know."

"Fortune favours the bold," someone replied.

Oxtail soup, sweetbreads and mushrooms, devilled eggs. More champagne. A fine crack spiderwebbed the plaster beside my head—had it been there a moment ago? I wasn't certain. I waited for more fissures to appear.

Dr. Dewhurst was explaining his methodology to a medical man visiting from Denmark. "We only treat the genteel classes with formulae that have already been proven safe and effective on the poor."

"But, sir, needn't you care most for the lowliest of your patients?" the man wondered.

Daniel leaned back in his chair and clasped his hands across his belly. "Society is like a great tree," he said. "What tends to those blossoms on the upper branches will inevitably sift some pollen onto the lower flowers, so that all produce fruit according to their natural capacities."

"The Great Chain of Being!" Christa sighed. "All of us in our God-given places."

She was in the midst of pouring drops from a little glass bottle into her champagne. "Mrs. Dewhurst, you'll exceed your dose," Daniel warned her, and reached for her wrist, but she scoffed at him and emptied the glass in one swallow.

A silver tray was wheeled round with twenty different types of cakes.

Christa turned away from our table to speak to the Danish doctor's wife. Mr. Thornfax nudged Daniel, took something from his pocket, and opened his palm beneath the table so the doctor could see. It was his watch case, twisted and scorched. "That's the work of your boy Rampling," he told him.

"Whyever would Tom Rampling ruin your watch?"

Mr. Thornfax spoke softly: "'Twas fused to the blast cap he manufactured for Watts. A mechanism for delay. For sabotage."

Daniel swallowed. "I don't believe it of him."

"You will let me know his whereabouts when next he turns up?"

"Surely—no real harm was done by it, Thornfax? I will deal with the boy."

"'Tis for me to deal with, Dewhurst. My business. As we agreed."

Daniel stared at him.

"I insist," said Mr. Thornfax.

Daniel dropped his eyes and reached a trembling hand to lift sugar cubes into his tea.

A whispering struck up inside the walls, a sound just below hearing that rang the crystal and vibrated the silverware and made the quartet's melodies nothing but noise in my ears. Daisy lay at the bottom of the Thames, half interred by now in silt. Her open eyes were watching the hellish green shadows and the little fish come to feast on her flesh. Or she lay in the dust by a country crossroads, face down perhaps, waiting for the sun and the buzzards to do their work.

Another memory from Holybourne came to me: red ants swarming over a bird's nest, bristling and bright, devouring the hatchlings alive. The terrible beauty of that furious, bloody-minded tide. Mr. Thornfax was like that, in his spry little *Heroine* on the glittering ocean. And he was not alone in his self-interest and cruelty. I saw him as one of thousands, millions—hungry, war-making men swarming over the world, multiplying their horde from the helpless and hapless.

Daniel was taken up in the frenzy, and Archibald, too, in his way—how else to account for his excitement over yesterday's explosion?—and so would I be, once I had attached myself to Mr. Francis Thornfax and become the Lady Rosbury. I was halfway there already with my flashing jewels and my lips wet with champagne.

I watched my sister's heavy lids, her dull gaze upon the cakes, the smile not reaching her eyes. For a moment I envied her the numbness laudanum gave her, and I found myself wondering whether her little bottle might have something left in it for me. We were the queens, she and I, tucked deep away in the anthill. The fat white queens, nectar-drunk and bloated on the spoils.

"Your brother-in-law gives his consent to our marriage," Mr. Thornfax was saying to me, leaning in just enough to include Daniel in the conversation. "But I should like to know it has your approval too."

"M-my a-p-proval?" I said, struggling to hold him at the centre of the whirlpool so that, while the room bulged and wavered and revolved, his golden head stayed in focus.

"Will you marry me, sweet little Miss Somerville?"

With a suck of pressure everything came to a standstill. I felt it in my eardrums: a pop like going up in the balloon at Kew and coming down again. I took my hand from his and placed both my hands together in my lap.

How could there be nothing in Mr. Thornfax's face to betray him? I forced myself, then, to look at him—to really *look*, to search that handsome face for a sign. I examined the clear blue eyes. The broad, unlined forehead with its feathery brows. The straight, regal nose. The generous lower lip and the upper lip with its strong, shapely bow. If I'd imagined a sleepless night would manifest in shadows under his eyes or a bleary look—if I'd thought the revenge he'd taken on Daisy might reveal itself in a hardness or tension somewhere—I needn't have wondered. The man was as perfect as ever.

Daniel nodded encouragingly at me from behind his teacup.

"Ask m-me who I think is behind the B-Black Glove," I said, "and then you shall have m-my answer."

The teacup clattered into its saucer. A beat of shocked silence, then Daniel said, "Leonora!"

"Ask me who I think m-murdered your father."

"Leonora, how dare you?" Daniel said.

Mr. Thornfax's growl cut him off: "A word, Miss Somerville?" He hoisted me out of my seat and hauled me several paces away. The guests sitting nearby winked and lifted their glasses to us: the young lovers, swept up in our prenuptial passion.

Daisy was dead, and Tom Rampling would be caught and killed, too, and I was in Hell. I had seen the etchings in Dante's book in my aunt's library. I knew that, at any moment, a snake might slither from a gentleman's open mouth. A lady's rib cage might crack apart to reveal a pulsing nest of maggots where a heart should be. These could be mere shells of people, dried husks the infernal wind would strip, any moment now, to skeletons.

Mr. Thornfax put his arm round my waist and bent his head to my neck. The cool, firm pressure of his lips at my throat did not signify passion. I knew it now: his most ardent caresses at the opera had been staged, measured precisely for their effect on those around us. What I'd felt in Tom's arms—that leaping heat, that thrumming pleasure—that was another thing entirely.

"The bargain of a tongue-tied wife rather depends on her remaining silent," Mr. Thornfax murmured. "You may think whatever you like of me in private, and I will oblige you by being your rogue. Only I hoped we might step out in society together. I shouldn't like to be forced to keep you shut away at home."

It was Hell, but Francis Thornfax would survive it, I thought. Like a worm he would thrive on the rot and decay. I pulled back from his embrace. "The L-Lady Hastings will never allow it," I told him.

"The Lady Hastings may have refused my invitation today, but she's already given her consent to the marriage. I had her reply last week. We are engaged, sweet Leonora. I am engaged to a lovely, sad little mutemouth of a girl, and all London loves me for the charity of it."

"I have written to her. I have t-told her everything!"

His eyes narrowed. "That is quite enough on the subject now, Miss Somerville. You begin to bore me."

"Oh, my poor head! I am dreadfully unwell." Christabel lurched into us, digging her fingers into my arm until I yelped. "Miss Somerville, I beg you, come to the ladies' salon at once and help me douse my temples." Without waiting for Mr. Thornfax's leave she dragged me on a weaving path among the tables.

We found the salon through the lobby, tucked beside the cloakroom. Christa rounded on me the moment the door closed behind us. "Are you truly so stupid as to accuse the Lord Rosbury of being a criminal?"

"You d-don't know what he's done," I said.

"Of course I don't know, and neither should you. It isn't your concern. You're to be his wife, not his solicitor."

"Would … would you have me live b-beyond the law?"

Christa's eyes narrowed as she advanced on me, swaying slightly. "I don't give a fig where you live so long as it isn't at Hastings House."

I blinked, taken aback by the poison in her tone.

My sister put a hand on a chair back to steady herself. She tilted her head and regarded me a moment. Then she laughed. "How fitting if Thornfax should turn out to be a cad."

"I d-don't understand."

"Did you think I would forget, little sister?" she snapped. "Do you think five years is enough to cure heartbreak, to soothe the pain of happiness utterly destroyed?"

"You mean Mr. Clayton?" I said. "Christa, that marriage would have been ruinous for you."

"Oh, how skilled you are at parroting the Lady Hastings when it suits you!" she spat.

I gasped. I hadn't realized I'd switched into Aunt Emma's voice.

"Yes, indeed. Mimic appointed herself judge and jury over my lover, and I lost him. What gave you the right? I wonder. Who were *you* to decide *my* happiness?"

It was the most she'd ever said to me about her old beau. I'd hoped that, after all this time, I had been forgiven for Mr. Clayton. Clearly I was wrong. Tears leaked from my eyes.

She straightened and patted her hands over her bodice where it flared at her hips. "Well, I will not judge Mr. Thornfax, and so you shall have him, like it or not. Even if it means your absolute ruin." She cast me a smug look. "Perhaps especially if it means your ruin!"

"You don't m-mean that," I whispered.

Christabel smiled. "No one cares about you, Leonora. You may think yourself the axis round which the world turns, but you will find yourself quite forgotten once married."

"Christa. Have m-mercy."

"Mimic has no mercy," she retorted. She dug her handkerchief from her sleeve, tossed it at me, and watched, hands on hips, while I dabbed at my eyes.

She whispered, "It is perfect if he is a cad. It is exactly what you deserve." Then she turned and flounced from the room.

NINETEEN

I stood many minutes before the gilded mirrors in the salon trying to compose myself. The hard fact of it was that my sister was right: Mimic had no mercy. I'd shown no mercy to George Clayton on the night our aunt had come to Holybourne to meet Christabel's suitor and we were all seated in the parlour.

"Coombs has taken a man's bollocks for less than what you owe him!" Mimic had blurted, out of the blue. It was a deep male voice, rough and disdainful.

I could hear the voice even now, alone at the mirrors in the ladies' salon. I could still recite Mimic's whole speech, even after five years—the whole conversation I'd heard while eavesdropping on Mr. Clayton and his friends in the barn. The fact that I was only twelve when I said the words and had no idea what they meant had done nothing to alter the devastating results of Mimic's performance that night.

"You had better sew things up with this country chit and get that pretty fortune of hers back to London, and fast. Your flat's already been ransacked, you know. And that whore you favour, Sissy Gordon—"

"Stop!" poor Mr. Clayton had begged me then. He'd fallen to one knee in front of me, right there in the parlour at Holybourne, with Christa tugging frantically at his arm.

"—Coombs's men have beaten her within an inch of her life for lying to cover your tracks."

Shaking off my sister Mr. Clayton lunged forward to grab hold of my slipper. "Please, Miss Leonora, no! You—you don't understand. Please stop."

"You will take your hand off my niece," Aunt Emmaline ordered.

Mr. Clayton released me and jumped to his feet. "My good Lady Hastings, I can explain—"

"You will not explain," Aunt Emma interrupted him, all quiet menace. "You will gather your coat at once and you will not return to this house. Nor will you attempt to contact Miss Somerville again."

Christabel had wailed and flung herself at our aunt. "Wait, wait, please!" she'd pleaded. "He's done nothing wrong. He was framed, you see. He has told me everything. He's been honest with me from the start!"

"Whoring and gambling? Debts and deceptions?" Aunt Emma snapped at her. "I doubt he's given you the whole story, foolish girl."

"It isn't true! She's lying," Christa shrieked. "Mimic is lying to you!"

But Mr. Clayton had already fled the room. Over the sound of my sister's sobbing we heard him away at the stables, calling for his horse, and none of us ever saw George Clayton again.

When two of Mr. Thornfax's guests came into the salon to re-pin their hair, I forced myself to receive their tipsy congratulations politely before fleeing the room.

Passing back through the lobby I heard angry voices and turned to see someone struggling to get past the doorman. My heart hammered hard at the sight of that white, pinched face and disordered hair.

"Tom!"

Surprised, the doorman released him as I approached.

"Tom, you m-mustn't be here!" I tried to steer him back to the entrance, but he shook me off.

"No, Leo, you won't stop me. He has gone too far this time. He must be called out." Tom's voice was strained with fury; his whole body trembled.

"P-please, no." The discovery of Mr. Thornfax's watch case had already signed Tom's death warrant. The man would be only too happy to have the excuse of a public assault. I grabbed Tom's arm, not caring who might see us, and held his face with both hands, trying to force him to look at me. "W-wait. Listen!"

But he shoved past me—"I am sorry, milady. I am sorry for it all"—and strode toward the hall, clearly intent on confronting Mr. Thornfax.

"Thomas Rampling, leave off at once! That door is suicide for you, and you know it will not bring Daisy back to life." Even as I spoke I sagged with relief; Mimic had struck upon the Lady Hastings at her most forbidding, and Tom paused and turned.

"You will give us privacy," I snapped, and the hovering doorman scuttled from our sight. I seized Tom's wrist and dragged him to the cloakroom vestibule.

"You know, then? You know he's murdered Daisy?" he whispered, white as ash.

Abruptly Mimic abandoned me again. I could only nod.

The horrified grief in Tom's eyes frightened me and set my tears to flowing again. I clutched his shoulders. My face went up to his and I kissed him deeply, desperately, as if trying to breathe back into him the life I saw drained from his face.

Tom pushed me away. He heaved a dry, retching sob, and another—awful sounds, like drowning. He wheeled round, pushed open the service door, stumbled outside to the gutter, and vomited there.

"Everything I've done." He choked, head down and gripping his thighs for balance. "Everything I've tried—in the end I've made it all worse. In the end I am just like *him*."

I rubbed his back and began to protest, but he interrupted me: "What are you doing out here? He'll search for you, milady. You need to go back inside."

"I won't. I c-can't go back—I can't m-marry him, T-Tom!"

Putting a hand to the bricks for support, Tom wiped his mouth. Then he straightened and, almost unconsciously, he tugged his collar and vest straight and smoothed his hands over his coat. Catching himself up, ordering himself, putting himself to rights. It was as if the violent upset of the past few moments had never happened. His face became smooth, remote, and expressionless.

"I've brought something for you," he said, and opened his satchel and took out a soft leather pouch. Inside, wrapped in a soft cloth, was the music box I'd so admired at his grandmother's flat.

I touched the beak of one crystal bird, stroked the other's back. The fact that he'd brought it with him suggested he hadn't planned on returning home. "Did you set out to flee, or to c-confront the L-Lord Rosbury?" I wondered.

"Both, I think. I don't know. The police found his watch case in the wreck." Tom's mouth twisted. "I was there. I watched the inspector receive it from his sergeant and polish it like a penny on his sleeve."

"The p-police found it? Then w-why h-haven't they arrested him?"

"The inspector returned the watch to him in person and apologized for interrupting his tea." Tom gave a bitter shrug. "No one will ever believe ill of Francis Thornfax. The man is utterly immune. And now he knows I betrayed him."

"There will be more violence. There will be more p-poor ch-children—you can't r-run away now!" Even as I said it I flushed with shame for accusing him of cowardice, especially when the accusation was a cover for my own rising panic at the thought of not seeing Tom Rampling again.

He cupped my elbow, a brief, soft stroke of his fingertips on my arm. "They told me Daisy would be the last, at least.

And when I heard the inspector wish the Lord Rosbury luck next month with his anti-opium bill in Parliament, I finally knew why."

"I d-don't understand." My tears had begun again.

"Dewhurst's new drug is a highly concentrated form of opium. It is expensive to produce, and no one will want to buy it so long as other opiates are available. Thornfax, meanwhile, has narrowed his fleet to a single ship, a smaller and faster vessel than any of her competitors, and lined with concealed cargo-holds."

"I defy any wharf-hound to discover my *Heroine*'s secrets!" Mimic cut in, so that I copied Mr. Thornfax's arch tones.

Tom gave a grim smile. "Exactly. 'Tis the perfect monopoly: Thornfax smuggling the opium into a dry market, Dewhurst selling it to 'patients' gone mad with yearning for it. All they needed was a British government convinced that opium was ruining society."

"The B-Black Glove."

"Yes. A fiction, of course. But the newspapers have swallowed the story whole, and so the public believes that London shall continue to be terrorized by gang violence until our streets are freed of the drug entirely."

I had an odd mental image, suddenly, of Archie and his fellow journalists as noisy jays flocking at the scene of the train derailment, flitting from corpse to corpse, picking bits of news-story from the wreck to feather their nests. I shuddered. I was glad my cousin had not invented the Black Glove—how devious of Mr. Thornfax to suggest such a thing to Aunt Emma that day we lunched with her!—but it was likely that Archie's news-stories had nonetheless furthered Mr. Thornfax's cause. "You must go s-straight to the p-police," I told Tom. "Someone m-must believe you."

"There's no proof. Just the word of a lord against the word of a lockpick."

A lockpick and a mad girl, I thought. He was right. We had more deaths and more violence on our hands now, and still we were no further ahead than before the train explosion.

Tom touched my arm again. "Milady, if I'm not going to challenge Rosbury I must take my leave."

"No!" I said. My mind was made up before I realized what I was considering. "W-wait here. Two minutes." I turned and slipped through the door before he could reply.

I would never find my things, I thought, as I surveyed the forest of garments in the cloakroom. But I could not bring myself to leave the music box, so I slipped it into the pocket of a gentleman's greatcoat and pulled the coat on over my dress. I removed Mr. Thornfax's necklace to the pocket as well, and I wound a lady's fringed shawl over my head. Coins for fare, I remembered, and groped among the hanging coats until I heard the telltale jangle from a pocket.

"Milady," said Tom, as I flew out the door again, but I brushed straight past and led him at a trot through the twilit mews and out into Whitehall Yard. He caught my sleeve again. "Miss Somerville, stop! This is—"

"Call me Leo," I told him. I was breathless but calm. "Or Luck, if you p-prefer. Not Miss and not Milady. Not any-m-more." I saw a cab ahead and hastened to hail it.

Tom cupped my face in his hands. "Leo. You cannot come away with me."

I laughed. I couldn't help it; he sounded so strict and courtly in the gaslight. "I am not c-coming away with you. You are coming with m-me."

"Where?"

I took advantage of his surprise to climb into the hansom, and he followed. "To find proof," I told him.

TWENTY

At dusk the wharf buildings became great blotters sipping ink from the street. Night engulfed their lower stories but couldn't yet reach the rooflines that leapt into the indigo sky.

Tom moved as naturally in darkness as in daylight. He unlocked the warehouse and led me, swiftly and silently, through the black maze of storage to the secret interior door. In the laboratory he lit a lantern and held it aloft. Then he cursed. He plucked something from the counter, opened a cabinet beneath, and cursed again.

"W-what is it?" I bent to look, but he caught my waist to hold me back. On the shelf was a small glass jar filled with a pale yellow syrup.

"You wanted proof? Here it is, then." He opened his palm and showed me a short copper cylinder with a wax seal. A length of cotton wicking was coiled round it. "This is a blast cap, packed with fulminate of mercury. When it meets a spark it burns in an instant, hot as lightning.

"And that"—he pointed to the jar of syrup, one arm still

protectively across my torso—"is enough nitroglycerin to send half the city up in flames. Thornfax lost an entire ship last year to a single ounce." He shook his head in disgust. "How easily I was gulled into believing they were finished with this!"

"This is what D-Daisy carried on the t-train?"

Tom nodded grimly. "Watts mixes it with clay to make it more stable, but it's still unpredictable as hell." He set the lantern on a hook and gingerly closed the cupboard door. "My greatest fear was that it would find a spark from somewhere other than my ignition device before Daisy was safely away. The fear was misplaced, of course. It was Thornfax I should have feared all along."

I looked round the lab. The low light flickered across the marble and steel surfaces, illuminating the rows of apothecary bottles like votives in a cathedral. Except for the jar of syrup concealed in the cabinet, the room was perfectly orderly and benign. And couldn't there be a plausible explanation even for the explosive oil? Nitroglycerin was being tested as a treatment for heart patients, after all; I'd heard Daniel discussing it with his colleagues. Tom was wrong, I thought. What we'd discovered was no proof—at least none that would incriminate Mr. Thornfax.

"Records," I said. "Where is Dr. D-Dewhurst's journal?"

Wary of the explosive, Tom had me stand in the doorway while he made a search. The medical diary was gone, and there were no other papers or records in the room.

"Mr. Thornfax's d-desk," I remembered. "The drawers!"

I held the lantern while Tom took out his wallet of picks and crouched over the lock. It took nearly fifteen minutes of careful effort, and then we found only duty bills, sales slips, and banknotes. The fact that Mr. Thornfax was importing opium and profiting enormously at the Mincing Lane auctions was not in dispute, however. We needed something more, something to tie him directly to the explosions.

Tom opened the second drawer more quickly. I marvelled, watching him probe with the picks, at how his deft fingers had learned, and were now remembering, the delicate mechanism of the lock.

In this drawer was a box of fresh stationery. I knew at once what it was, and my hand trembled as I lifted the top sheet of paper. White, with a fine black border. A tiny black glove-print at the top.

Tom's eyes widened, and he returned my smile. "Ah, Miss Luck," he said. "Clever girl."

"Mr. Rampling. Just the man I hoped to see tonight!" Mr. Thornfax's voice came from directly behind us. And behind him, their rumbling voices echoing in the dark warehouse, were Watts and Curtis.

Tom planted himself in front of me. I shut the drawer with my hip and crammed the sheet of paper into my coat pocket next to the music box. Then I turned to face my fiancé.

Mr. Thornfax's face registered only the briefest flicker of surprise as he recognized me. He smiled, showing his white teeth. "Miss Somerville. What an amazing coincidence! I spent the last hour making excuses for your abrupt disappearance from our engagement party. And not ten minutes ago I had the most heated discussion with your brother-in-law. The good Dr. Dewhurst was under the impression that I'd spirited you off for some malevolent purpose and kept demanding to know where I was keeping you."

He sounded so cordial and genteel that, when he held out his hand to me, my fright and shock moved me automatically to take it. Tom squared his stance to block me from stepping forward.

"Of course," Mr. Thornfax went on, as though Tom weren't present, "I assured him with blameless conscience that I hadn't the faintest idea what he was talking about."

With a single stride he closed the distance between us. Before I saw Mr. Thornfax lift his fist he'd already hit Tom—a hard punch to the jaw that sent Tom's body thudding sideways into the panelled wall.

I cried out and knelt beside the slumped form, but Mr. Thornfax snatched my arm and hauled me back to my feet. "Curtis, help the poor lad up," he said.

Tom was lifted. His head lolled, and Curtis yanked at his hair and slapped his cheek to rouse him.

"My darling Miss Somerville," Mr. Thornfax crooned. "Would it bother you so terribly much to be parted from this boy? I hate to think you've developed an inappropriate affection for him."

At that moment, I think, I could still have fooled Mr. Thornfax. I could still have managed to convince him I was in the warehouse by happenstance or innocent folly, and I could have calmed him, flattered, and cozened him into delaying whatever vengeance he was planning against Tom. Instead I panicked. "D-don't hurt him!" I cried. "He didn't want to c-cross you. He acted only to s-save D-Daisy's life!"

Mr. Thornfax laughed, and the sound raised gooseflesh across my arms. "Ah, yes. Daisy. The Juliet to his Romeo, isn't that right, Rampling? I am sorry that your efforts to save your sweet little dope-fiend failed so miserably."

"How dare you!" I said. "You m-m-murderer!"

"Leo, stop," Tom begged. He turned to Mr. Thornfax, hands raised. "Please, milord. She has nothing to do with any of it."

"'Leo,' is she? You *are* on familiar terms." He turned to Watts and Curtis. "I believe we've found our abductor and seducer, gentlemen."

I moaned with fear as Watts drew a revolver from under his coat. "Daniel w-will know where w-we are—" I tried.

"No, he will not know." All pretense of civility suddenly dropped like a discarded cloak from Mr. Thornfax's voice. He drew me tight to him, pressing until I struggled for breath. "And even if he suspects, he will not act. Dr. Dewhurst is a mild man who hates a confrontation more than anything.

"Curtis!" he barked. "Find some rope and bind her." He hurled me into his desk chair.

"No! I am accountable, not her." Tom tried to hold Curtis's arm and was tossed backward against Watts, who wrapped him in a chokehold and pressed the gun to his ribs.

"Indeed you are accountable, as you declare with such chivalry," Mr. Thornfax told him. "Fortunately you will have an excellent chance to make the account square."

Curtis tied my wrists together behind me and knotted the rope to the chair. I was weeping now, trying to stifle the sounds so Tom would not feel even worse. Curtis did not look at me as he worked.

Mr. Thornfax gestured toward the laboratory next door. "Mr. Rampling. Watts here will supply you with the materials he has prepared. In forty minutes' time he will be an eyewitness to a great catastrophe at the British Parliament. We will all witness it, for it will light up all London like Christmas!" Mr. Thornfax's smile managed to convey boyish excitement as well as bloodthirstiness, and his men sniggered in response.

Watts shoved Tom toward the lab. A moment later they reappeared, and Tom had a fresh welt on his cheek. Watts held a newspaper-wrapped cylinder and the copper lightning cap with its coiled wick. "The cap were in his pocket, sir. He'd stole it already," he reported.

Mr. Thornfax drew out his pocket knife.

"S-stop!" I cried.

He cast me a look of great disdain. "Miss Somerville, I intend no violence. I mean only to ensure against sabotage." Taking the blast cap from Watts he unwound the wick and cut it to a length of four inches. Then he handed it back to Tom.

"He'll be k-killed!" I said.

"He will have only seconds after he lights the fuse," agreed Mr. Thornfax, "but he will die happy to have secured your safety. That is, so long as we see the evidence of his work within the specified forty minutes."

"Lord Rosbury." Tom stood straight, ignoring Watts's gun. "No one will be inside Parliament tonight except guards and clerks. Shouldn't we make more ... more of an impact if we wait until morning?"

Mr. Thornfax clasped Tom's shoulder. "Ah, my boy. I do appreciate your strategizing on my behalf, truly. Your impulse to wait is wholly selfless, wholly in the service of the Black Glove, I am sure. And yet I am decided. Parliament, you see, is largely a symbolic target. 'Twill confirm suspicions that the very fabric of our society is threatened by the lawlessness of the opium gangs, and that passing the ban is the nation's only hope.

"But your cause needn't be so involved as all that. For your motivation I think you need only look there." He jerked his chin toward me, and Tom's tortured gaze followed. "She will be freed when it is done, and killed if it is not."

Watts thrust the explosive and lightning cap into Tom's hands. Then he took out his gun and prodded Tom into motion.

"See him as far as the Embankment, then take your distance," Mr. Thornfax ordered.

When they had gone he turned to me and shook his head. "Your silence. That is all I ever wanted from you. Your pretty face, your respectable name, and your silence."

"Who c-could be s-silent?" I sobbed, "when you are a m-m—"

Mr. Thornfax put his shoe to the corner of my chair and tipped it onto two legs so that I hovered, gasping and off balance. "Or in lieu of silence, the ravings of a madwoman," he said. "Who would ever believe talk of conspiracy and murder coming from the lips of Mad Miss Mimic? I was perfectly safe, you see?" He released the chair, and my head snapped forward on my neck as the legs hit the floor. "But you thought of a way to interfere anyhow."

Mr. Thornfax gripped the chair's arms and leaned into my face. "I am going home, Miss Somerville. After Mr. Rampling has completed his task Curtis will take you home, too. Tomorrow I shall call early at Hastings House—frantic for your safety, having searched half the night and slept not a wink—and we shall be joyously reunited. In two weeks we shall be married. And then I think my new wife will be more than ready to begin a course of Dr. Dewhurst's experimental medicine."

He gripped my head with both hands and kissed me. I felt his hard breath in my throat. His lips and teeth pressed into my flesh until I tasted blood and whimpered with the pain. When he released me he was grinning, and his eyes gleamed with cold elation.

Mr. Thornfax gathered his hat and gloves, motioned Curtis into the warehouse, and closed the secret door. I heard their muffled voices and a single pair of footsteps receding. I was left a prisoner under guard.

TWENTY-ONE

*T*hus began the longest, most torturous effort of my life. I worked at the knotted cord long after my fingertips had lost all feeling. Every hint of give in the bindings sent my heart pounding, and I froze, holding my breath, whenever I heard a cough from Curtis or the sound of his pipe being tapped out against his boot. I was unable to loosen the knots completely, but I set to twisting my wrists until at last one hand had made enough room for the other to squeeze free. I turned to untangle the rest, wincing at the bracelets of raw skin and my torn, bleeding fingernails. Then I forced myself to sit still, with my hands clasped again behind me, while I thought of what to do next.

Perhaps it was the act of pretending to be bound when I was no longer. Or perhaps it was the sight of Mr. Thornfax's silver-tipped cane propped by the door where he'd forgotten it. Whatever the incitement, Mimic sprang suddenly to life.

"Curtis, I need you!" I called, adding an edge of panicky urgency to Mr. Thornfax's suave baritone.

I scrambled round the corner into the laboratory just before the office door opened.

"Milord? Where are you?" Curtis sounded uncertain.

I searched in the wan moonlight and lit upon a heavy marble mortar. I clutched it in both hands and pressed myself next to the doorway. "In here, man! Help me!" Mimic-as-Thornfax shouted.

The moment Curtis's head appeared past the doorway I struck at it with the mortar. He fell against the wall with a grunt, blood spreading on his temple. I hit him again, panic redoubling my strength. The mortar rolled from my hands, and I fled out into the enveloping shadows of the warehouse.

I made it to the southeast corner of the building, feeling along the wall and skirting the piled crates whenever my knees struck them. My legs shook in delayed reaction to the violence I had committed. Then I heard Curtis shout Mr. Thornfax's name, and I saw his hulking form emerge from the doorway behind me. He held aloft the lantern. Its swaying light showed me his face, gruesome and half-blinded by blood, and the gun clutched in his other hand.

Something soft brushed my shoulder and I stifled a scream. A canvas sail-bag on a hook.

Curtis swung the gun in my direction. "Who's there?" he demanded.

I shrank into the space under the bag. Curtis took several lurching steps in my direction. Then he stopped, wiped at his brow with his wrist, and shook his head as though trying to clear it.

I understood then that he hadn't seen me in the lab before

I hit him with the mortar. He'd truly been fooled by Mimic's ruse, and now his injury was befuddling him still further. In fact, I thought with a surge of desperate hope, Curtis was afraid. When he'd called out just now I'd caught the note of fear in his voice.

So Mimic decided to bring Daisy back from the dead.

I began with a cry, a shuddering wail of despair that rose from a low moan into a shriek. "How could ye?" I said next. "Oh sir, how could ye do it?"

Curtis had jumped back at the first sound, but now he thrust the gun forward. "Who is it? Show yerself!" he blustered.

"'Tis only poor Daisy, sir. Only that me poor spirit hungers an thirsts, so." As Mimic spoke I tore the pins from my hair and shook it forward, covering my face. I shrugged from my coat and knotted its sleeves around my waist to mask my white skirt. Fumbling with the buttons I tore open the bodice of my dress to expose my shoulders and chest.

"I watched you die," Curtis said. "I dropped you off myself. You was cold as …" He faltered as I came to my feet in the shadows beyond his lantern.

"Cold! Ah, it's so cold!" Mimic-as-Daisy sang out, elongating the *o* into another hollow, harrowing wail. "Won't you come warm me, sir?" I took a heavy step forward, hunched, and swayed just at the edge of the light.

Curtis blinked and boggled as if forcing his eyes wider could make Daisy disappear. But I wasn't going anywhere. The big man's quaking and panting—a shallow, wet panting like an unhappy bulldog—sent a glow wicking through me, a surge of something like real power. Curtis backed up and must have tripped on something, for his arms wheeled wildly and he dropped the lantern. The gun went off—I screamed, and Mimic kept my scream going long after I knew I hadn't been shot, modulating the pitch into a piercing, inhuman sound.

The lantern rolled, but before it sputtered out I saw Curtis scrambling backward on all fours, mad with fear. He stood, stumbled, found his feet again, and fled.

I waited until the frantic tread stopped echoing through the warehouse and I saw the outside door swing closed behind him. Then I stumbled along the warehouse wall toward the longest crack of moonlight until I found the dockside door.

I circled the building and peeped round the corner. A figure materialized suddenly from the darkness and sprinted across the street toward me—Tom! It was Tom! Elated, I was just about to step out to greet him when he ran directly past without seeing me and slammed full-force into Curtis, knocking the big man hard against the boards.

"Where is she?" Tom said. "What's he done with her?"

"God forgive me!" Fear and confusion still laced Curtis's voice. "'Twarn't my doin'. 'Tain't fair she be hauntin' me for it."

Tom shook him. "Where is she?"

"She's dead, God forgive me! The girl is dead."

"Stop him!" Watts's nasal shout came from up the street. Tom dropped Curtis. I shrank back as his footsteps fled and Watts pounded up. "What's the matter with you?" he said to Curtis.

"M-my head." Curtis sagged against the warehouse wall.

Watts cursed and leaned forward, hands on his thighs. "That wily young bastard knows every alley in the city," he panted. "Slipped me not four blocks from here and led me on a merry chase. We're better to hold the girl for Thornfax, at least."

Knowing I had only the time it would take for Curtis to collect himself and confess my escape, I turned and ran back the way I'd come. Keeping close alongside the brick-wagons and containers, I crept toward the foot of Nicholson's dock.

Minutes passed. Even as I scanned the piers for a sign of Tom, willing him to catch sight of me, and listened hard for signs of Watts's pursuit, I found myself becoming strangely calm and clear-headed. All of these hulking silhouettes of industry seemed to offer not menace but shelter, now. Even the shriek of a rusty, far-off winch seemed benevolent. So this is how a person grows brave, I thought. In escaping greater danger the lesser dangers are a relief to fear.

A sudden flare drew my eye. "Leonora!" Tom's shout came across the piers, but I could make out nothing between the ships' hulls. A bright arc cut the night, and a trailing plume of blue light—there he was, at last, beside the *Heroine*! He'd hurled something onto the deck.

"It's too late. Run, Leo!" Tom was waving his arms wildly at me. Then he disappeared, and I heard a splash—had he fallen? I searched, and saw him surface in the moonlit water, swimming fast, his wet hair slick as sealskin. "Miss Somerville! Seek cover!" Terror turned his shout into a yelp.

I saw another flash of light—Watts firing from the pier behind Tom—and the shots cracked out across the water. I dove to my knees behind the lip of a cargo sled, afraid my white bodice would reveal me to Watts as it had shown me to Tom, more afraid still for Tom in the open water.

Then the whole river lit up like noontide.

I was thrown flat onto my belly. Pain bit across my chest and burrowed through to my spine. The hard-packed mud suctioned to my cheek and breast as if it would swallow me. A roaring torrent of heat and light shot past my ear. Suddenly upended, the massive iron sled loomed above me and teetered a long moment before settling, miraculously, on its narrow edge, where it shielded my body from the onslaught of flying debris.

Dazed and deafened by the blast I rolled to my back. Pain stabbed through me with every breath, and I found I could not move my left arm. I watched the scene unfold above me soundless and vivid as a dream. Hell had broken open and was mounting its vengeance upon Heaven. A column of fire wide as the Thames thrust furiously into the sky. Silhouetted against it, the great steam-winch broke silently from its crane and plunged into the heaving river. Silent, the crane itself shuddered and tipped from its moorings; I felt its impact through the vibrating earth at my back. Glass showered from the shattered windows of the warehouses. A burning barrel rolled past my feet.

I struggled to sit up, to stand. At the centre of the inferno teetered the incandescent shell of the *Heroine*. The adjacent ships were burning, too, and many buildings smouldered and glowed where debris was landing on their roofs. I could hardly bear the heat, let alone the pain, but I clutched my arm against my body and stumbled down to the water's edge. Fiery timbers bobbed everywhere on the churning surface.

It seemed an eternity until I spied Tom. He was floating face down, his shirttails billowing behind him. I tore the coat from my waist and, one-handed, lowered myself into the river.

At first the icy water was welcome relief to my scorched face, and by clinging to a broken crate I managed to propel myself the short distance to Tom's side. But I could not hold both Tom and the crate with one arm, and my sodden skirts wrapped round my legs, dragging me down.

We were not far from the shore. I kicked hard against the wet weight of fabric, against the suck of the black water. Although I knew Tom was not breathing, I fought to hold his face above water. I shouted his name again and again, my own voice silent in my deadened ears. I forced myself to focus only on his mouth, on keeping the bluish lips from going under. I refused to look at the white, closed eyelids for fear that horror and grief would drown me before the river did.

My injured arm twisted in Tom's shirt, and when I cried out I choked on a mouthful of foul, silted water. The explosion had crumpled the timber wall along the bank closest to us, and a section of it heaved loose in a torrent of muck. Waterlogged, it sank beneath us, dragging us out and down in its wake. The bank slid and melted and became a sinkhole, too slippery for a foothold and now, in any case, too far away.

I could feel the river's insistence against my body from toe to neck. As if in a dream I heard its dark invitation: *Come away, come down.* I kicked at it in fury and screamed, but though I felt the rawness in my throat I could not hear my own voice. All this time, my damaged ears could hear nothing. And now, as my head bobbed under the firelit surface, I saw nothing, either. The whirling pyrotechnics vanished above me, leaving a blessedly cool darkness.

Only for one moment, I thought. I'll rest only a moment. The river sighed against my face and the pain drained from my body. I stopped moving and allowed myself to sink.

But sink I did not. Instead I was wrenched upward by strong hands. I surfaced, spluttering and bleating at the renewed agony in my shoulder. I saw a policeman in the water beside me and more policemen crowding the bank. Then my arm was twisted again—I was certain this time the limb was torn from its socket for good—and the blessed darkness rushed back in to claim me from the pain.

TWENTY-TWO

The silence and the darkness—and the dreaming—
went on for a long time. I dreamed I lay in a white bed
with my arm bound immobile across my chest. I dreamed I
floated on the Thames, watching the stars perform a lantern
show for my amusement. I stumbled through dark caverns,
clinging to damp walls. I saw Archibald Mavety pacing on
the pier and shouting words I could not hear. I walked a sunlit
footpath with Tom and felt—but did not hear—his whisper
in my ear. I fought a black, slithering dragon and choked on
its sulphurous breath.

I dreamed my bedclothes were on fire and half-woke with
painful coughing. A white-whiskered man pinned my wrist
to the bed and pierced my skin with a syringe. I thrashed to
escape, and my aunt Emmaline leaned over me, stroking my
forehead. Then I slipped back into sleep.

The next time I woke, I was just clear-headed enough to
recognize my surroundings. I was in my old bedchamber at
Aunt Emma's house in Kew. My hearing had recovered too,
except for a strong ringing, and my aunt was arguing with the

whiskered man: "I know 'tis uncomfortable for her, but she is strong."

"But the pneumonia—"

"Her coughing has lessened; you said yourself that her lungs have cleared. Doctor, if she is to get well, she must *wake up*. I won't have my niece recover only to condemn her to a life of morphia enslavement!"

The doctor sighed. "Laudanum, then. At least for another week or two. The coughing has slowed the healing of her clavicle considerably. 'Twill be another month before it stops paining her altogether."

But the laudanum sickened me so that I could not keep any food in my body. Aunt Emma spooned broth and laid compresses on my aching head. Finally she took the bottle of medicine away and replaced it with an endless rotation of garden powders and teas of spearmint, boneset, ginger, and eyebright. My fractured collarbone did hurt, especially when I coughed, but after a week or so I felt less nauseated and began to sit up in bed for short periods. Bess bathed me with a damp sponge and leaned me over a basin to wash my hair. She threw open the windows on breezy days so I might smell the nearby hayfields.

Still I would sleep whole days, shutting out the light with the coverlet pulled up over my head. It made my nights more restless, but I preferred the darkness to the oppressive sunshine. Time crawled on, day blending endlessly and monotonously into night.

Aunt Emma took to visiting my bedroom just to sit and speak to me. She spoke to me of the robins who had made a nest outside her parlour window, and the fledglings who fought for space in the nest and hopped to the rim and flew away. I would wait until she left the room, then turn over and go back to sleep. She would come back and wake me and tell me of the lavender plants that scented the garden path and the old, blind hound that wandered in from the gamekeeper's cottage.

Over and over I would sleep, and my aunt would wake me, and we would talk. On her many, brief visits to my chamber I felt too weak and ill for conversation, so Mimic stepped in for me with a surprisingly close approximation of my own voice. She even stammered on occasion, for authenticity.

Often I caught Aunt Emma peering into my face with concern. She always looked away immediately. Once, though, she said, "You are not yourself, my dear."

I assumed she meant Mimic, and heat came into my face. But Aunt Emma said, "Your spirits are even lower than this illness warrants."

Neither my aunt nor my maid spoke of the events at the Thames, and I knew they meant to wait until I would ask them. I put off asking. I felt the memories pressing at the edges of my mind, and I knew that my constant headaches stemmed in part from the shock and sorrow I was refusing to face.

One morning I turned my head to find, perched on my bedside table, Tom's music box. One of the crystal birds was missing and, when I turned the little knob, the clockworks did not move. I shoved it under the blanket, willing myself back to sleep. But sleep would not come. My pillow dampened with the tears that leaked from my eyes.

Later, when Bess came in with my breakfast tray, Aunt Emma drew up a chair. She waited until we were alone, cleared her throat, and nodded at the music box where I'd replaced it on the table. "They found it inside a gentleman's coat beside the river," she told me. She smiled. "It was eventually deduced that you'd taken the coat from Whitehall. You will recall the leaf of stationery in its pocket? Well, my dear, that scrap of paper has induced great excitement amongst the police detectives. Your cousin Archibald is making quite a nuisance of himself about it, too. He's convinced it somehow connects the Lord Rosbury to all the explosive attacks."

I stared past Aunt Emmaline to the leaves on the tree outside trembling against the cloudy sky. I knew from many hours of practice that if I concentrated I could transform the pattern of greens, blues, and whites into the dappled surface of a pond.

"I've read and reread the letter you wrote to me before … all of this. The one in which you lay out the case, as it were. You suspected Thornfax, and it seems now you had good reason. No one has been able to locate him."

I knew that I could pretend my body was floating just under the pond's surface, borne along by the water, looking up at the light but hearing nothing. And I knew that eventually this fantasy could lull me back to sleep.

She tried again: "The Dewhursts have taken their children to France. Daniel's medical licence has been suspended, and Christabel couldn't bear the scandal." Aunt Emma paused and slipped a hand into the pocket of her housedress. "There's also this." And she laid Mr. Thornfax's diamond-and-amethyst necklace on the bedcover.

I recoiled as though she'd dropped a snake into my lap.

"It was found among the rubble and taken into evidence,"

she explained. "But half of London saw you wearing it, so I didn't need to press very hard for the police to hand it over."

"I don't want it," I said. I looked back to the leaves outside, but the fantasy of the pond surface was ruined.

"I know you don't want the man," she said, "but think what these jewels could buy—"

"Sell them, then," I told her, "but I do not want the money, either."

She slipped the necklace back into her pocket, sighed, and took my hand. "Speaking of money, Leonora, I want you to know that I've made a decision. I have transferred the deed of Hastings House to your name. I've also established an allowance for you that should quite suffice to let you live as independently as you like." Her hand, trellised with blue veins, squeezed mine, and she traced a fingertip over the healed rope wounds on my wrist. "You are young, my dear, but you have more than demonstrated that you know how to take care of yourself!"

My tears began to flow again. I took the music box from the table and cradled it in my lap.

"My dear girl. Oh, my dear." She had not witnessed me cry since the rescue, and the sight was obviously upsetting to her. "I shall have it repaired for you!" Aunt Emma leaned to take the box from me, but I gripped it harder.

"It cannot be repaired," Mimic said for me, through my sobs. "He is the only one who could have fixed it, and he is gone."

"Who is, my dear?"

"T-Tom Rampling!" The name was a ragged moan of pain.

My aunt sank onto the bed beside me, wide-eyed with surprise.

"I loved him, Aunt." Suddenly, I no longer knew whether it was Mimic or I talking. "I loved him. He was g-good and brave, and clever, and he made such beautiful things. I lost him in the river that night. I let go of him, and he drowned."

It was neither Mimic nor I talking—not in the old sense, anyhow, not separate or taking turns. Something inside me had thrown open a door. Something had thrown open a door and hurtled through it and was tearing down the passage-ways, battering the walls with its wings and shrieking for the open sky. Something shattered the glass, burst through the window, and filled the whole house with unbearable light.

"You were trying to save this boy, this Tom Rampling. Is that why they found you in the water?"

"I loved him, and he is dead. I can't bear it!" I squeezed my eyes shut and slid down until the bedclothes covered my face.

My aunt stroked my hair, clucking and murmuring comforting words, but now that I had confessed them my feelings would not be appeased. The bed shook with my sobbing. My injury throbbed savagely, and I wheezed and grew light-headed, and still I could not stop.

"Laudanum," I begged at last. "Please, let me go back to sleep!"

She refused at first, but eventually she brought me a glass. Between hiccups I gulped down the medicine, and Aunt Emma stayed at my bedside until sleep finally came.

The London Examiner

MAY 20TH, 1872

Evidence in Thames River Case Points to the Lord Rosbury

ARCHIBALD MAVETY, SPECIAL REPORTER

THE WHEELS of justice turn slowly, they say—and nowhere more slowly than the Thames River inquisition. Rumours continue to fly regarding the whereabouts of Mr. Francis Thornfax, Lord Rosbury, whose clipper *Heroine* has now been pinpointed as the primary target—or should I say, the source?—of the explosion.

Rosbury's name is associated with the anti-opium bill to be put to the vote next week in Parliament. Popular opinion would lay both the attack and the gentleman's subsequent disappearance at the feet of the Black Glove, the secret organization behind so much public terror this last year. But this writer must insist, as I have done so often during these past weeks of wild speculation and conflicting reports, that all the facts be taken into level account. As is now public knowledge, the distinctive sheet of stationery recovered from the scene of the Thames explosion bore the imprint of a previous note written atop it: the note delivered in advance of the Black Glove attack on the passenger train only days earlier. The stationery was found in Lord Rosbury's own warehouse—a point of evidence that, alone, should argue for Thornfax's complicity in the Black Glove's activities. Futhermore, comparative analyses performed for this newspaper by two independent experts have subsequently proven that the note was written in Lord Rosbury's own handwriting. Can there be any doubting that man's involvement, if not his guilt entire?

Meanwhile the courts plod on in his absence, hearing one witness after another with nothing better to offer than 'I was at x and overheard y.' Let us hope, dear readers, that the relative peace that has descended upon London since the Thames incident continues, and that I am correct in believing the Black Glove has fled, once and forever, along with the sole author of its threats and warnings.

TWENTY-THREE

A few days later it was decided I was well enough to have visitors, and I was dressed and bundled with blankets into a chair in the parlour. In fact there was only one visitor: my cousin Archibald, who coughed into his fist as he entered the room. He schooled his features as he took my hand, but I'd seen his shock at my sickly appearance.

Aunt Emma had gone out for the morning, so my cousin and I were left to make our own conversation. He tried to inquire about my recovery and my stay at Kew, but Archie had always been dreadful at small talk. Not even waiting for my answers he fell to his knees in front of my chair. "Oh God, Leo! I am so, so sorry for it all," he exclaimed, and I was surprised to see real tears in his eyes.

"Whatever is the matter?" I said. Had he allowed my name to be smeared in the papers after all?

"You—you nearly died because of me!" he choked. "I had the facts, I was suspicious as all hell of Thornfax, and yet I did nothing."

"No one knew what would happen—"

He cut me off. "I *waited* for something to happen. It wasn't until the countess brought me that letter you'd written to her, and then Dr. Dewhurst enlisted my help in search of you after you disappeared from your party, that I even really considered you might be in danger."

"But you saved my life." I remembered, suddenly, what I thought I'd only dreamt: my cousin shouting from the pier at the Thames. "I saw you that night. You brought the police." I held my smile steady until the shame and worry creasing my cousin's brow began to soften. "You didn't send me to the Docks that night, Archie," I continued. "You were caught up in the plot like everyone else. I was worse than anyone. Do you know at some point I suspected you of making it all up about the Black Glove? I even wondered if you were writing those notes yourself after each explosion. No, the truth is that all the damage, all the d-death"—my voice caught, and I veered away from the thought of Tom—"was my own doing. My own fault." I tucked my right arm under the linen sling supporting my left. Despite the blankets on my lap I felt cold.

Archie snorted, shook his head, and got to his feet. "That's ridiculous, Leo. This falls squarely at Rosbury's feet, and you know it." All signs of his own remorse had evaporated.

"Where is he?" I asked. "Why haven't they found him?"

"I wish you didn't care." He settled himself on the chesterfield and picked up my aunt's Harlequin statuette.

"Is he still in London, do you think?"

"I shouldn't think he'd linger so close. He has accounts and trusts all over the world. He could live like a king anywhere he wanted and not be bothered by suspicion."

"But the police must be attempting to bring him to justice."

"I doubt they'd try him for murder in any case. Mischief, maybe. He may be a rogue but he's still a lord."

I sighed, and Archie must have mistaken it for relief, because he gave me a sharp look. "You *are* finished with him, aren't you? You haven't fooled yourself into thinking he can be redeemed, or anything stupid like that?"

I scowled at him. "I may have been stupid for a time. But I've read your reports. Your newspaper should thank me for snatching the Lord Rosbury's stationery. It's made you quite the detective hero."

"Yes, that was a brilliant stroke, Leo! Can you believe the man was arrogant enough not to bother even *trying* to disguise his penmanship? Well, of course you believe it. You knew him better than anyone." Harlequin turned somersaults in my cousin's restless hands. "D'you know I've been promoted thanks to all that? I might be sent to America for a feature on the Indian wars. Only last month a troop of Cheyenne braves sabotaged a Union Pacific rail line."

"Give me that, will you? You're likely to drop it any moment."

Archie passed me the figurine, and I laid Harlequin in my lap.

"The countess wants …" Archie hesitated and then donned his most determined journalist's face. "I need to ask you, Leo: What happened with all this business of Dewhurst's hired boy? This Tom Rampling character?"

The mention of Tom's name brought hot blood to my cheeks and a painful tightness to my chest.

Archie saw it and rushed on: "I don't want to upset you. It's only that Rosbury's man Watts died in the explosion, you know, and his driver—what's his name, Curtis—keeps insisting that all the Black Glove business was carried out by Watts and Rampling alone."

A series of racking coughs overwhelmed me. When I could finally breathe again I said, "It hardly matters now, does it?" I was exhausted by the conversation. I wished nothing more than for my cousin to say goodbye so that I could crawl back upstairs, sink into my bed, and go to sleep.

Archie took a letter from his pocket—my letter, the one I'd written to Aunt Emmaline before the train attack. "You wrote about sabotage," he said. "You seemed to think Rampling was working *against* the Black Glove. But the police have found no proof to support that notion."

"There *was* proof," I corrected him. "They found …" But Mr. Thornfax's pocket watch had been returned to him, I remembered. The police had discovered it in the train wreck but, assuming the Lord Rosbury could have had nothing to do with the derailment, had delivered it back to him directly. I'd watched him display it to Daniel at Whitehall, listened to him declare to Daniel that Tom was his to revenge himself upon—

"Ask Dr. Dewhurst," I said to Archie. "He knows. If you want to keep playing the detective, write to Daniel and ask him about Lord Rosbury's pocket watch. Perhaps his guilty conscience will prompt him to tell you the truth about"—I could not bring myself to say "Tom" or even "Mr. Rampling"—"his poor assistant."

"I *knew* Dewhurst knew more than he let on!" Archie

exclaimed. "Of all the craven, self-interested—I'd like to go straight to France myself and beat the truth out of him, or drag him by the ears back here to testify!"

The idea made me smile. "You don't seem exactly suited for a sheriff's role," I said.

"Oh, I'll adapt. Detective, sheriff—the lines are all blurred for a journalist. I'll play any role to get at the truth."

"To get a good story, you mean. 'Tis not the truth that sells your newspapers."

Archie's grin was quizzical. "I didn't think it was possible to trump my cynicism, Leonora, but I believe you've just done it. Journalism calls for sensationalism, I'll grant you. But it also demands a real social commitment. I've dug out the truth about Rosbury's dealings, haven't I?"

I shrugged. "Truth is a storytelling technique like any other."

His eyes narrowed. "You sound like the countess. But that's not her voice; it's your own, or very nearly. In fact I haven't heard you stammer once since I arrived. What's happened to you, Leo?"

"The lines are all blurred," I said, in a perfect imitation of Archie. Then I switched back to Leonora's voice. "'Tis the same for me, I suppose: a series of overlapping roles."

"But which one is you? Which is the true Miss Somerville?"

I laughed and saw my cousin wince a little: there was no humour in the brittle, weary sound. I looked down at Harlequin in my lap, stroked his checkered belly, and scraped my fingernail over the enamelled teardrop on his cheek. As near as I could tell, the true Miss Somerville no longer existed.

TWENTY-FOUR

*T*here are things I cannot say in any voice. I was born Leonora Emmaline Somerville, but I am not at all sure that is still who I am. They called me by that name at Hastings House, but I shall not live at Hastings again, with its cold floors and colder memories, even if I am to become its owner. The revisions to my aunt's will have freed me from the need to get married, so I will not seek refuge in a husband's name, either. After my adventure with Mr. Thornfax marriage seems a dubious sort of refuge in any case.

Aunt Emmaline says your story determines who you are. Well, I suppose I am now come to the end of mine. It is remarkable how the human body will knit itself back together, no matter how tattered the human heart. My collarbone healed, and the congestion in my lungs ebbed until I could once again breathe deeply without risk of a coughing spasm. My appetite returned enough that I could take regular meals downstairs with Lady Hastings. I walked the gardens—first on her arm or Bess's, then alone—and over the days and weeks I developed a favoured circuit of the grounds. I would start at the orchards, where the apples and pears were ripening and the beehives thrummed with midsummer fervour. I would make my way down through the hayfield to the pond, where lines of frogs, like tipped dominoes, plunged into the sludge at my approach. Then back along the rush-choked creek—if I was lucky I would startle the heron and witness how he beat his great wings into the sky—and up to the barn, to dandle the kittens and stroke the ponies' silken noses.

Aunt Emmaline had decided that the real test of my recovery would be a visit into town. This I delayed as long as I could, preferring the secluded universe of Kew, but one evening she declared she had business in London the next day and would not go without me.

Next morning Bess packed my cases, did my hair and, with Aunt Emma's assistance, helped me to dress properly. Then she fluttered about with needle and thread, taking in my gown where it sagged and gaped.

I asked for a mirror, and Bess brought one—reluctantly, I thought. She propped it against the wall. "You will be yourself again, Miss Somerville," she assured me.

I laughed, thinking of Mimic. "Leave me a moment," I said.

My amusement died as I stood in front of the glass. My left arm, newly freed from its sling, hung weakly at my side. I had to force my shoulders straight, as they seemed to want to hunch around my damaged collarbone. I was so wasted from the pneumonia that despite Bess's efforts my clothes still hung on me.

And my face! I did not recognize my own face. I was pale as death despite my walks in the sun, with concave cheeks and grey shadows under my eyes. The rouge powder Bess had applied only accentuated how starkly the bones stood out. I scrubbed at the powder. I tried bending over at the waist to bring the blood to my face but suffered a wave of dizziness upon righting myself. I tried a smile and shuddered at the ghoulish effect. It reminded me of something, and I stood a moment, hands on hips, trying to think what it might be.

Daisy. Not the Daisy of my invention, that theatrical ghost girl with whom I'd frightened Curtis into letting me escape. The real Daisy. The sick one, languishing in the surgery at Hastings House. Withered, hollow-eyed, flayed from the inside with craving for Daniel's drug. I remembered leaning over her body in that bed, wincing at the smell and thinking how easily our fates might be reversed. Perhaps, I considered now, it was not a question of reversal, exactly. Perhaps there was only a downward force, a greedy, hungering force in the world like a vacuum. It would grasp anyone it could and drag her into its vortex and suck her life away. Perhaps anyone who strayed from the story of her life even by a single page—or a single word—could be caught like this and dragged down.

Paradoxically there had been real pleasure in Daisy's eyes that day at the surgery. I remembered feeling uncomfortable at the soaring, sensual pleasure the girl evidently felt with Dr. Dewhurst's medicine in her blood. I wondered if perhaps I had felt moments of such pleasure—perhaps under Mr. Thornfax's gaze, under his touch? At the opera, maybe, or at Whitehall. The joy of dissolution.

I leaned closer to the mirror, thinking that the greatest strangeness in my new appearance was my eyes. I imagined at first that the irises had changed colour. But it was less tangible than that: a depth, I thought, a darkness. A drowning. Could a drowning reveal itself in one's eyes?

Nearly nine weeks had passed since I was rescued from the Thames. Only at that moment, gazing at my reflection, was I able to take the full measure of how that night had changed me. I decided I was glad of my ravaged appearance. It mirrored the state of my mind, of my heart. At least I was not wearing a mask.

The ride to the Kew railway station in Aunt Emma's open carriage was a sustained assault on my enfeebled senses. The road was hot, dusty, and pitted, jarring my bones. My bonnet offered scant protection from the bright sunlight, and the driver's shouts to spur the horses set off a dull throbbing in my head. To stave off the headache I pretended not to be me. I envisioned myself a girl new to England, excited to travel, to gaze for the first time on the iron daisies and domed glass at the ticket-house, to sip my sweet tea from a paper cup on the platform. I conjured a fear of wasps, and begged my aunt to wave them away from me with her hat. I laughed when she knocked one of the creatures to the floor and stomped it, valiantly, under her shoe.

Ever since Mimic had come under my wing—since the moment I'd confessed my true feelings to my aunt, the moment I had begun to speak as Mimic, and she as me—I'd found it a simple thing to adopt a "character" in this way when it suited me. I chose close to my own age, sex, and upbringing, so as not to be obvious.

In my new role I was terribly proud to be seen in the Lady Hastings's company. The train cars had been coupled incorrectly, and we had to walk partway down the platform for First Class. The porters leapt down and swarmed to transport our luggage behind us, and many faces pressed against the windows to gawk at us. Aunt Emma's London driver, Provis, met us at Addison Road and brushed the coal-smuts off our cases before lifting them onto the trap. And how people stared! I supposed Londoners had always turned their faces toward the well-to-do and watched us go past. But now I noticed their fascination; I felt it as though I were performing on a stage. "Swells," I heard a woman call us, murmuring to her son, and I asked my aunt for a coin to give the boy.

Enjoying the sunshine now, I scanned the lawns and walks of Kensington Gardens as we rode, fascinated by the promenading ladies with their Brussels lace parasols and the gentlemen in their fine linen suits. A new fad had struck during my convalescence. Many of the ladies carried a straw with a little wire loop at the end; this they dipped into a cup and raised to their lips to send streams of shining bubbles into the air. I looked at them, and they looked at us in our carriage, and a crowd of passersby watched us watching each other. A man along the Ring Road selling iced lemonade at a stand carried a live ferret on his shoulder. In my excitement I pointed at it and laughed before remembering myself and pressing my hand to my lap.

My aunt laughed, too. She leaned over and kissed my cheek. If during the past weeks at Kew she had ever noticed the occasional slight changes in my manner and speech, she had not commented. But now she said, "You are a wonderful actress, my dear."

I coloured and stammered an apology.

"No, I am in earnest," she said, squeezing my hand. "I have always said your mimicry would serve you well, have I not?"

"But 'tis not sincere," I reminded her. "It is a lie."

She pursed her lips. "Sincerity is a myth, and a dangerous one, in my opinion. We are taught to be sincere in order to keep us from saying what we think. And what sort of sincerity is that?" She leaned in to whisper in my ear: "When you are weak, you can seem strong. When you are strong, you can seem weak. In this way you shall outwit those who would dominate you."

"Is that why you took to the stage?" I said. "All those years ago, before I came to you at Kew. Did you learn to act in order to ... avoid domination?"

Aunt Emma looked out over the pond with its gliding swans. "I was a widow—young, fair, and obscenely rich. I had to do *something*, or be swallowed up by my suitors."

"I am young, fair, and obscenely rich. Mightn't I take acting lessons?" It was a joke. But the moment I said it I knew it was exactly what I wanted to do.

"You hardly need lessons!" my aunt said. "But I do know some gifted instructors." She stroked a lock of my hair from my cheek. "I am glad to see you make up your mind for something, Leonora. I've worried you've been at loose ends since your illness."

"Only take care to know your own mind, before you make it up," I reminded her, parroting her voice.

She laughed again, a carefree sound that rang out over the path and drew even more looks our way. I memorized the sound, tucking it away for future use.

Aunt Emma spoke to Provis, and the carriage wound its way along the rose gardens and over the stream and out through Victoria Gate. I didn't feel quite up to seeing Hastings House, so we chose a roundabout route through Cambridge Square and went clip-clopping past a public lecture taking place outside the Mesmeric Infirmary. MEDICAL AND DENTISTRY NO PAIN HYPNOTISM, proclaimed the banners. A white-coated man with a woolly, pointed beard was bleating at the crowd: "Opiates are enslaving the souls of our countrymen!" I heard, and, "Morphine is an unnatural answer to a natural problem!"

The carriage slowed to a crawl in the High Street, the walks swarming with afternoon window-shoppers. A gentleman stood outside of Pierce & Co. in a sky-blue top hat asking passersby for their opinions on his purchase. "Very fine indeed!" Aunt Emma called to him as we passed, and those on the ground broke into applause at her approval. Another gentleman waved at us, and we stopped to greet a Mr. Brewster and his wife, both enormously fat and sweating through their clothes. They were old friends of my aunt from the Adelphi, and she introduced me and told them I would one day be an actress too. Mr. Brewster reached obligingly for my hand but said, "She's too frail for it, Countess. I can tell you at this moment, just setting eyes on her. You forget, I believe, the sheer hard labour of undertaking a stage role."

"Ah, but my dear fellow," said Aunt Emma, sitting up in

her seat, "you forget, I believe, the first rule of the theatre: Never judge an actress by her appearance!"

He laughed and touched his hat, and his wife laughed, too, and we called our goodbyes and drove on.

Provis pulled up in front of a narrow shop in Mayfield Street. The shingle above the window was decorated with carved clockworks and the words DECLAN FITZHUGH, MASTER WATCHMAKER. Aunt Emma reached down and drew from her travelling bag my broken music box. "Take it in," she ordered gently. "I know Fitzhugh. He is skilled enough to fix it. I will wait for you there"—she pointed to an alehouse several doors down—"and order your tea."

I stroked the music box, wondering if I didn't prefer it damaged. Surely with Tom gone, the tinkling tune would sound like a dirge to me. And even if the single remaining bird could be reanimated, wouldn't it look horrifically lonely pecking at its seed?

But my aunt nodded encouragement, and I knew how badly she wanted me to get over my heartsickness, so I gathered my skirts and allowed the driver to hand me down.

A red-cheeked, whiskered man in a brown suit looked over his glasses and greeted me in a broad Scottish brogue. I said hello and handed him the music box. He turned the box over, peered at it through his glasses, and chuckled. "'Tisn't me area of expertise, but I've an idea who may help ye," he said. Setting it on the counter he pointed to the back of the shop, to another man bent over a work desk. "A lass here for your assistance," he called.

The clocks studding the walls filled the narrow shop with a muted cacophony of ticking. The seated man was surrounded by towers of miniature wooden drawers; I wondered how on earth he remembered what was in any of them. He wore a cap turned backward and, over it, a leather strap with a heavy magnifying lens masking one eye.

I approached slowly, reluctant to trouble his concentration. His work surface was scattered with minuscule screws, dials, gears, and wires, some of which were sorted into rows by size. He was attempting to set a spring into a tiny brass mechanism. The long, fine-boned fingers handled the tools so deftly that in spite of the lens he wore, I had the impression he was feeling how it should fit together more than seeing it.

All at once my blood pounded in my ears. My vision swam. I sagged against the counter, gripping my hands into fists, screwing my eyes shut against the sudden assault of memory—the feeling, as though it were only yesterday, of fingers like those stroking my cheek, caressing my neck, brushing my lips. I couldn't breathe.

This had been a mistake. Coming to town today, pretending to be well. Acting as if life could go on for me. As if my world hadn't ground to a halt the moment I lost my grasp on Tom Rampling's collar in the black water of the Thames.

I wheeled round and, stumbling blindly, made for the shop door.

"Milady?"

I turned. The man was on his feet, tearing the lens and the cap from his head, dropping them to the floor.

It was Tom.

TWENTY-FIVE

I took a step toward him, and my legs gave out under me. My knees hit the floorboards. I caught myself on my palms.

Tom rushed forward and sank to the floor before me. His fingers traced a trembling shape in the air before settling on my shoulder. "Miss Somerville?" he said. "Are you … well?"

"Tom," was all I could manage.

"For a moment I thought you were a ghost!" he said.

"I am," I said. "I have been." His soft, musical voice, his hands on me—he was real. He was alive. A sob burst from my throat, and I lunged forward and buried my face in his chest.

"Is't all right, then, Mr. Rampling? Is the lass taken ill?" Mr. Fitzhugh hovered beside us, but some gesture from Tom must have put his worry to rest, for his steps retreated again.

Tom cradled me a minute there on the worn wooden floor. Then, very gently, he set me back from him. He helped me to my feet. He straightened my bonnet and smoothed my hair. "Did the Lady Hastings send you to me?" he said.

"The Lady Hastings?"

A beat, and then we spoke together:

"Do you know my aunt Emmaline?"

"Did she send you here to see me?"

I gave a weak laugh. So she'd known Tom Rampling was employed here. Of course, she must have known. She must have found him for me. She must have engineered this whole journey. "I've been ill," I told him. "I think my aunt wanted to spare me the shock."

He smiled then, finally. "She seems to have failed at that." He pulled a stool over to the counter and nodded at me to take it; for himself he fetched his workman's stool from the desk.

Shaken, still shaking internally, I held my arms crossed tight. I was half afraid my ribs would fly apart at the violence of my heartbeat. The racket of ticking clocks seemed louder and more urgent than before. "Tom, tell me," I said. "Tell me what happened to you after the river."

He cleared his throat. "Firstly, milady, I owe you my thanks."

I shook my head. "I needed fishing from the water myself. If you weren't already drowned, I would have drowned us both."

"The police did me the favour of resuscitating me before shutting me up at Newgate."

"Newgate … Prison?" I gasped.

"For nearly a month—until the countess and your cousin, that reporter fellow, found me. They had Dr. Dewhurst send a letter from France. Even though he's implicated in the matter, too, his testimony was enough to see me released." Tom paused, looking at me through his lashes as if to measure my reaction.

My head spun. I found I could not react, could not speak. There are Tom's grey eyes, I thought, with their lavish fringes. There is that still, solemn face with its depth of hidden feeling I had only begun to fathom—Tom Rampling could have been hanged! Even if Curtis's testimony had been questionable, London was so eager for a villain, so desperate to put a face to the Black Glove—Tom could have been condemned on suspicion alone.

"The Lady Hastings wrote me an introduction," he continued. "She arranged this apprenticeship."

"The Lady Hastings," I repeated, stupidly.

"Yes. I owe her both my life and my living. And I know that of course she did it all at your behest."

"No."

"Miss Somerville. I must offer you my thanks—for your gift, also."

I was shaking my head.

"Rosbury's—your—necklace. The countess insisted that you wanted me to have it. After everything I'd done—putting you at such risk, your injuries. It was most generous of you. Most kind."

I burst into laughter. I couldn't help it, though it sent colour into Tom's cheeks. It was either laugh or weep. "I hope you sold it away at once," I said, when I'd recovered.

His colour deepened. "Yes. Milady, I never told you: my mother died in prison, years ago. Her husband—he was not my father. Well, he wasn't really even her husband, to own the whole truth." Tom inhaled, and squared his shoulders. I saw that he needed me to know this. "He's been at Marshalsea these last five years."

"Debtor's prison." There was no threat of laughter now.

He nodded. "He loved cards too well, and betting on horses. I saved my wages as best I could, but when I went to Newgate I needed nearly the whole sum to leave behind for the care of my grandmother. With your necklace I paid Father's debt entire, and the interest as well, and—well, I didn't want him living with Grandmamma and me, exactly"—Tom flushed again and rushed to finish—"so I paid a year's rent on a room for him, too."

Did he feel so indebted to me for those loathed gems of Thornfax's that he must offer this accounting of the sum? Was he so eager to clear himself of any obligation that he'd confess all the flaws of his birth and parentage? It wasn't even a confession, exactly: the speech had been tight-jawed, nearly belligerent, as though intended to shock me or to send me away. "Tom. Did my aunt not tell you I have been at Kew all this time?"

"When Hastings House was vacated I assumed you'd gone to France with the Dewhursts. Or you would go when you were well enough."

"Did you not think to visit me?"

Solemn grey eyes searched my face. "No, milady," he admitted.

I stared back at him. I was still stunned by the notion that he might have been incarcerated forever, or executed—that he might have survived the drowning without my knowledge, only to be killed before I ever discovered him—and now it seemed to my stricken mind that if I took my eyes off him he would be gone again. If I looked away, if I even so much as blinked, Tom Rampling would dematerialize and I would awaken in my cold bed alone. I will wake, I thought, and my mouth dried with my fear of waking. I had suffered through this dream before.

"Miss Somerville, are you well?" he said, very softly, as if I might collapse again any moment.

I forced myself to look away, to prove I was not asleep and not deluded. Tom was here, and Tom was … changed. Tom had a living now. A proper job, using his best skills, and a clear route to steady advancement in the craft. I looked around me at the cases of pocket watches and the shining clock faces on the walls. One shelf held several glass and metal sculptures that I recognized at once as siblings, or descendants, of my music box. Here Tom could make his beautiful devices without want of materials and sell them at fair value.

Returning at last to his face I saw that he'd been watching me take it all in, and I saw that he was proud of his work here and wanted me to appreciate it. "This is where you belong," I said.

"Yes," he said, and his eyes shone with satisfaction.

A contradictory feeling ranged through me: a broad happiness, a sharp yearning. "I love it here, too," I said.

Tom's eyes darted away, and when they returned the satisfaction was cloaked. His face was perfectly still. He said, "Have you come to say goodbye, then, milady?"

He didn't want me here in this shop. I was invading the space he'd found for himself, for his future. He hoped for closure only, not friendship. After all he hadn't sought me out, had he? He'd never troubled to visit me at Kew.

"Miss Somerville. It's all right," he prompted, as if to reassure me of his feelings when I took my leave.

I fought to keep my tears in check. "Leo. I asked you, once, to call me Leo."

"Leo."

Was that sadness in his voice? I could not tell, and my confusion made me suddenly angry. "I thought you drowned in that river, Tom. I thought you were dead. All this time I have been grieving you. I've been half-dead myself with grieving you!"

Tom's eyes widened. "I am sorry for your suffering. I didn't know—"

I leapt to my feet. "I did not tell the countess to come to your aid. I was ignorant of all of it! I told her to take those awful jewels away from me. That is all. You needn't *thank* me as though I've been lounging about at Kew and tossing alms in your direction!"

The bell chimed; I saw Mr. Fitzhugh hastily exiting the store. I'd spoken quite shrilly—I'd been shouting, almost. Well, it was too late to stop now. I turned again on Tom, and the remembered horror of his death struck through me again, stoking my outrage. "I grieved you." I gasped, and said it again: "I *grieved* you!"

"I am sorry."

"Would you be sorry at all if I did go to France with Christa and Daniel? Would you grieve me?" My face flamed. Even as I spoke them I could hear how childish and undignified the words were. I sound like my sister, I thought, dismayed: my voice, but Christabel's sort of words.

Tom sat down, leaving me standing before him. He folded his hands in his lap and looked at them. "The Lady Hastings informed me of your new circumstances, your allowance.

You have a future. You won't have time for a … dalliance with someone like me."

"A 'dalliance,' Mr. Rampling? Is that what you believe it was?" Shrill.

He frowned. "That is not what I—"

"Would you grieve me?" I insisted.

"Oh, Miss Luck." He sighed. There was a long pause. My heart thumped in my ears, syncopating with the hectic chorus of the clocks, so that I wondered if I would even hear him when he did continue. He kept his eyes on his folded hands.

When he spoke again, it was barely a breath. "I began to grieve you from the first moment we ever spoke. In the parlour at Hastings, that day you fetched me for Hattie. Do you remember? We spoke, and I … I smudged your face with my filthy hand, and I loved you at once."

It was barely a thread of sound, but I heard it like a shout: *I loved you.*

He looked up at me. "I loved you. But I knew from the beginning that I could never have you."

I started to protest, but he held up his hand to stop me. "My story runs a different course than yours. It began differently—I should say it was written in a different language, even."

"We can rewrite it," I whispered.

A wan grin. He shook his head. "We added a chapter, perhaps. But no. We cannot rewrite our stories. I should not wish to."

I was silent.

"So do you see, Leo? I grieved you too. Right from the beginning, I grieved as I loved, all along."

I did see. I swallowed my tears before they could stab at my eyes. I offered him my hand. I made him a curtsy when he took my hand, and then I said, "Goodbye, Mr. Rampling."

"Goodbye, Miss Somerville," he replied, and smiled at me, and bowed.

I turned and walked a straight, steady line out of the watchmaker's shop.

Aunt Emma always likes to say that the story makes the character. If offstage you learn your character's story by heart, then onstage you can become her. "Your story," she says, "determines who you are." Tom had spoken in the past tense when he said he loved and grieved, as though he were telling of an age gone by, of a previous lifetime. To him our story was already told and concluded.

He had closed the book.

TWENTY-SIX

I found the countess in the alehouse's leafy back garden sitting at a filigreed iron table spread with plates of fruit, buttered rolls, and cold ham. I took the chair opposite hers and busied myself with sugaring my tea.

She reached across and touched my cheek. "I hope you know I did not do it for a joke," she said.

"The music box errand?" I said, and frowned. I had forgotten the box on the counter at Fitzhugh's. It was just as well, I decided. If I couldn't bear the memento when I believed Tom dead, I could only imagine how unbearable it would be now that I knew he lived, yet didn't care for me.

"No, not the errand," Aunt Emmaline said, "though I did want to shield you from the strain of nervous anticipation. No, I meant withholding my knowledge of Mr. Rampling's fate. You must understand that I needed to know the boy first. We needed to see his name cleared, of course—but then I also needed to judge his character."

"And shall you pronounce your verdict?" I was speaking in a strange, flat voice; I couldn't place it in my memory.

Her brows lifted. "Do you feel I've meddled in your affairs?"

I stirred my tea. "I have no affairs. I've been asleep for months. Longer. I've been asleep my whole life, when I come to think about it."

My aunt tried to take my hand and sighed when I pulled away. "Leonora, really, you are much too hard on yourself," she said.

"And now that I've awakened at last it appears I am made of solid gold, like Midas's daughter, and am therefore untouchable."

"Midas's niece, you mean." Aunt Emma's lips pressed together. "You *do* feel I've meddled."

I sighed, suddenly ashamed of my ingratitude. "No. You took care of me, and you cared for Mr. Rampling, too. You called Daniel to task, and it saved Tom's life."

"Thomas Rampling is truly a remarkable young man. He was positively eloquent in Parliament, you know, when they asked him to testify in the opium ban debates. He warned them how addictive and dangerous the new alkaloids of morphine can be."

"Did the ban pass, then?"

She shook her head. "Other witnesses spoke too—doctors and importers mostly—and they convinced the House it would be altogether too costly and difficult to enforce a ban."

"Lord Rosbury's new ship was designed to be secretly stuffed with opium," I told her, and despite everything my chest warmed with sudden pride at Tom's valour in destroying the *Heroine* under her captain's nose.

My aunt echoed my thoughts. "At least Mr. Rampling's actions curbed the supply."

But Tom Rampling, I remembered, wanted nothing more to do with me. "Isn't it more likely he's driven up the prices at auction?" I said. "In the end he's probably made men like Rosbury all the richer."

"Not Rosbury himself, though." An amused note crept into Aunt Emma's voice. "It turns out your Mr. Rampling was the one who told the police to search the pockets of that coat for the Black Glove's notepaper. If Francis Thornfax was ever really in the running for your affections, my dear, I'm afraid he is quite out of the race now."

Her joking nauseated me. I lurched to my feet, gripping the table as the blood rushed from my head.

"What is it? What's the matter?" She began to rise, too, but I held up a hand to make her sit.

What was the matter? I could have married Mr. Thornfax, I told my aunt. I was fooled and flattered. I had enjoyed his company and his attention, and I had especially enjoyed the sense of power I'd won at his side, my sense that on the Lord Rosbury's arm I could have anything I wanted. And because of my enjoyment I became part of his crimes. Because I stood by I was partly to blame.

And now? Now, I told Aunt Emmaline, the world seemed a smaller, meaner place than before. Robbing Mr. Thornfax of his prized ship, forcing him to run away— these small triumphs would never make up for the lives lost to his murderous schemes. I knew that Tom Rampling would carry young Will's death with him, and Daisy's, and poor Hattie's, for as long as he lived. I knew he would blame himself for bringing those victims to Mr. Thornfax and to my brother-in-law. And he would blame me for being blind, for standing by. He did blame me. And I blamed myself.

"Well, that makes an unhappy ending, then," Aunt Emma commented, when I had finished.

I sat down. There was nothing else to say. We ate in silence; I picked at my food and washed each bite down with tea.

Finally my aunt put down her fork. She touched her serviette to her mouth. "Did Mr. Rampling tell you that he blames you?"

"Of course not. He told me that I have money, and that our stories are different and cannot be rewritten."

She snorted. "And you believed him?"

I hesitated. "He said he would not wish to rewrite them."

"He would not wish to rewrite *yours*." Aunt Emma clucked her tongue. "Ever the gallant knight, isn't he? Do you know what I had to say to persuade him to accept the money from Rosbury's jewels?"

"You told him I wanted him to have it."

"Well—yes, I did." She ducked her head, and I couldn't help but smile at her shamefaced expression. "Oh, dear," she said. "I wounded his pride, I'm afraid."

"His pride," I repeated. Tom Rampling wasn't proud. Was he?

"Did you make him a speech, at least?"

"Pardon me?"

"It was Mr. Rampling's duty to release you from any tie to him, and it sounds like he performed his duty admirably."

"Very admirably." I could hear the bitterness in my voice.

"But you did not do your duty. No"—she held up a finger to stop me from interrupting—"I don't mean your duty to him, or to me, or to anyone else. I mean your duty to yourself. You did not make him a speech."

"What sort of speech?" Bitterness gave way to impatience now.

She folded her hands in her lap and narrowed her eyes. "You say you want to be an actress. I'm sure you can think of something. Now go on, before you develop stage fright!"

So I walked back to the watchmaker's shop. Mr. Fitzhugh brushed aside my apologies and told me I'd find Tom out the back door, in the mews.

Tom was sitting hatless on the curb, elbows on his knees, watching a groomsman down the way roll a hoop to his small son and daughter. I sat myself down beside him, and he jumped and turned his head. My apology for startling him died in my throat when I saw that his eyes were raw with tears.

Hope sped my pulse at the sight. "You're weeping," I said.

He braced himself to get up, but I seized his wrist and held it. I watched his nostrils flare as his face struggled for composure, as he tried to mask all sign of the emotion I'd glimpsed, to recover his dignity. To recover his pride, I thought, realizing my aunt was right. I released his arm, suddenly regretting my thoughtless intrusion.

But Tom stayed seated beside me. "Grieving," he admitted, with a wry shrug. "As I said before."

Grieving—as you love? I wanted to ask. If only he would tell me how he felt! But I had a speech to make him, I remembered, and I wrapped my arms round my knees, wondering how to begin.

"You said goodbye to me," he reminded me.

"I retract it," I answered. "I am not going to France." An inelegant beginning for a speech, but now I'd started I didn't want to lose momentum: "I want to study to be an actress. I am going to take acting lessons. For the stage," I added, as he stared blankly at me.

I cleared my throat and tried again. "You said I had a future, thanks to my aunt's money. Well, you have a future, too, now: an apprenticeship, a fine living, the patronage of the Lady Hastings. Very soon you will likely meet a nice girl and marry her and have a houseful of beautiful little children." What on earth was I talking about? This was a dreadful speech. I felt slightly hysterical. "But in the meantime I shall be in London, and I won't be living at Hastings House or attending balls or taking gentlemen's cards. I shall be learning to be an actress, and I'll come to visit you often in the shop—I shall bring you watches and things to fix, if I have to—because I can't bear not to see you." Here my voice cracked, and I gulped back a panicky sob. I'd lost the theme of my speech entirely.

"Leo," he said softly.

"My story already has you in it, Tom Rampling!"

"Leo."

"It's too late to switch to another chapter. You're already a character—you're the hero, in fact."

"Leo, I don't—"

"You're the hero!" I yelped.

Tom reached over and covered my mouth with his palm. "You've lost your stammer," he said, as if he'd only just noticed. "Is your Mimic at your service, then?"

I nodded. My tears flowed freely over his hand.

When he released me he swiped his thumb across my cheekbone and then put the thumb to his lips to lick the tears from it. The intimate, unthinking gesture produced another hot flicker of hope within me. But Tom frowned. "You deserve more than a common lockpicking criminal."

I sniffled. "Well now, I'd hardly call you common. You single-handedly destroyed half the merchant ships in Britain."

A startled chuckle escaped him.

"I've had my fill of lords, Tom," I said. "I'll take my chances on a lockpick."

He shook his head and started to look sad again, but I leaned in and pressed my lips to his. Tom held rigid at first, resisting me, but after a moment his hands came up to tangle in my hair, and he pulled me against him, returning my kiss, multiplying it. His mouth was warm, the scent of his breath sweetly familiar. I felt as if I was drawing life from him, filling and unfurling, as if Tom were strong sunlight and I a spring leaf.

He bent his head to rest his forehead against mine. "Miss Luck." He sighed. "I dreamt and dreamt of this but I never dared to hope."

"Say it again."

"I never dared—"

"No, the name." I touched his chiselled cheekbone, his temple where his pulse beat just under the pale skin.

"Miss Luck?" He kissed me, and his voice broke lower. "I can hardly say it enough. You are fortune and favour"—another, deeper kiss—"and rapture and bliss. I shall have to take you in small doses or be overcome." He bent to kiss the spot where my neck met my new-healed collarbone.

The unexpected caress in such a vulnerable place made me stiffen and then heat all over with pleasure. "Am I your remedy, then?" I joked.

"You are my remedy," Tom replied, but it was a whisper, solemn as a vow. He felt me shiver and gathered me, gently and protectively, into his arms.

"And what of the Lady Hastings?" he said, into my hair. "After everything she has done for me I wouldn't dare to disappoint her."

"The Lady Hastings grew impatient with the wait," came Aunt Emma's voice behind us.

We scrambled apart. She was standing in the doorway with Mr. Fitzhugh, who was leaning comfortably against the frame, arms crossed, as though they'd both been there some minutes already.

"Do lift my niece from the pavings, would you? She's been quite ill, you know. Though judging from her colour at the moment"—she peered into my flushed face as Tom hurried to assist me—"I would say she is well on her way to recovery."

Aunt Emma tucked my arm through her own and led us back into the shop. I blinked in the room's dimness after the bright mews.

The four of us stood amid the clocks' chatter, waiting for one another to speak.

"I swear to you, Lady Hastings," Tom said, at last. "I will strive my whole life to become worthy of her."

Mr. Fitzhugh coughed, and Aunt Emma arched an eyebrow. "It seems your apprentice shall beat my niece to the stage, Declan," she said.

"Weel now, yon lad's not typically given to dramatics," the watchmaker told her. He took off his glasses and wiped them, with exaggerated motions, on his shirt. Then he put them back on and peered at Tom in mock concern. "I wonder what ails him."

"Give him strong tea when we are gone," said my aunt.

"Oh, won't you have mercy?" I protested. "He doesn't know, yet, how you tease!"

"Forgive me," she said, utterly unapologetic. "Mr. Rampling, let us not speak of our whole lives. Let us speak only of today. And of Thursday, when I hope you will have finished repairing Leonora's music box, and you and Mr. Fitzhugh might come to dine with us in Gordon Square, in order to deliver it."

Tom took Aunt Emmaline's outstretched hand. "It would be my pleasure, Countess," he managed.

"Please come even if it's not repaired," I added, to make sure there was no misunderstanding.

"Order a fortifyin' supper," Mr. Fitzhugh suggested. "These younglings need meat ta their bones. Too much faintin' an swoonin', elsewise."

Suddenly every timepiece in the shop began to strike five o'clock, an explosion of sound that made Aunt Emma gasp and clutch Mr. Fitzhugh's arm while the rest of us laughed. I looked at Tom—his warm, smiling mouth, his grey eyes incredulous with happiness—and I knew he heard in the din what I heard too. It was the whole world chiming us a new hour, a new era. A new beginning.

AUTHOR'S NOTE

Mad Miss Mimic is a work of fiction grounded in historical fact. While I invented the particulars of Leo's story, I tried to be as accurate as possible about life in 1870s London for an upper-class girl. But in this novel I also wanted to take Leo places a "typical" Victorian heiress would never go, so I spent countless hours in libraries and archives researching the history of speech disorders, medical practices, opiate addiction, clipper ships, explosives, and criminal underworlds. Luckily libraries and archives just happen to be some of my favourite places in the world!

DEADLY MEDICINES: OPIUM, MORPHINE, HEROIN

In the nineteenth century, opium was perfectly legal and freely available at apothecaries' and chemists' shops. The liquid tincture favoured by Leo's sister, Christabel, called *laudanum*, was sold under such popular names as Godfrey's Cordial and Mrs. Winslow's Soothing Syrup as a remedy for everything from ladies' headaches to babies' teething pains. Morphine and codeine were isolated from the opium molecule in

1805. The hypodermic syringe came along in 1853, and over the next decades doctors began to inject their patients with morphine for faster, more dramatic pain relief. If you had money you could buy your own syringes, and morphia addiction, commonly called *morphomania*, spread like a plague among the middle and upper classes in the late 1800s.

In 1874 an English doctor named C. R. Alder Wright discovered a new way of processing morphine that made its effects much quicker and more powerful. Dr. Wright published his findings in a pharmaceutical journal but did not pursue the manufacture or marketing of the drug. Twenty years later, the Bayer company (mainly known nowadays for Aspirin) patented the compound, called diacetylemorphine, under a name that captured its "heroic" effects: *Heroin*. Heroin was sold across Europe and the U.S. as a cough remedy and pain reliever. It was even prescribed as a cure for morphia addiction! It took many years for the medical world to grasp just how dangerous and addictive heroin actually was. Faced with increasing reports of overdose and withdrawal sickness, Bayer quietly pulled heroin off the shelves in 1913.

That initial 1874 discovery of what would later become heroin is the sort of historical detail that novelists adore. I knew right away that my Dr. Dewhurst would be experimenting with morphine derivatives and testing them out on "patients" like Hattie and Daisy who had nowhere else to go. Whether doctors actually used orphans and paupers for medical experiments is uncertain—if they did, they certainly didn't keep records!—but codes of medical ethics were a lot looser and less rigorously enforced in the Victorian period than they are today.

Dr. Dewhurst doesn't call his new wonder drug "heroin," of course, but I couldn't resist sneaking the name into the novel somewhere, so I christened Mr. Thornfax's new clipper ship the *Heroine*.

STUTTERING (AND MIMICRY)

Stuttering is a speech disorder that affects 5 percent of the world's population in childhood and 1 percent in adulthood. This means that in 80 percent of cases a stutter spontaneously resolves by adolescence. While physical in origin (a "locking" reflex in the vocal cords), stuttering is made worse by stress, including stressful speaking situations. Singing, reciting poetry, and imitating other people's speech (e.g., acting in a play or performing stand-up comedy) is known to temporarily relieve or eliminate stuttering. The fact that Leo's ability to mimic voices also allows her to speak stutter-free is therefore medically plausible even if I did make it up.

My portrayal of Leo's suffering under various "therapies" for her stutter is not an exaggeration. In the 1800s treatments for stuttering ranged from surgical removal of part or all of the tongue, to electrical shock and other "punishment" therapies, to regular doses of laudanum or morphine for the stutterer's "nerves." Leo's love for opera and poetry and her eventual path to "finding her voice" was inspired by the work of a contemporary poet whose work I greatly admire named Jordan Scott. Jordan grew up with a stutter, and his book *Blert* explores what he calls the "poetics of stuttering." You can hear him read aloud from this book online in the film *Flub and Utter* (links under "For Further Reading" below).

EXPLOSIVES, TERROR, AND CRIME

Nitroglycerin was developed in Sweden by Alfred Nobel, founder of the Nobel Prize. He set up a laboratory on a barge in the middle of a lake after an explosion at his first workspace killed his younger brother. Nobel patented the blasting cap in 1864 and dynamite in 1867. In my story Mr. Watts more or less copies Nobel's recipe for dynamite: he stabilizes the nitroglycerin by mixing it with clay, forming it into sticks, and attaching it to a blast cap. The timer Tom Rampling makes from a pocket watch would not have been impossible from an historical standpoint: after all, the first adjustable mechanical alarm clock was patented in 1847 in France.

The Black Glove and its terror attacks are products of my imagination, not of history. Britain's first direct experience of terrorism was the Irish-American bombing campaign of 1881–85, after which the Explosives Act was passed in an attempt to control the possession and sale of dynamite. Mr. Thornfax's plot to monopolize the opium market wouldn't have worked in real life, either. Although various proposals to restrict or ban addictive drugs were debated in Parliament throughout the late 1800s, both opium and cocaine were still legal in Britain at the start of World War I.

Leo gets into serious trouble when she wanders into the wrong neighbourhood. London in the 1870s housed a massive underclass of desperately poor citizens crowded into slums and forced to survive on begging, prostitution, and larceny. Criminal gangs like Mr. Sears's and Mrs. Clampitt's in my story offered some shelter and protection to orphans and street children in exchange for the spoils of their thievery. (Punishments for children were slightly less severe than for adults.) The prevalence of petty crime in "rookeries" like Spitalfields and Seven Dials is evident in the long list of Victorian slang terms for different types of thieves, including *roughs, mobbers, fingersmiths, sneakthieves, cutpurses, hoisters, house-breakers, snide-pitchers, toy-getters, duffmen, welshers, skittle-sharps, magsmen, busters, screwsmen,* and *pocket-pickers.*

FOR FURTHER READING

Brown, G. I. *The Big Bang: A History of Explosives.* Stroud, U.K.: Sutton, 1998.

Dormandy, Thomas. *Opium: Reality's Dark Dream.* New Haven: Yale University Press, 2012.

Kelly, Jack. *Gunpowder. Alchemy, Bombards and Pyrotechnics: The History of the Explosive That Changed the World.* New York: Basic Books, 2004.

Lavid, Nathan. *Understanding Stuttering.* Jackson, MS: University Press of Mississippi, 2003.

Parssinen, Terry M. *Secret Passions, Secret Remedies: Narcotic Drugs in British Society 1820–1930.* Philadelphia: ISHI, 1983.

Scott, Jordan. *Blert* (poems). Toronto: Coach House Books, 2008; *Flub and Utter* (film). www.flubandutter.nfb.ca/#/flubandutter; *Stutter Featuring Jordan Scott* (film). www.vimeo.com/7384677.

White, Jerry. *London in the Nineteenth Century: 'A Human Awful Wonder of God.'* London: Jonathan Cape, 2007.

Finally, if you'd like to read more fiction with words like *slumduggered* in it, I highly recommend anything by Charles Dickens, and especially *Oliver Twist.*

ACKNOWLEDGMENTS

My thanks to all the readers of this book in its various drafts for their feedback and encouragement—particularly to editor Melanie Little; to my agent, Monica Pacheco; to my parents, Bart and Marianne Henstra; and to Lynne Missen, Brittany Lavery, Sandra Tooze, Chandra Wohleber, and Vikki VanSickle at Penguin Random House Canada. To those who cheered me along with good writing company, especially Kathryn Kuitenbrouwer, Suzanne Alyssa Andrew, and Heidi Reimer. To the staunchest supporters of my early writing efforts, including Mary Tangelder, Stan Kaethler, Jessica Westhead, and Jennifer Burwell. To my sons, Rowan and Marlow Vander Kooy, for promising to read the book even though it "looks pretty girly" and to give all their friends free copies. And to Neil Vander Kooy: you were my first reader, my first listener, my first everything.